ALL THE HIDDEN MONSTERS

AMIE JORDAN

Chicken House

2 Palmer Street, Frome, Somerset BA11 1DS
www.chickenhousebooks.com

Text © Amie Jordan 2024

First published in Great Britain in 2024
Chicken House
2 Palmer Street
Frome, Somerset BA11 1DS
United Kingdom
www.chickenhousebooks.com

Chicken House/Scholastic Ireland, 89E Lagan Road, Dublin Industrial Estate,
Glasnevin, Dublin D11 HP5F, Republic of Ireland

Cover design and illustration by Micaela Alcaino
Typeset by Dorchester Typesetting Group Ltd
Printed in Great Britain by Clays, Elcograf S.p.A

FSC
www.fsc.org
MIX
Paper | Supporting
responsible forestry
FSC® C018072

1 3 5 7 9 10 8 6 4 2

British Library Cataloguing in Publication data available.

PB ISBN 978-1-915026-11-8
eISBN 978-1-915947-42-0

PRAISE FOR *ALL THE HIDDEN MONSTERS*

'This is one of my first YA crime books and now I know it won't be the last! I had the best time following Sage and Oren as they team up to solve the twisty supernatural mystery in the streets of Manchester. The unique spin on a fantasy world within our own had me hooked (and desperate to solve the mystery alongside our duo!). This book is the perfect combination of fantasy, true crime and fun-filled chemistry.'
ALEXANDRA CHRISTO, author of *To Kill a Kingdom*

'I adored this book! It was the perfect blend of a twisty mystery, found family and inventive world building. Think *Legends & Lattes* with murder.'
AMY McCAW, author of *Mina and the Undead*

'Fans of *Big Bad Me* and *Mina and the Undead* will devour this! Pulse-pounding, paranormal fun.'
KAT ELLIS, author of *Harrow Lake*

'A brilliant mix of the supernatural and classic crime, something I've not seen done before, and which breathed fresh life into familiar tropes. Zippy dialogue, a fast pace and winning characters – a sure-fire hit!'
GINA BLAXILL, author of *Pretty Twisted*

'In *All the Hidden Monsters*, there is both a gripping plot AND flawless character arcs that make you stay up way too late reading compulsively! Full of adventure and action, perfectly paced, at times dark, sometimes emotional, and gripping throughout! Can't wait to read more from Amie.'
BEN OLIVER, author of *The Loop*

'The supernatural murder mystery I didn't know I needed.'
ANEESA MARUFU, author of *The Balloon Thief*

'A gorgeous, slow-building story about self-acceptance and accepting the possibility of being loved by others, which slapped me right in the feels.'
JESS POPPLEWELL, author of *The Dark Within Us*

Cosy crime is well and truly dead. This is the start of the best new crime series I have ever read, and the murders keep on piling up. In a world below our own, anxious young werewolf Sage, and Oren, a warlock with a bad attitude and unbelievable good looks come together in an epic enemies-to-almost-lovers investigative thriller. Throw in a charming poltergeist who loves to cook, and you've got a funny, serious, scary and passionate fantasy – and you'll *never* guess who's on the killing spree Upside and Downside . . .

BARRY CUNNINGHAM
Publisher
Chicken House

For the twenty-year-old me –
told you you'd prove them wrong.

And come he slow, or come he fast,
It is but death who comes at last.
Sir Walter Scott, *Marmion* (1808)

I

OREN

'Single victim. Female. Young . . . mid-twenties. Throat cut. Defensive wounds to arms and torso. No transformation.'

Oren circled the body, examining all angles.

Still in human form, she was lying on the floor of her Upside apartment living room, ruining a perfectly good rug with her blood. Her shoulder-length blonde hair was stained red at the tips, and her eyes were still open, staring vacantly at the memory of the last thing they saw.

He crouched and held a hand over her chest, a few centimetres from her non-beating heart, and closed his eyes. 'Body core temperature cooling but not cold. Dead less than an hour.'

He sighed and got to his feet.

'Blood spray on the walls indicates throat was cut before she fell . . .' He paused, glancing at his notebook open on the coffee table. 'Or . . . staggering back from her killer.'

Blue ink transcribed his musings, fading and changing itself with every fresh observation.

'Partial footprint in the blood. Mug of coffee: mostly

drunk. Apartment in good condition. Bedroom untouched. Kitchen,' he poked his head through the doorless arch into a small workspace, 'in order. Noticeboard – nothing of interest.'

At least, not to him.

He walked back into the hallway. Keys sat in a dish on a small table beside the door, a few bits of junk mail discarded beside it. He turned the letters over, examining both sides, then threw them back down.

'What a Thursday you've had, Lucinda Hague.' He waved a hand and his notepad appeared on the table. 'Front door undamaged. No forced entry.'

He went back into the apartment, stood for a moment.

Something felt . . . off.

He turned on the spot, sniffed.

Nothing.

He sniffed again.

Still nothing.

Interesting.

He couldn't put his finger on it . . . Why was this bothering him? At first glance it really did appear to be a human crime, the fact the victim was a Downsider mere chance. And there was nothing at the scene to give away supernatural secrets. He should walk away and leave the humans to deal with it. They'd never know the unlucky Lucinda Hague was a werewolf, the only Downside race that could live Upside permanently. He pitied them. Saw their desire to try and live human lives as a denial of what they were.

He frowned. He didn't like being unsure. Roderick – his so-called captain at the Arcānum, the elite force of warlocks that kept the peace in the supernatural world – would write it off quickly if he couldn't produce anything concrete.

He tutted, irritated. Roderick had given him an hour before he tipped off human authorities to a disturbance at the address, and he'd used most of that.

Time to go.

He gave Lucinda Hague one final, impassive glance, then shrugged, and slipped from the room.

. . . And heard a heartbeat humming like the wings of a trapped bird.

He paused.

He usually tuned out emotions. Had honed his skill set over many years to control his over-heightened senses, and he'd almost missed it.

He wrenched open the apartment door so quickly she dropped her umbrella in surprise.

A girl trussed up in layers against the cold, her thick coat buttoned high over a scarf, stared at him. Her dark, wind-whipped hair was falling out of its scruffy bun, untamed and as wild as the look of fear in her brown eyes.

2

SAGE

The stench of blood was so strong Sage thought she might be sick. Or pass out. Or maybe both.

And then Lucy's apartment door had flown open and a tall, young man – dark coat unbuttoned over a grey T-shirt and jeans – not a man, a warlock, and absolutely not the friend she'd come to visit – was glaring down at her.

'I'm looking for . . .' Her voice trailed off.

Lucy, the first friend she'd made when she'd arrived in Downside, eight years old and newly orphaned in the were-wolf attack that'd killed her parents and little brother.

Lucy, who had heard crying and crept into her room and answered all her questions about this insane new reality she'd been thrown into.

Lucy, who had run from Downside the morning of her ˗hteenth birthday, and never been back.

Lucy, who had pushed her to turn up unannounced to demand why her old friend kept cancelling plans and seemed to be cutting her off.

Lucy . . .

Oh, God, the blood!

Salt and iron, pine-laced. Absolutely, definitely, one hundred per cent werewolf blood. She could taste it, so warm and fresh and tangy that involuntary bile started to rise up her throat.

She looked back down the corridor . . . but nothing. Of course nobody else could smell it. The rest of the apartments were inhabited by plain humans, with muted senses and no idea of what lay behind this door.

'I can smell . . . blood,' she managed to choke out, her heartbeat thrumming in her ears.

'Obviously.' He sniffed pointedly, scenting her, marking her as werewolf too.

'You knew her?'

Knew who? Lucy?

Knew?

The breath left her body in one quick *whoosh* as the word washed over her.

She felt something in her hair before she realized it was her own hands pushing wisps from her face, tightening her bobble, anything other than acknowledge the truth: another person she cared about was dead.

The faces of her lifeless parents flash again, her little brother's hand reaches out across the sleeping bag, the sound of final rasping breaths . . .

The magnolia walls and identical wooden doors started to sway.

She looked up at him again, took in his bright blue-green eyes, his hair, half-black, half-white, and grey flecks in between, as if he'd started the ageing process far too early. He must've been sent by the Arcānum to the scene of a supernatural crime . . .

Scene of a crime.

Lucy . . .

She almost laughed out loud. Delirious, hysterical, denial-filled laughter.

Lucy couldn't be dead? She couldn't be—

Suddenly she was barging past him and into the apartment.

She'd only been there once before, but it was as she remembered it. A white corridor with a few framed pieces of artwork, and some hooks for coats. She barely noticed any of it, her sights fixed on the living room door ahead.

'I wouldn't do that if I were you.'

She pushed open the door and stared at the body on the floor.

For a moment, her brain simply had nothing to say.

Completely blank. Unable to compute.

The hair stood up on the back of her arms, pressing against the inside of her sleeves: a sensation like electricity crackling over her skin. Or maybe *it* was trying to get out. The monster in her.

No.

No, that godforsaken wolf wouldn't be making an appearance. Not today.

She didn't realize she was shaking until the hand that rose to cover her mouth began to tremble.

Suddenly, she couldn't breathe.

The air felt so thick and heavy, and every breath made her feel dizzier. She wanted to keel over and vomit all over her feet.

Everything was speckled with blood. The floor, the walls, the ceiling . . . The body of her friend was drowning in it. A single half-footprint marked in the mess. She wanted to turn and run from the horror. Glassy eyes. Gone.

She looked up to see that he'd followed her. His trainers looked too white. Too clean. The only thing in the whole room without crimson stains.

He didn't even falter at the horror all around them as he grabbed her elbow and steered her back into the hallway and out of the apartment. She felt a pulse of power ripple down the corridor, saw the slight haze of magic meld itself to the walls and the doors, extra reassurance that no humans would hear them.

'I asked you a question.'

She blinked. What question?

'You knew her?' he repeated impatiently. 'Speak.'

The force of authority in his tone shocked her mouth into motion. 'Once.' She supposed she didn't know Lucy very well at all any more.

'We were in the same Downside orphanage. She left when I was eleven. That was seven years ago and I've barely seen her since. Every couple of years, maybe.'

'You don't seem too upset.'

It wasn't the question she'd expected next . . . Maybe it was shock, or maybe she'd just seen worse. More memories flashed.

Skin ripped and torn. Blood and bone. Light hair stained red.

'I think,' he said softly, 'that plenty of killers return to the scene of the crime. Get a kick out of it.'

She flinched, so appalled by the accusation she didn't notice his hand shoot for her again, laced with more of that faint, glimmering, golden mist. From the other hand, a small blade exploded out of thin air.

She yelped in terror as a vice-like grip wrapped around her wrist, and suddenly his perfectly sculpted face was centimetres from hers, immaculate white teeth showing as the steel blade pressed against her throat. 'Why did you kill her?'

'I didn't!' she gasped. 'I swear, please, I—'

'Were you jealous?' She could feel the sharp edge pressing into her neck. 'That she built a life here and left you behind?'

She started to sob in earnest. 'No—'

'Then who was it?'

'I don't know!' she practically screamed, trying desperately to claw his hand off her wrist, but it was no use. The magic enveloping their hands made her feel like she was scratching against glass. Not even wolf claws would break through. She realized now that was the point. 'I don't know anyone who'd want to hurt her!'

'Not a single enemy?'

'None!' she cried. 'She was just a journalist. She volunteered in her free time. Helped people. She was good, and kind, and—'

He dropped her hand, and stepped away.

She stared at him, horrified, cradling her wrist in her other hand.

'I know it wasn't you.'

What?

What?

He shrugged. 'Shock produces the truth more often than not. And quicker. I just wanted answers.'

She gaped at him.

Bastard. Absolute bastard.

She'd have said it to him, too, if she wasn't still so shocked she thought she might crumble to her knees.

'The human police will be here soon to wrap this up. You should go.'

'Humans?' she repeated faintly. 'You don't think this was a supernatural murder?'

'That's none of your business,' he said. 'Present yourself at the Arcānum headquarters tomorrow at noon to give a statement. I'll have some questions about her background.

The journalism. Volunteering. Whatever.' He put his hands into his coat pockets. 'Go.'

She looked past him one last time at the body of her friend, aware that it was the last time anyone who knew her in life would see her face.

3

SAGE

Sage barely remembered the journey home.

She'd rushed out of the apartment – the cafes, restaurant and pub outside all oblivious to what she'd just witnessed. Fled from it all – from the warlock. From Lucy.

She ran around corners and across roads, barely looking, hardly noticing the agitated beeps of cars she stepped out in front of, or the disgruntled mutters of bodies she collided with. The heavens had opened again, and this time it was as if they'd been waiting all day just for her.

The city centre was always busy but the humans Upside were weeks from Christmas. It was heaving. Full of determined shoppers with little regard for how much they needed to *get out of her way*. She just wanted to get home. Where it was safe and warm and not covered in blood.

But at last she saw it, like a precious lighthouse that signalled land to sailors lost at sea. She stumbled past Afflecks Palace, towards the sanctuary of the neon-blue light of Dive Bar that told her she was nearly safe, past the famous mosaic on the side of the old building: AND ON

THE SIXTH DAY GOD CREATED MANchester. She grimaced. If there was a God, He'd created a hell of a lot more than that.

Inside Dive Bar, Big Jon waved a scruffy rag as he polished glasses behind the bar, but nobody else noticed her arrival. Music blared, and a pool tournament was underway in the corner, so Sage managed to slip through without being heckled. A rare treat. The floor was sticky with stale ale, and the air stank of the cigarettes that were supposed to be banned indoors.

Beyond, the barrel room was humid, the walls covered in snaking pipes full of amber liquids, the thudding music rattling the metal canisters. The ancient trapdoor was heavy, the old wood rough and splintered, the hinges rusting, and as she pulled it open, the faint iridescent hum of magic that held the gateway locked to human touch rippled over the surface.

She climbed down the spiral staircase, into the darkness. Her lungs burnt, her throat raw from the icy air. She was drenched, sobbing. The cold had already seeped into the marrow of her bones. Her very soul felt frozen. And shame prickled at her cheeks when she remembered how scared she'd felt trapped in that warlock's grip. She had a beast inside her and hadn't even tried to use it to defend herself?

'All right, Sage?' Stellan, the gatekeeper, winked from the shadows as she reached the bottom. As always, he sat dutifully beside the staircase, the only light flickering from a single candle. He was a ghost, a medieval knight, and still wore the clothes he'd died in. The soft chink of the torn chainmail hanging off his chest tinkled through the darkness. A murky tunnel stretched beyond him, lined with rows of electricity cables that siphoned power from Upside.

She shook her head. She couldn't speak. She'd made it to the underground city, hidden entirely from humans and carved out by magic. She was Downside.

Home.

'P?' She let herself into their apartment.

Her best friend smiled as she walked through the kitchen wall.

Her light blonde hair was plaited back and her clothes, torn and ripped in places as they had been when she'd died, like Stellan, were still stained with blood. She looked . . . muted, like the colours were there but worn out and faded, and fluid enough that Sage could just see through her when she moved.

But P's expression was bright and her eyes warm as she floated down the hallway towards the living room. It was cosy and welcoming, fairy lights draped over picture frames and vases of flowers that filled her nostrils with sweet scent. Sage's eyes lingered on a small frame in the top corner of the bookshelf. Herself. Young and smiling, an even smaller boy next to her with identical brown hair.

'There's minestrone in the kitchen,' P said. 'I'll dish

you up a bowl.'

Sage stared at the sofa, and the rug on the floor in front of it. P would go mad if she pulled off her squelching trainers and got wet footprints all over it. But at least it wasn't a footprint in blood.

The force of it could've knocked her to the floor.

'Sage?' P's voice was closer again, and she looked up to find the ghost hovering in the kitchen doorway, a ladle in her hand, with a face of concern.

Lucy had been one of Sage's first supernatural friends, but nobody got her better than P.

And so it all came out, in between gasps of air and tears and snot and everything else, as she broke down at last and described what she'd found in Lucy's apartment. And had she been telling anyone else, they would've thought it was all about Lucy. But P understood that it was just as much about the other bodies covered in blood. Even greater and more painful losses that she had already experienced in her short life. Losses that'd landed her in that orphanage in the first place. In that apartment with P. That Lucy was just the tip of an already sizeable iceberg Sage fought every day.

Some days, it was all she could do to keep the guilt at bay. To wake up and walk around pretending her nightmares hadn't plagued her with those terrible memories. Left her with more questions about why she'd survived and her family had died. Her parents, her little brother. Was it luck, or fate, or punishment? Some days, she didn't see any point in rising from her bed at all.

It was P, and P alone, who'd refused to let her drown.

And that was what she was doing now. An expert in saying all the right affirmations at the right time. Until at last all her tears were spent and she felt some semblance of peace again.

Then she spewed some anger about that warlock.

P nodded along, eyes wide. 'Report him!' she said firmly. 'They're arrogant arseholes at the best of times but they can't go round treating people like that, Sage! Not when you just found . . . well . . .' She sighed and shook her head. She offered another tissue from the box she'd produced from somewhere or other. 'Go shower, you're all damp. I'll bring you the minestrone and some crusty bread to dip. We'll watch bad human romcoms until we feel better.'

By the time Sage woke the next morning, it took a few minutes to remember the horror of the previous night. And though it made panic well in her chest again, it was softened by the following memories of the quiet giggles of she and P, dreamy-eyed over a young Patrick Dempsey, and she was able to push it back down.

'I have sausages,' was P's greeting the millisecond she emerged from her bedroom. 'And toast. Or I can do bacon if you want?'

P was the best cook. The best. Restless and with endless hours to fill, she cooked so much they had to give most of it away, brandishing Tupperware with an expression that dared anyone to refuse. But their friends Juniper and Willow, Rhen, Danny and Cypress regularly turned up for the handouts.

'Or eggs—'

'Toast is fine,' Sage yawned as she threw herself on to the sofa to pull on her trainers, quietly grateful P had thought to put them under the radiator to dry. 'I'll eat as I walk.'

And P . . . said nothing.

Sage rose, and went to the kitchen door.

It was immaculate, as always. The surfaces gleamed, as did the sink taps. P was almost as obsessed with cleaning as she was with cooking. Everything was as it usually was but . . . P was by the cooker, hovering a few centimetres off the ground as she prodded sausages sizzling on a griddle, steam curling in tendrils right through her, making her translucent arms look opaque.

'What's wrong?'

'What do you mean?'

'I just said toast and you didn't try to insist I have something with it.'

P tried to school her face into a look of innocence, as if she wouldn't have ever said such a thing. They both knew that was a lie.

'P?'

'Oh.' She dropped the spatula into the griddle, flustered. 'Fine. Danny called about an hour ago.' She grimaced. 'Word is spreading, about Lucy. All the werewolves are talking. Wanted to know if you'd heard. If you thought it was true she was murdered.'

Sage swallowed. 'I can't.'

'I know.' P nodded. 'I said you hadn't mentioned anything. That I'd tell you when you woke up.'

'Have you heard . . .' Sage said awkwardly, 'anything from your . . .' Her voice trailed off, still unsure, despite the tightness of their friendship, how to put it. 'I mean, has she . . .' She sighed helplessly. 'You know?'

P shook her head. 'Nobody's seen her. They don't think she stayed. They think she chose to pass on.'

Because everyone had a choice, when their time came. To remain as a ghost, or to pass on. It was a permanent decision, and once made there was nothing that could ever change it. It was the decision P had had to make. She had stayed.

Sage nodded. She hadn't expected it. Lucy had been so keen to escape Downside and supernatural life that she was unlikely to opt for eternity as a ghost.

P handed her a little foil package with a bleak smile. 'You'll be early if you go now, it's only eleven.'

'I want to stop by the captain's office before I go find that warlock—'

'Oh, Sage,' P whined, and she knew that familiar look of pity from her friend. 'Is it worth it, today?'

But something had been bugging her as she lay awake into the early hours, plagued by the memory of Lucy's vacant eyes. She hadn't realized what it was in the horror-struck moments she'd stood in between the carnage, but something in that room had felt . . . off.

She grimaced. She did have a reputation for turning up unannounced at the office of the Arcānum captain . . . in fact, Roderick had expressly forbidden her from doing it again. But this time, it was serious. Lucy was dead, and she was pretty sure that she could help. This time, he'd have to listen to her.

The new headquarters of the Arcānum had recently moved into their neighbourhood, and was inside a tall, modern-looking building. Part of some scheme to revamp the warlocks and their image.

Ha.

Anyone who believed that hadn't met Roderick.

The sky, a fairy glamour of the real sky above ground, was watery pale. It was early enough for Downside to feel not asleep, but still bleary-eyed. The high-street shops had unshuttered, ready for another pre-Yuletide rush to descend upon them that afternoon, but it wasn't too busy yet.

In the residential areas the festive spirit felt more real. Not the manufactured idea in shop windows, designed to encourage spending on trinkets nobody really needed. The supernatural world celebrated Yuletide: the far older winter festival steeped in legends of old gods and ancient traditions that plenty of newer human traditions were built upon.

Downside still idolized Odin, a bearded old man who

rode Sleipnir, an eight-legged horse, through the skies — sounds familiar, huh? Indeed, some Downside occupants had lived long enough that they still remembered when Odin was the only old guy that delivered presents.

The occupants of the apartment blocks and houses around her had risen, fireflies flickering in windows. Yuletide tradition had trees decorated with fruits and candles, though thanks to a unionized strike by the water nymphs who ran Downside's emergency response unit, a compromise had been made after one candle fire too many. Fireflies were now used instead.

Holly and mistletoe were crucial Yule decorations, so the city was covered in them, and singing was important too. Sage loved it all. Downside children left boots stuffed with hay and carrots outside their front doors and on window ledges for Sleipnir, which Odin would swap for gifts. Even in Downside, her heart remembered her own childhood Upside, their Christmas tree and stockings on the mantle, a brother complaining about the wait to open presents and a mum and dad who—

No.

Lock it away.

She crossed the street, passing a block of apartments that towered into the fake sky when a voice called her name. She looked up to see a window tossed open three floors above, the face of a girl with long, dark braids hanging out, one giant golden paw waving to get her attention. At once, her heart dropped. If Danny had called P, did all her friends know about Lucy already?

'The theme for the pub quiz tomorrow, it's first-gen Pokémon.' Juniper pulled a face. It seemed word had only spread through the werewolves for now. Sage swallowed the lump in her throat gratefully. 'Make sure Harland comes or we're toast.'

Juniper was right. Their part-time flatmate would be their only hope of victory, and they took quiz night at the Faun's Head seriously. She couldn't manage to open her mouth, not without unleashing the emotion lodged inside her chest like a dead weight. She nodded, and gave what she hoped resembled a smile as the sphinx dived from the window, eagle wings carrying her off into the distance.

The Arcānum headquarters came into view. All smooth edges and shiny panels. She could see the gloomy sky reflecting off it before she'd even got close. Before it sat a large courtyard, with pristine hedgerows she could see being tended to by the old minotaur that'd run Labyrinth Landscapers, Downside's premier horticulture company, for decades. A large, illuminated fountain took centre stage. Mermaids, beautiful and long-haired and graceful, using trumpets to spray water over the giant golden A elevated in the centre.

She rounded the fountain and headed for the wide doors with another sigh, hopeful that for just this once, Roderick would shut up and listen to what she had to say.

4

SAGE

The captain of the Arcānum threw down some papers and folded his arms across a broad chest.

'How did I know you'd turn up today?'

She cleared her throat. 'I came about—'

'Lucinda Hague,' Roderick finished her sentence, gesturing with his chin. 'Oren's updated me. That was you, then?'

She spun. There, hands in pockets leaning against the wall, still in the white trainers that'd bothered her so much in Lucy's apartment, was that warlock.

Her own senses, even more sensitive than any warlock's, hadn't realized somebody else was in the room? That his magic could mask him like that was . . . frightening. He smirked like he knew it too.

Her cheeks flushed. 'It was me, yeah.'

'What do you want, Sage?' Roderick demanded. His dirty-blonde hair was tied back and his eyes were hard. Like he knew he was in for a long day and wasn't pleased about it. Even less that she'd shown up to make it longer. 'You were due in Oren's office at noon.' He looked pointedly at the clock on the wall that said she was forty minutes early.

Oren pushed off the wall and sat on the chair opposite Roderick's desk, brow raised expectantly.

Now she wasn't drowning in the scent of blood, she could smell his aftershave. Expensive-smelling and hints of cedarwood and—

Sage!

If her cheeks had been burning before, flames were licking up into her eyeballs now.

'Just hear me out—' she started, but Roderick cut her off.

'How many times do I have to tell you, you're not a bloody warlock!'

Oren snorted. 'This is her?' His accent was only slight, but gave away that he came from somewhere far away. 'The werewolf that keeps asking for a job?'

Her stomach squirmed.

The Arcānum was a warlock institution. Their magic powerful enough to uphold law and order throughout the supernatural cities of the world. Roderick had refused to let her join. But she'd never given up. As a human child, before that night on the moor when she'd been changed – all she'd ever wanted was to grow up and become a police officer. And maybe have a police dog. Well, the dog had been the biggest pull actually, but the conviction that she wanted to catch bad guys had never really gone away. Especially since the perpetrator of her own family's deaths was never identified.

'There isn't anything to say I have to be,' she shot back. 'I looked up old records—'

Roderick looked like he might explode. 'You did what?'

She'd argued her case enough times that she didn't quite begrudge Roderick his look of fury. But she was desperate. Desperate for her life to be more than stuck Downside. Go Upside, join the human police, was all Roderick had said. But she couldn't leave P.

'There's no rule that says the Arcānum must be magic,' she went on. 'Centuries of warlocks just adopted that concept.'

Oren started to laugh under his breath, but it wasn't kind.

'Because you all die in the end!' Roderick stood, his hands flat on his desk. 'It's too time-consuming to train you when you barely provide a half-century of service!'

She was horrified to realize there was a lump in her throat, but she refused to cry again. 'Lucy was my friend,' she said quietly. 'I just want to help find her killer. That's why I'm here.'

Roderick closed his eyes, as if summoning his last ounces of patience. 'There's nothing to find. Nothing definitive at the scene. It doesn't meet the threshold to be classified as a supernatural crime, so the humans—'

'You're wrong!' She didn't mean to shout. She froze the moment she did. But in her panic that they'd miss the vital information she'd turned up to tell them, she was struggling to stay calm.

'Excuse me?' Oren's head lifted slowly, as if her statement was a personal slight.

She swallowed. When she opened her mouth nothing came out. She cleared her throat and tried again. 'I didn't realize, at first. I thought . . . because Lucy was . . . the blood . . .' She took a deep breath. Saliva was welling under her tongue again, like the moments before vomit rises up your throat. She could barely say the words. 'There was silver in that room.'

It was the only thing werewolves feared: had such a detrimental effect it was banned entirely from Downside. The times she hadn't been able to dodge shaking hands with someone Upside wearing silver rings, she'd come away with blistering burns across her fingers. Werewolves knew. Knew what was silver, and avoided it.

A beat of silence.

Then Roderick rolled his eyes, ready to dismiss her again.

But Oren leant forward, frowning. 'What do you mean?'

Roderick stared at his arcānas, aghast that he was even entertaining her.

She looked between them, pretty aghast herself. Took another deep breath.

'I can't walk within a few metres of a jewellery store Upside without feeling the effects.' She had this one chance; she had to make them listen. 'The second I walked into that room the air felt so thick I could barely breathe. I was in shock. I didn't realize what I was feeling right away. It must've been . . . tiny . . .' She frowned. She hadn't quite figured it out herself yet, but she knew she was right. 'But every werewolf knows how it feels. The breathlessness. The dizziness. It's different. I'm telling you. Whoever killed her knew what she was and used silver to do it. They weren't human.'

'Bullshit.' Roderick waved a hand impatiently, as if he could wave her out of his office entirely. 'The room was a bloodbath. You saw that as well, right?'

'It could've been used to slow her down,' she argued. 'Stop her protecting herself—'

'Stop, Sage!'

'No!' she yelled.

And she knew at last she'd gone too far. His expression was clear: there wasn't anything she could say to convince him otherwise.

She looked down at her feet. 'I just . . . wanted someone to know.'

The tears she'd been keeping at bay were at danger point, ready to spill down her cheeks before she could hide them.

She turned for the door.

As her hand felt the cold metal of the door handle, Oren answered. 'I'll take the case.'

'What?'

She whirled, sure it'd be some fresh joke at her expense. But . . . no. He didn't look happy about it. And he wasn't even looking at her. 'I told you something felt off, Roderick.'

'I can help,' she blurted. 'I can—'

'Oh, no.' Oren was laughing that cruel laugh again. 'I don't think so.'

She looked at Roderick. 'Call it a practice run.' She could feel herself starting to plead again. 'She was my friend. If I get anywhere, if I help to solve it, surely I'm worth a trial period—'

'*If I help solve it,*' Oren said with a sarcastic laugh.

But Roderick's eyes narrowed.

'Fine.' He looked between them. 'You want to take this case, Oren.' He smirked. 'She's given you your only "lead". And the gods know she won't leave it alone until she tries to solve this case. She can partner you. Let me know how you get on,' he finished with an air of dismissal.

Oren held up a finger. 'We have a deal, Roderick. I work alone.'

'Deal's off.'

'I don't think so.'

'I think so, unless—'

'Be very careful,' Oren let out a hiss so fierce that Roderick stopped talking, 'what threats you make.'

Something had slipped between them that she'd missed. But the sound of the warning made her stomach squirm. Her eyes flickered between them.

'Wait outside, Sage. He'll be with you in a minute.'

She almost choked on thin air. '. . . For real?'

'For real.' His smile didn't reach his eyes as he glared at Oren.

Not daring to stay and risk what she'd just gained, she ran from the room.

She didn't even try to eavesdrop. Didn't want to know what furious discussion was happening behind that door. Her heart was beating like she'd just run five times around the city. She'd . . . She'd got the chance! She could've screamed! If the lifeless face of her old friend wasn't still burnt into her eyelids.

Then the door flew open and Oren was there, his expression so furious that her excitement evaporated at once. As he slammed the door she saw a fleeting glimpse of Roderick's smile as he turned back to the papers on his desk.

'Um,' she said quietly, her face burning again. She'd . . . well, she didn't know what she'd expected. She hadn't expected Roderick to cave.

Her entire body cringed.

'Just . . .' He shook his head, and she could see his teeth clenching behind his jaw. 'Follow me.'

She managed to nod. He strode off down the long corridor, two warlocks practically flattening themselves against the wall to avoid his warpath.

Out in the pristine courtyard, he rounded on her again. She was trying to work out what to say. How to apologize.

But without waiting or warning he reached out a hand again. She flinched, memories of a dagger exploding from that hand the last time it came near her.

The flicker in his eye was resentful. 'I'm not going to hurt you.'

Though his expression suggested he hadn't quite decided.

The hand barely touched her before she was dragged into bone-crushing darkness.

5

SAGE

She almost lost her balance entirely.

Her feet touched the ground almost as soon as it'd shifted under her. They weren't outside the headquarters any more.

Oh, God, they were outside Lucy's apartment, and it still reeked of werewolf blood.

This time it wasn't even fresh. Just . . . dusty. Dry. It made the back of her throat itch.

'What the hell was *that*?'

'Shifting.' He looked unaffected by the insanity of breaking all laws of time and physics.

She cleared her throat. 'I didn't realize that was a thing for warlocks.'

'It isn't,' he said. 'For most warlocks.'

'But it is for you?'

He almost imperceptibly rolled his eyes. 'I'm very powerful.'

Of course he was.

She tried to be nonchalant about his kind of warlock

magic, but it wasn't seen often. So much of Downside possessed their own kinds of magic and used it openly and in ways that made everybody's lives easier. A table wiping itself down in a cafe. A dustpan and brush sweeping a floor by itself. But this magic set her teeth on edge with apprehension.

Criss-crossed across the door was police tape branded DO NOT ENTER over yellow and black stripes. Sage swallowed.

'Why are we here?'

'How well did you really know her?'

'Not well,' she admitted. She knew he was watching her reaction. 'Not any more.'

'Will you be able to go back in?'

Go back in? She blinked.

Oh, shit.

He was actually doing this . . . He was taking her back in there?

Well, she'd learnt to cut herself off from the things that caused her pain. It had been the only way she'd managed to survive.

'I'll be fine.'

It was only half a lie.

He nodded, waving a hand as the tape loosened itself from the door frame and the door lock clicked itself open.

She paused just inside the lounge, looking again at that rug covered in blood. This time without Lucy's body. Taken away by the humans who'd thought they'd found her first. There were little numbered stickers where the forensics team had photographed what they considered evidence.

And there it was again. Instant nausea and dizziness. In a sadistic kinda way, she could've burst out whooping.

She'd been right. It was only faint. She almost couldn't believe it . . . A pair of silver earrings could have her keeling over, so how was she still standing? What exactly was it?

She looked over the blood-sprayed walls.

Shut it down. Block it out. Just a victim. A stranger.

'All right, then.' Oren strode to the centre of the room, holding out his arms like they were about to play a game. 'You wanted to join the Arcānum. Assess this crime scene. I estimate death around three to three-fifteen FYI, and you'd turned up by four.' He was watching her with a cold expression. She'd wanted this chance for so long, this one opportunity to try. 'Shall I start you off?'

'No.' She held her breath and stepped into the room. 'So, she lay here.'

'Oh, well done.'

She gritted her teeth. The worst part was that she didn't entirely blame him. 'Look, I'm sorry, all right? I didn't mean for . . . this outcome.'

'It's a bit late for that now, isn't it? I'm stuck with you.'

'That's your own fault.' The scorn made her embarrassment go nuclear. 'If you've given Roderick a reason to blackmail you, that was stupid! I get this situation isn't ideal, but not once have I mentioned that bullshit stunt you pulled with the dagger yesterday, when I have every right to be pissed off too. Yet I'm still able to be civil . . .'

Her voice trailed off. The expression from when he'd stepped out of Roderick's office was back but . . . worse.

'Let me be clear,' he said softly. Shit . . . were his teeth elongating? Only slightly, but, yep . . . they were definitely fangs! And she realized: he had a monster hidden inside, just as she did. 'Roderick is a grade-A bastard and he's fed up of you. It's the only reason I'm putting up with this charade. Seeing his face if you earn yourself a trial period on his watch will make my decade. But I work alone for reasons you evidently don't comprehend.' His face was close to hers again. 'You wouldn't speak to me like that if you did. This is my only warning to you.'

She had no idea what any of that meant. Her heart was pounding again. A mixture of anger and anxiety. Because he was right. This was a charade. And who was she kidding? She was so out of her depth.

But if she walked away she knew Lucy would just become another case file. Another number. Who she was, what she'd been when she lived . . . it'd all disappear with the future she should've had.

Sage wouldn't allow it.

She couldn't.

She swallowed and said evenly, 'Wolves are pack animals.' The only explanation she supposed she could give. That he might prefer doing things alone, but solitary life just wasn't in her nature, in her blood. He might not want her offer of help, but it was a request for . . . tolerance. Peace for now.

He was silent for a moment.

And then he sneered in her face. 'Pack mentality isn't a strength, Sage. It's a weakness. You embarrass yourself.'

She hated him. He was a bastard.

But she refused to let a single tear fall. So she lifted her chin, turned her back on him, and circled the room.

She breathed slowly, forcing herself not to be overcome by the dizziness clouding her brain, but allowing it to guide her.

She wandered around the room. Around the sofa, past the coffee table, its surfaces and a mug, empty but for the last few dregs, covered in a thin layer of dust – part of the human police force's hunt for prints. On a shelf above a TV, plastic flowers with a thin coating of dust sat on either end, alongside a few candles, and a framed black-and-white photograph of a young couple that were now probably ancient. Grandparents, maybe. She looked down at the TV stand, the remote control discarded at an angle where Lucy had last thrown it, never expecting that she wouldn't use it again. She wasn't sure why it struck her, that remote control, but it made her chest tighten. If she knew she was living out the last afternoon of her life, would she take more care with how she left her possessions? She wasn't sure.

She pushed down the nausea and dizziness as she moved into the kitchen and opened the cupboard doors. Basics. And the same with the fridge.

Hm.

Oren was still, arms folded. Waiting. The fangs were gone and his expression was schooled back to impassive.

She checked the bathroom and bedroom, poking her head through each doorway and taking a deep breath.

Nothing.

'It's in here.' She forced herself not to shudder as she came to a stop in the living room again. 'The silver.'

He looked around. 'You're certain?'

'You . . . can't sense it?' she asked, confused. 'I thought I was just confirming something you suspected?'

He shook his head. 'I can't sense silver at all.'

'But you said something was off—'

'What else can you smell?'

'Nothing. Well, except for werewolf, warlock and blood. That's us accounted for. But . . .' Her eyes went wide.

He nodded. 'No scent of a human attacker. That's what bothered me. It just wasn't enough for Roderick to class this as a supernatural case.'

'But how's that possible?'

'There are ways to conceal scent with magic.'

'You're saying the killer must've been magic? Supernatural?'

He shrugged. 'Technically the killer only needs a magical

accomplice. But magic is involved somewhere. Therefore I guarantee the humans won't find a single trace of DNA either.'

She stared at him as the reality crashed down. An impossible task. 'Your magic could probably kill me without making all this mess too, right?'

He didn't answer.

All the possibilities ran through her mind. She voiced some of them out loud, trying to make sense of it all.

'Even a necklace' – she edged into the corners of the room, monitoring her body's physical reaction – 'would be enough to . . . knock her out . . . smother her.'

She frowned. She just couldn't figure—

Her eyes fell on the mug on the table.

Oh, God.

She let out a faint sound, hand coming to her throat. 'It can't . . .'

'What?' Oren's head snapped towards her. 'What is it?'

But she was already heaving, a hand over her mouth as she spun away.

Lucy wouldn't have ingested it knowingly. She just wouldn't.

'The mug,' she rasped. 'In the coffee.' The thought of it inside her, going down her throat, burning at her insides. She felt like she was going to faint, be sick everywhere and then fall to the floor and die.

Then Oren was there, holding a bucket she'd never seen

before, magicked out of thin air and shoved in her face as vomit exploded from her mouth. She grabbed the bucket as she sank to her knees.

The images raced through her mind of the moment Lucy must've realized she'd somehow ingested silver. Her heart hurt, her head hurt, her stomach and her throat. Those last moments as she lay dying in agony, for her killer to then slit her throat?

She could see Oren from the corner of her eye sniffing the mug. Then in a puff of gold mist, the mug, and its contents, disappeared entirely. Instantly, the nausea subsided.

She wiped her mouth, and the bucket in her hands disappeared too.

She expected to see some cruel amusement on his face, but even Oren looked grim as he stared down at her.

'I'm guessing it was used to stop her transforming,' she said quietly. 'The silver alone was enough to kill her.'

He nodded slowly. 'So why make the mess?' His eyes moved across the bloody room again, and he frowned.

'Silver to debilitate, and magic to conceal evidence, but neither used to make a clean kill. To kill a werewolf,' she said slowly, more to herself than Oren, 'which could easily be passed off as a human crime . . . None of it makes sense. Unless . . . the killer wanted this murder to stand out.' She looked up at him. 'She's not . . . the target.'

At last there was a ghost of a smile on his lips. 'Go on?'

'She's a message. A warning. But for who?'

6

SAGE

Sage ordered a cider and took the bottle of Rattler to the corner her quiz team usually took over every Friday evening.

There was a loud but friendly argument raging across the room regarding the fairness of the fairy in their company using their wings to get a better height and angle on the dartboard.

Usually Sage would've laughed. She didn't think it was fair at all. But she stared quietly at the bubbles in her bottle instead, distracted. Her mind raced. The silver in Lucy's coffee: the killer must've used magic to stop her sensing it. It must've been a matter of grains, less than the tip of a teaspoon of sugar. But enough to kill her.

The pain.

The burning.

She wiped a tear from her cheek. She still felt sick.

'Y'OK, love?' Elaine, the landlady, asked. Behind the bar she just looked like any middle-aged woman: greying roots and glasses. It was only as she stepped around the bar and revealed her goat legs that you realized: of course all the staff in the Faun's Head were fauns. She gave a sad, pitying smile. 'We heard about that young werewolf, Upside.'

It wasn't a question, exactly, just acknowledgement that she understood.

Sage didn't know what to say. If she opened her mouth she'd cry.

As if to save her, something pearlescent and slightly fluid rushed in. Elaine sighed and backed away, the sound of her hooves tapping gently on the stone floor, perhaps relieved that someone had arrived to keep her company.

P's face was slightly wild.

'Did you find it?'

P nodded. 'Sage—'

'Wait.' She held up a hand. She knew she'd have to tell Oren.

Leaving Lucy's apartment, he'd muttered about autopsy reports, because Roderick would refuse to accept silver in the coffee on her word alone, although he said he had also sent the mug contents to be properly tested. He'd sworn under his breath at the prospect of having to get a human report. And when she'd asked if Roderick had contacts, he'd admitted he did, but it could take some time.

She hadn't dared suggest it to his face, she wasn't sure how he'd react to . . . less legitimate methods. But the moment they'd stepped foot back into Downside, and he'd stomped away, she'd flicked open her own phone and called the one person who might be able to find what they needed without being detected.

And P had pulled it off perfectly.

Sage grimaced as she scrolled for the new contact he'd saved into her phone.

'This is insane,' P whispered. But her wide eyes had turned bright too. 'I can't believe it, Sage, this is your chance, at last—'

'Don't hold your breath,' Sage sighed and held her phone to her ear.

'What?' He didn't even say hello.

Rude.

'Don't go mad—'

'I thought you were at the pub . . .' She wasn't sure how it sounded like a threat, but it felt like one.

'I am. But I asked my housemate to go Upside . . . find the autopsy report. Anyway, I'm going to put you on speaker—'

'No need.' A familiar voice made them both jump.

She whipped around to see the warlock beside her. He looked thoroughly irritated.

P let out a small, shocked squeak. And the whole room stilled.

She hadn't known shifting existed until that afternoon, so she understood that not many Downsiders would be used to seeing a warlock fabricate in the middle of the room.

'You live with a ghost?' he said, looking at P.

She gestured to a chair, trying not to look too much like she was pleading. The room was staring. 'This is P. She doesn't need a bedroom so we keep each other company at reduced rent. And she cooks. We're all winners.'

'Cooks?'

'Poltergeist,' P said brightly, although Sage could tell her friend was forcing it. The only explanation for how a ghost could touch anything.

His eyes dropped down to the bloodied clothes that were proof the accident that had killed her had been particularly traumatic. 'Ah.' He nodded. 'Unresting soul. Makes sense.'

P looked at her with a 'this guy is an arsehole' expression. Sage wholeheartedly agreed.

'You live alone?' P asked coldly.

'I prefer to do everything alone.' He gave Sage a pointed look, but took the chair. The room's buzz returned. 'Roderick's put Sage with me to ensure she finally quits.' No mention of the blackmail, she noticed.

'You'll make her quit just to prove a point?' P's indignation saw her rise almost half a metre off her own seat.

He rolled his eyes. 'I'll find that killer with or without Sage's help, it's up to her if she stays around.' P opened her mouth to retort. 'What's "P" short for? Poltergeist?'

'Patricia,' she grumbled, deflating. 'After my grandmother.'

'Patricia is awful.'

Arsehole, indeed.

'What did you find Upside, P?' Sage cut in.

P's expression changed at once.

'They did the autopsy early this morning,' she said quietly. 'They were discussing it when I got there. I went into the office and looked through the notes while they were in the meeting room. It's there. The pathologist has noted it in her stomach and kidneys. There's a rare condition called argyria which is a bodily reaction to prolonged exposure to silver. In humans it happens slowly. But they don't know how werewolves react to it so must've assumed it wasn't relevant to her death . . .' She shook her head. 'The point is, you were right, Sage. She ingested the silver before she died. That would've killed her without . . . everything else.'

She sighed a breath of . . . not relief, but she was grateful for the extra confirmation.

Her stomach churned again.

'I can go back tonight,' P added. 'Once the station is empty. Take copies of everything.'

Sage looked at Oren. She could tell he was trying not to look pleased. The knot in her chest loosened slightly. 'So . . . not in trouble?'

'If you hadn't pulled this off, you'd be in immense trouble, Sage.' He scowled at her. 'Don't do it again without telling me first.'

She smiled.

He didn't smile back.

Beyond him, the door opened and Harland strode in, unwrapping the badly knitted scarf – one of P's latest fad hobbies – from around his neck.

His face was bright, and he gave Elaine a thumbs up as she held up a bottle of his usual dark liquor: Wolfsky whisky.

'Upside won't rest until we all freeze to death.' He shook off his coat to reveal a lime-green hoodie, some manga character branded across it. 'It's started snowing up there—'

He spotted Oren, and froze.

Harland attended a human university Upside, then on weekends he told his human friends he was going back down south to visit family, and stayed Downside with them. He was eighteen and also a werewolf, but with his soft baby face, he passed for younger. All their male friends were like this – tall and gangly, full of teenage spots and long limbs they'd grown into far too fast to have worked out how to move them smoothly yet. Compared to Oren – well, he made them look like boys. Nervously Harland pushed his glasses up with a finger. Sage knew someone like Oren would be obliterating whatever tiny specks of confidence he had.

'I'm leaving.' Oren stood, looking at Harland's outfit with no attempt to disguise his disgust. 'Be at the Arcānum headquarters tomorrow for nine sharp. I don't like being kept waiting.'

'It's Saturday,' P said, taken aback.

Oren looked blank. 'I don't care.'

Without another word, he disappeared out into the night. At least it was a normal exit, this time.

Harland stared at them. 'What have you done?'

7

SAGE

She flinched. Was a second person accusing her of killing Lucy?

'What do you mean?' Sage demanded. 'Just because an arcānas was here doesn't mean I've done anything wrong.'

He looked at her like she was an idiot. 'You do know who that is?'

She looked at P, who shrugged.

'Oren Rinallis?' He pointed at the door. 'As in, the *Rinallis family*?'

P still looked blank. But it'd stirred something in Sage. Some distant memory of a history class from Downside high school.

'Remind me,' she said slowly.

Harland swung his rucksack under their table and sat in Oren's seat. 'His family is only important on the other side of the world. He's the rebellious one. He's the one that left home, or maybe they kicked him out. Who knows? But, Sage, they say he's an assassin!'

She blinked, and waited. But his earnest expression

didn't falter. She started to laugh. 'Harland,' she said. 'He's got an attitude problem and a big ego but—'

He shook his head vehemently, pushing his glasses up. 'That story a few weeks back. The witch coven in Ireland?'

Actually, that was quite bad. It was on the front pages of *Downside Daily* for at least a week.

Thirteen witches, all killed. A whole coven wiped out. The piece had hinted the punishment fit the crimes, but still . . .

She swallowed. 'Ireland has their own branch of Arcānum.'

'Someone was sent from England to deal with it. That's what I heard.'

'That doesn't mean it was him, Harland.' P was trying not to look too sceptical, since Harland embarrassed easily.

'That famous case of a chupacabra pack that ran riot killing human livestock? It was Rinallis who tracked them all down. That's literally in textbooks. And he killed half a wolf pack in Scotland *single-handedly* about ten years—'

'How do you know all this?'

'I study history,' he reminded her sheepishly. 'And . . .' He paused, and his cheeks really did go puce, like he knew he was about to get laughed at again. 'You know what they say.'

This time it was P who snorted. They'd heard him pitch this theory too many times. 'The Cariva isn't real, Harland. Everyone knows that.'

He blustered. 'We don't know that! That's the point of secret societies!'

'The Cariva isn't a secret society, it doesn't exist. It's a story to scare kids into behaving.'

A collection of the worst warlocks that ever existed. She supposed Harland had interpreted that as assassins. Oren was many things, but an assassin? Nah.

He wouldn't want to mess up his hair.

Harland looked unconvinced. But the shrug of his shoulders was defeatist. 'So why was he here?'

Sage told him everything. About how she'd met Oren. About what had happened to Lucy. Seeing her there, on the floor.

'Oh, Sage.' He hurried to put his drink down.

'It's fine,' she said quickly, shaking off his hug. 'Don't worry about it.'

She really liked Harland, but as a friend, and he was so desperate for any girl to notice him that as soon as one did, she got the feeling he'd never let go.

'So does he know who did it?' he asked.

She shook her head and picked up her phone. She'd snapped a quick shot of that footprint in the blood before they'd left, the only link to Lucy's killer they had.

P took the phone from her and frowned down at the little screen.

'Ergh, no.' Harland leant in to take a look too, then jolted, hand over his mouth. He heaved as if he might be sick. 'Blood . . . makes me feel funny.'

P handed Sage's phone back over just as the door opened again and the rest of their friends walked in.

Cypress, a kelpie, came first, shaking her long dark hair, the colour of her mane when she transformed into her truest form: a water horse. And not far behind her was Rhen. A selkie in Downside was a cruel irony. He looked as human as she or Harland, except for when splashes of water got on his skin and he started to turn into a seal. Which meant he couldn't often go Upside – to a city where it rained more than half the year.

But she only had eyes for Danny. Tall and as gangly and spotty as Harland, his face was pale and drawn, with slightly-too-long hair framing his face. She'd known him longest, had lived with him in the werewolf orphanage where she'd met Lucy, and he had known her too. She barely even noticed Juniper and Willow trotting in on their golden lion legs. When Danny looked at her his eyes turned watery, and hers did too.

She rose for him, holding her arms out. Their embrace was long and silent, but it said everything that needed to be said. When she pulled back, all of their friends were waiting for them, not wanting to interrupt the unspoken words. Elaine appeared with a tray full of drinks none of them had ordered.

'A toast,' she offered. 'On us. For friends lost.'

Sage mouthed the *thank you* she couldn't bring herself

to say out loud.

The landlady nodded and left them.

Harland gestured for Rhen and Cypress to take their glasses, moving the two with straws in front of the sphinxes, and even P had been afforded her own empty glass to raise. Sage and Danny accepted the glasses Harland held out to them.

Harland raised his own glass, realizing without needing to be told that he was the only werewolf there that could manage speech. 'To friends lost,' he said, and the rest of them followed.

'To friends lost.'

As Sage moved the glass to her lips, she paused. 'To Lucy,' she whispered before she sipped.

She heard Danny whisper it back beside her.

8

OREN

He stood in front of the obnoxious gold fountain that loomed over the courtyard outside Arcānum headquarters and waited for her.

He couldn't believe he was still playing along with this bullshit.

She had five minutes before she was late, and he was hoping she was so he could leave without her.

He'd almost gone back and had it out with Roderick, demanded someone else take the girl on but . . .

His blood still boiled at those subtle threats his captain had muttered as she'd fled that office. One day, before he left the city for good, he'd end Roderick's ability to sneer. And breathe. And exist. Yet, as furious as he was about the whole situation, it was nothing compared to what Roderick would feel if he was forced to give the girl a job at the end of this case. He'd consider that decent payback for now.

He'd have to control his temper today, but he knew it was showing on his face. He'd glared at the pukwudgie outside his joke shop on the high street so darkly, daring him to even *try* shifting along in front of him, and the bent little man had blanched. He'd felt a pang of satisfaction for it too.

Then he saw her, hurrying up the street towards him, and forced the grumble back down his throat.

Her dark hair was tied in a ponytail that bobbed as she moved, her brow furrowed in concentration and determination.

That instantly irked him.

He hadn't wanted to admit he was impressed with that little stunt the poltergeist played last night. That'd irked him too.

'Where have you been?' he demanded.

She had the audacity to glance pointedly at the old clock face on the front of a nearby building. 'It's two minutes to nine. I'm technically early.'

'And you are technically annoying. Did the poltergeist get the full report?'

She nodded, raising her shoulder that carried a rucksack. Her cheeks were pink, and he could see the smallest speckles of sweat on her nose from rushing to get there in time.

'I have another Upside job for her,' he said brusquely. He resented asking for help. But it would make this whole painful experience so much quicker.

The girl blinked. 'Um . . . You're sure?'

'Would I say it if I wasn't?' She was clearly biting back a

retort as her jaw locked. He didn't care. 'You said Lucy was a journalist?'

'You want P to go to her office Upside?'

He nodded. 'The humans will have been all over it yesterday. But it's the weekend, so it should be quiet. It'll be harder for us to turn up and repeat all the same questions without arousing suspicion. Whatever she was working on that could've pissed people off. Bought her some enemies, perhaps. Sources, clients, informants. Just whatever she can find. We have to start somewhere. Tell her to come here, after.'

She nodded and called her dead housemate. What a weird little set-up that was, huh?

He watched her relay the orders down the line, and heard P's voice call him something unsavoury.

'Did you know warlocks can hear almost as well as were-wolves,' he said loudly.

'What's he gonna do? Lock me in a prison cell I can walk out of?' P scoffed. 'I'll see what I can find. But just so we're clear. I'm going for you, Sage, not him.' And she cut the call. Sage knew he'd heard, and she clearly didn't know what to do with her face.

'Soooo . . .' She drew the word out awkwardly. 'Where are we going today?'

'The Arcānum archives.'

'What archives? What's in them?'

He could barely contain his impatience.

'The Arcānum holds files on every single supernatural occupant of the city – Upside and Down. We're lucky that Lucy lived Upside. We make a point of gathering as much information on those werewolves as possible. Helpful, in cases like these, at least.'

From the look on her face, and the way she flinched, she'd evidently had no idea that level of surveillance took place.

'We can't leave supernaturals loose Upside without some idea of what they're up to.' He shrugged. 'What did you expect?'

He wasn't that interested in her answer. 'Follow me.'

She trailed him around the fountain and back towards the large doors into the Arcānum headquarters.

'We lost, last night,' she said. 'The pub quiz.'

The conversational tone was forced. She was trying to gauge how receptive he was going to be to her presence today. As if he might've changed his mind about wanting her there overnight. Ha. He couldn't stop the sneer curling his lips as he glanced back. Her cheeks pink from the cold were now red.

He felt embarrassed for her.

'I don't care.'

'I won't bother inviting you to the next one,' she muttered.

'Good.' He snorted as he pulled open the tall wooden doors and stood back to let her pass through. 'I've heard you werewolves have your little groups. Like miniature packs that socialize together, into films and reading or whatever. Quiz nights, apparently.'

It was pathetic. The thought of all the faux enjoyment and laughter. Drunk teenagers were not funny.

He led her through the wide entrance hall without waiting to check that she was following.

'A book club is hardly anything to laugh at,' she snapped. Despite the fact it was astonishing she even dared to snap at him, he realized he liked it when she did. It was a sign he was getting under her skin. Some small retribution for managing to force herself on him. 'And it isn't just were-wolves. I know for a fact the hydras also have a book club on the other side of town and I also know that the witches hold a bi-weekly gardening club. I think you'll find it's just called having friends.'

'Sage, that gardening club is a cover to grow illegal herbs for potions.'

Another glance over his shoulder and he could tell from her face that she did know that, actually. But she hadn't realized he did.

'If you know, why don't the Arcānum stop them?'

'We will if they start hurting anyone.' He shrugged. 'At the moment they're brewing potions that get people high and selling them as headache tonics. They're not addictive. If they were poisoning people, we'd step in.'

'Sorry?!' she said incredulously, her echoing footsteps faltering on the marble as she almost paused where she walked. 'You know that the witches are running an underground drugs cartel and you're simply monitoring the situation?'

He pulled an impassive expression, gesturing with a hand for her to keep moving. 'It's a lot of effort to go to when they're not harming anyone.'

She looked aghast.

He almost laughed as he veered left through a long corridor that sloped downwards. There were a few doors, but not as many as in the brightly lit corridors above. This corridor hadn't been granted the privilege of modernization like the rest of the headquarters.

The sounds of grunting and yells came from behind one door and he couldn't resist a glance at her alarmed expression. She was so out of her depth it was painful. If he took her into those training rooms, she'd be crying in minutes.

He passed through another set of double doors into the archives. Nobody sat at the tables reviewing files, and the room was empty. Good. He wasn't in the mood for skittish warlocks and awkward glances this early in the morning.

The air here felt old. The dust that hung in it was heavy. Would be heavy even for a human; was heavy for him, never mind her werewolf senses. He could taste the texture of the thick, ancient papers at the back, and the leather of centuries-old ledgers. He wondered what the air tasted like for her.

He set off deeper into the archives, past rows of book-cases and shelves, stuffed with boxes of whatever-the-hell else, and scrolls of yellowing parchment.

His eyesight was keen, but he couldn't see in the dark. He squinted down the long stacks, lit by dim lamps on the walls. He would usually light a ball of magic to help him on his way but . . . he frowned. He felt it made him look inferior. Her werewolf sight meant she could see perfectly well even in pitch-darkness.

'I sent the coffee mug to Forensics . . .' he said as they walked. 'His office is at the end of the archives.'

'Great,' she said with sarcastic brightness as not one, but two closed doors came into view. 'More charming warlocks.'

'Oh, this one's an exception to all the rules,' he said. 'You'll like him way more than me.'

9

SAGE

'**D**amn, Oren!' a voice cackled.

Sage followed him into a surprisingly light office to find a warlock with cropped white hair and completely white eyes lounging on a navy velvet chaise longue. He wore a red corduroy suit and if that didn't already tell her enough about his extravagant personality, the ruffled collar of his silk shirt did.

'So it is true!' He stood to greet them. 'Word spread like wildfire but I didn't believe it. What did you do to piss Roderick off this week?'

'Told him he should give her a chance.'

He started to laugh. 'Right . . . oh?' He realized that Oren wasn't being sarcastic. He looked between them. 'Seriously?'

'She argued her case well, what can I say? This is Sage. Sage, meet Berion.' He gestured half-heartedly. 'I didn't expect he'd give her to me, but here we are.'

'Sage?'

'That's me.' She tried not to look too awkward.

'Hm.' He strolled over to another piece of velvet

furniture, this time an indulgent, salmon-coloured chair in the shape of a scalloped shell that sat in front of a shelf laden with delicate and expensive-looking trinkets. He shook off his suit jacket and threw it over the back. He twiddled one of the rings on his heavily bejewelled fingers as he assessed the novelty werewolf. 'You could've come off far worse.'

Her face exploded with heat.

But a broad grin split Berion's face. 'Darling.' He leant forward, waving a hand. 'I'm only playing, that was to embarrass him, not you. Don't look so afraid!'

'Leave it out, Berion.'

Berion tutted, like Oren was spoiling his fun. 'So, how's it going?'

'You tell me,' Oren said.

Berion looked between them for a moment . . . or so she thought. Without any colour to his eyes, she wasn't sure when he was looking directly at her at all. Then he smiled and gestured towards another door in the back corner of the room.

'Sage, darling,' he gushed as he steered her forward, ignoring Oren entirely. 'Welcome.' He pushed open the door and a light flickered on by itself. 'My domain.'

The room was double the size of his already spacious office and looked exactly how she supposed a human laboratory should look. Except that among the rows and rows of bottles on thin shelves covering one wall, supernatural ingredients were mixed in with the human. Unicorn hair next to formaldehyde. Basilisk venom next to sodium chloride. Against another wall was a worktop with what looked like, well, miniature cauldrons. She could hear them bubbling away, bright-coloured splashes occasionally flicking over the sides, though there was no flame lit under them.

'What is all this?' she asked, gazing around the room. She stopped at the island in the centre of the room and looked over the various clear bags filled with random items and tagged with details of what was inside.

'I will have you know,' Berion gave a dark liquid in one of the cauldrons a stir with a spoon that hadn't been in his hands a moment ago, 'that before Oren arrived in Downside, my partner Hozier and I were Roderick's best agents.' He smiled at her again. The glint in his white eyes was cheeky. 'But I have other talents too.' He gestured towards his potions. 'I'm quite good at finding the evidence the rest of them are too impatient to work on themselves. So they send it to me.' He leant across the cauldron counter. 'That's how I ended up with this.' He held up Lucy's mug in a clear ziplock, and beside it, a small plastic screw-lid vial containing what looked to be the last few drops of coffee left in the bottom of the mug. 'It was you who suspected the silver in the mug, is that correct?'

She nodded.

He looked at her for a moment, and he had the grace to

look sympathetic. 'You were right. I just about managed to distil the tiny amount of coffee left in the bottom of the mug and was able to separate all the components. Your senses are especially keen, even for a werewolf. It's infinitesimal. It wouldn't have been difficult to block your victim from sensing it, with even quite weak magic.'

She stared at the bag in his hand. Then back at him.

He nodded. 'I'm barely using any effort at all.'

She hadn't realized she didn't feel nauseous at all until he said it. He slid a piece of paper on the island across the top towards her with the tips of his fingers. Handwritten notes in tidy, cursive lettering, confirming that there were traces of powdered silver in the coffee sample he tested. Signed off with the date and Berion's signature in the corner.

She looked back at Oren standing in the doorway, leaning with his arms folded against the frame. 'Will it be enough for Roderick to believe me now?'

Berion laughed. 'Tell Roderick to come to me if it isn't.'

She smiled at him. She was so relieved he wasn't like Oren. She didn't think she could handle two.

He put the coffee mug down and ushered them back into his more comfortable office.

'So you don't work cases any more?' she asked as Berion closed the door on his lab and headed back to his scalloped chair to retrieve his jacket.

'Oh, we do,' he shrugged. 'Sometimes. When Oren is

away and Roderick is desperate, but,' he let out an over-dramatic sigh as he straightened the lapels, 'I'm far too expensive to keep getting my clothes dirty.'

She grinned at him.

And then the office door burst open without a knock.

'They didn't have any of the yum-yums, so I got— Oh, sorry.' The small female warlock with red hair and two coffees in one hand, and a bag of what smelt like cinnamon buns in the other, paused in the doorway. She flinched almost imperceptibly as her dark eyes fell on Oren.

'This is Hozier, my partner,' Berion said. 'She controls the archives out there while I control the evidence in here. Her office is next door, if you ever need anything.'

'I heard there was a werewolf in the building,' she grinned in a conspiratorial whisper. Her accent, though subtler than Oren's, gave her a faint air of mystery. 'You're causing quite the stir.'

Sage felt her cheeks reddening again.

'Hozier gets the notification when a supernatural dies Upside,' Berion told her with a pointed tut at Oren, who clearly wasn't going to bother to explain.

'Notification?'

'When a Downsider, like your victim, goes to live Upside, they have to inform us.' Hozier put the coffees down on a little table beside a chaise longue. She was tiny. Barely taller than a ten-year-old, and there was something in the way she styled her eyes with black liner that made

~60~

Sage think of Egyptian pharaoh queens. 'A trigger spell is cast on their life force, so, in situations like this, should they die, it gives us a warning. Just enough time to make sure there's nothing to give away supernatural secrets.'

She'd . . . had no idea. She didn't know why she would know that . . . it made sense? She didn't know why everything kept surprising her.

Perhaps she'd just underestimated the work that actually went into keeping the order in their city.

'Time to go,' Oren said bluntly.

'We'll all be at the Warlock's Cloak for a few drinks tonight, Oren, if you fancy it,' Berion called after them as they stepped back out into the archives beyond.

'When do I ever fancy it?'

Berion sighed as if he'd expected nothing less. She wondered how many decades he'd been offering. 'Don't be a stranger, Sage.'

Oren shut his office door before she could reply.

'I liked him.' She nodded. 'I see what you mean, you and Roderick are just bad examples of warlocks after all.'

IO

SAGE

He didn't answer as she trailed him back down the long aisle of bookcases, back towards the filing cabinets at the front of the archives.

'Wait by the tables. I'll find Lucy's file.'

She nodded, rounding the last cabinet to see that this time, they weren't alone. A female warlock sat at one table, blue hair tied back in a plait, and a pair, two males, sat at another. All of them looked up.

The blue-haired woman rose at once, gathered her files, and left.

The other two, one with red eyes and the other with what looked like a birthmark covering half his face, watched as Oren turned and headed off to find whatever cabinet held Lucy's files.

'We'll go.' One of the warlocks rose.

She held up her hands, surprised. 'It's fine, we're—'

But he shook his head. 'We'll go.'

The door was barely swinging closed behind their retreating backs when Oren reappeared with a brown folder tucked under his arm, apparently oblivious to the fact his presence had just emptied the room as he picked at lint on his sleeve.

'What was that?' Sage asked.

The look he gave her said he was absolutely aware. That she should've been paying more attention.

'My reputation precedes me.' He threw the folder on to one of the abandoned tables, and a duplicate appeared on top of it for her. 'For some more than others. Clearly.'

She stared at him as he sat down and pushed her file towards her.

Oh.

The hairs on the back of her arms started to prickle inside her jumper again.

But she took her seat, painfully aware that they were alone in the archive, and said nothing.

She took the autopsy report P had retrieved from her backpack and held it out. He received it without thanks and flicked that open too.

'Tell me about her,' he said, glancing up from the notes.

She straightened. She'd forgotten he still wanted to interview her.

'She was a journalist for an Upside paper. *Manchester Evening News*. Last I heard, she volunteered at two different soup kitchens on alternating weekends and helped out with kids' clubs through her local church in school holidays.'

'Nothing to indicate she had any enemies?'

She shook her head. 'The opposite. She did as much to help the community as she could.' It hurt in her chest to talk about Lucy in the past tense. It still didn't feel real. 'I can't see how she could have made any enemies at all.'

'Scorned lover?'

'She was single.'

Oren pulled a face. 'It says in this file that her last boyfriend, human, left to work overseas a few months ago.' She tried to ignore the squirm in her stomach as she realized this was information she hadn't known. That Lucy had chosen not to tell her. 'Ended amicably by all accounts.'

'I didn't know she had a boyfriend,' she said quietly.

He glanced up at her again, but said nothing. His brow furrowed, he leant back in his chair and rubbed a hand absently over his chin as he contemplated.

Instead, she decided to broach the unanswered questions she had. 'Hozier . . .'

'What about her?'

'And the warlocks that were here when we came back out of Berion's office.'

He gritted his teeth at having to repeat himself. 'What about them, Sage?'

'They're all scared of you,' she said quietly.

'As they should be.'

She didn't roll her eyes. She didn't smile. She didn't say anything at all. The hairs on the back of her arms were still haywire.

'Berion wasn't.'

'Berion is stubborn, and so arrogant he'd rather die with his head held high than admit he's afraid of anything.' She thought it was pretty rich that he called anyone arrogant. 'Other than myself, and then Roderick, Berion is one of the most powerful warlocks in this city. Certainly one of the best fighters I've ever encountered in the training rooms.'

Training rooms? That room they'd passed on the way, with all the shouting and grunting, suddenly made more sense.

'Anyway. It' – he pulled a non-committal expression – 'gives Berion a false sense of security.'

She heard the veiled threat for what it was. 'And he's content to sit in that office?'

He really did smile then, and she caught herself by surprise to see how it lit up his face. 'I think he means it about not wanting to ruin his clothes. That outfit was tame. Trust me.'

'What exactly is it you've done, then? To have them all afraid of you.'

'What have you heard?'

Harland's words echoed in her memory. Chupacabras. Witch covens. Werewolf packs. P's incredulous glances on hearing that he could single-handedly kill them all. Her attempts not to laugh their friend down. But now ... sitting there ... she wasn't so sure about any of it.

He was watching her, and she realized the answer meant

something. Told him what she did or didn't know. Some kind of test.

She swallowed, and straightened. 'I'd rather hear the truth from you.'

Interesting. The flicker across his face revealed it wasn't the answer he'd been expecting. But somehow, she thought, it told him enough.

Her phone lit up with a buzz on the table. A message from P.

On my way.

He looked at the screen then back at her, and closed the file in front of him. Conversation, apparently, over.

'Secrets are secret for a reason.' He brushed it off with a sniff. 'Wait here.'

The abruptness annoyed her. But suddenly, she realized she was already a player in a carefully crafted game of words.

'You mean you don't trust me.' She knew that wasn't necessarily the reason he wasn't sharing every detail of his past with her, but she was still trying to gauge their positions. 'You won't spill the gory details?'

She knew at once she'd played it wrong.

He stiffened. She was sure it wasn't her imagination either that the temperature dropped several degrees.

When his head rose, the dark flash that crossed his face was gone so quickly she might not have even noticed it if she wasn't already gazing at him. He leant across the table between them, slowly, until his face was almost level with hers. She realized then exactly how small that table was.

'You think you have the stomach for my secrets?' he growled. 'The werewolf, rumour has it, that's too scared to change other than on a full moon? Well hear this: I've felt enough hot blood flowing over my hands to fill a river. Smiled into desperate eyes I've sentenced to die. Lit pyres. Smelt flesh burn. Killed plenty who *deserved* it. And when death comes, I never feel more alive. Is that what you want to hear?' He shook his head. He straightened up again and gave her a disgusted look. 'They're not *gory details* for the amusement of others, Sage. They're real people. Real monsters.'

Her cheeks burnt.

Her little brother in their camping tent, and her parents, attacked by a werewolf in the dead of night. All dead. Killed. While she alone had survived. She had lived. With nothing more to show for it than a wide scar across her left hip.

Had she reduced them to a gory detail?

No, Sage, stop. Don't cry now.

Oren had no idea about her past – about the traumas she had faced. On that night and others. Maybe lit pyres and burning flesh weren't part of her gory details, but she still had them. And he'd made her feel so small for trivializing it.

'Well, this looks sinister.' It was P. She looked around the darkened archives as she floated over. *What's wrong?* she mouthed.

Sage shook her head. *Later*.

'So?' Oren demanded, throwing himself back down into his seat. 'Did you find anything useful?'

'Obviously.' P dropped her papers on the table and sat. 'Or I wouldn't have wasted my time sneaking round corners and flying miles in the air so nobody Upside noticed magically floating papers.'

His sigh was impatient.

'Lucy's newspaper office was closed. I was able to work quickly without anyone noticing stuff moving. But before that, I went back to the police station to see if there were any updates since yesterday. It was a boon, really, a pair of officers were in the detective's office so I just' – she pulled an innocent expression – 'listened in. They have no leads. And no DNA. They're stumped. No surprise, really. The only interesting titbit is that they measured that partial shoe print and figured out it's a size ten.'

'That narrows it down to half the population,' Sage said. 'Unlikely to be female.'

'Other than the giant races . . . But they can't exactly wander around Upside, either.' P frowned. 'They'd already started to clear Lucy's desk but her desktop hadn't been wiped yet and whatever was taken from her drawers was in the editor's office.' She gestured to the stuff she'd collected. 'Printed everything off the computer and photocopied everything else.'

Oren frowned. 'You visited all these places when you

were alive?'

'Poltergeist,' she said, as if that answered everything. 'Ghosts attach themselves to places, can only go where they went in life. Poltergeists attach themselves to people so can go wherever they want.'

'Right . . . So you're attached to—'

'Sage, you told me Lucy always knew all the gossip at the orphanage,' P interrupted. 'It figures she'd make a decent investigative journalist. Some of her stuff is really good. Anyway. There was a desk calendar with appointments in, I photocopied that.' She pointed at another piece of paper. 'Subjects of articles, sources or whatever; I think with a bit more time this afternoon we'd likely match up some of the names in the calendar with unfinished articles she was working on.'

'Investigative?' Sage repeated slowly.

'Poking around, investigating, might be where she's made the enemies,' Oren nodded.

'Probably worth looking at recently finished articles too,' P murmured in agreement. 'I can help this afternoon, before you leave, Sage.'

Oren's head shot up from the printouts.

'Leave for where?'

Sage grimaced. She hadn't told him yet.

'I won't be here for a few days.'

'. . . Where will you be?'

'It's the full moon tonight. I leave this afternoon, I'll be back the day after tomorrow.'

His mouth dropped open. 'Are you serious?'

'Yes? It happens every month, Oren. Thought you knew that?'

He threw his hands out wide. 'You've gone out of your way to shoehorn yourself into this investigation, Sage, you forced Roderick's hand.' He sounded accusatory. 'Now I'm stuck with you and you're just telling me you're disappearing? This is a massive inconvenience, you know that?'

'And it isn't to me? Do you think I want to take three days out of my life every month for this shit?'

He shook his head. 'I can't hold off until you get back. A case can't halt while you prance around the countryside—'

P's gasp was high-pitched with shock.

'It's true!' he said furiously. 'This is exactly what Roderick meant when he said we don't need werewolves. An arcāna out of action is completely useless.'

It felt like a solid punch to the chest. She felt tainted, now more than ever. Like she had an affliction, a plague, that horrified everyone else around her. It didn't matter that she was just as disgusted by herself. More so.

She pushed her chair back. 'I'm going now.'

'What?'

'Sage,' P said quietly, eyes wide as saucers.

She shook her head. 'I'll be back in a few days. Do whatever you need. Fire me, if you want to.'

II

OREN

He barely saw her in the watery morning Upside sunlight. But when he did, he groaned.

He'd spent the rest of the day seething . . . and all of the night.

Sage had stormed out of the archive. Actually *stormed out*. And then P had silently gathered up everything on the table and followed her.

Not much shocked him any more, but he was shocked enough by the utterly petulant theatrics that he didn't try to stop them.

Then last night he'd received a text from P. A series of pictures of tidy, handwritten notes. The pair had clearly gone home and despite everything, sat down and meticulously worked their way through Lucinda Hague's articles and recent contacts, piecing it all together. Now he had a list of five names, cross-referenced against the electoral register for their contact details.

And so there he was. Upside, in a human residential area a few miles from the city centre, standing in a cul-de-sac of identical bungalows.

. . . And there was P sitting on the wall of the property he was about to visit.

'She asked me to be her eyes,' was all the poltergeist said. 'Nobody else will see me. We both know that I'll give her a better rundown, and I bet I take better notes than you, anyway.'

His teeth clenched.

For a century he'd managed to avoid having a partner, avoided having to take anyone else into consideration. And now he had two!

He resented this new-found feeling that he had to answer to anybody.

It was beneath him.

'Just stay out of my way.'

'Yes, sir.' She gave him a mock salute.

'Sugar, hon?' a voice called from the kitchen.

'Hon,' P snorted. He wasn't sure why the poltergeist didn't seem to take well to this woman playing host.

'Just one,' he said as a blonde head poked through the doorway.

The woman, around mid-forties with an unnaturally white smile, winked.

'Did she just wink?'

He couldn't answer or Cheryl would hear. The human who definitely couldn't see the poltergeist in the room.

Cheryl Wentworth, a woman Lucy had been in the middle of writing an article about. *How one woman's perseverance found her long lost-little sister*. She'd spent fifteen minutes explaining how she'd always remembered small flashes of a baby. Her mother had always told her it was a dream, or something she'd seen on TV. But she knew – just *knew* – there was more to it. When her mother died two years ago she'd found a birth certificate and adoption papers among other belongings, and she'd set out to find her little sister. Thanks to the online search campaign that'd gathered enough local attention to attract Lucy's newspaper, she'd finally been found. Charlotte. Though she went by her adopted name now. Fully grown, with a quiet but pleasant boyfriend and a job in sports therapy. She was not the baby from those memories any more.

He'd pretended to be interested.

He still didn't understand all the fuss around family. His own was thoroughly disappointing.

They were in a frilly living room full of ruffles on the curtains and sofa cushions. And an alarming amount of china animal figures in display cabinets. P had made a sound not too dissimilar to a dying cat when she'd floated through the wall and seen it all.

'I mean . . .' Cheryl said as she came back in carrying two cups.

'Not even on a tray,' the poltergeist muttered from the corner.

'. . . We were horrified when we saw it. My sister's staying with me at the moment — on and off with her boyfriend.' She rolled her eyes. 'Anyway, up popped her face on the six o'clock news. Put us right off our fish and chips. Murdered in her home like that. It's scary, y'know?'

'Your sister isn't home?'

'She's working away.' Cheryl smiled widely. The strength of her perfume was making him feel light-headed. 'You've just got me, I'm afraid.'

He accepted the drink with a polite nod, ignoring P's second snort as Cheryl settled herself down almost offensively close to him on the sofa. He waved a hand casually enough to evade her notice, and his notebook appeared on the shelves behind her, open and ready.

'When did you last meet Lucy?' He sipped at the tea. Too sweet.

'About four or five days before she died.' Cheryl shrugged. 'The Costa on Market Street? We met for a coffee and a chat, talk over a few details for her article.'

'Ask her if she ever talked about anyone else,' P said as she floated over to watch his notepad with interest.

He gritted his teeth. Of course, it had been his next question. 'Did she ever mention anyone, family, partner?'

She looked thoughtful. 'She said her ex moved abroad. I got the impression she didn't really have family.'

That wasn't a surprise. Her Arcānum records had shown she'd lost contact with her human family not long after her attack. She'd been a runaway, plenty of new werewolf kids were; scared and confused and fearing rejection, they ran. She'd been found and taken Downside not long after.

'Though,' Cheryl said slowly, 'she met someone after me in the coffee shop. A friend. Rob, I think she said.' She shrugged again, as if something as important as a name didn't matter. 'He must've walked in just as I left, I saw them through the window greeting each other. They looked, y'know, *friendly*.'

'Friendly?'

Cheryl's eyes twinkled. 'He kissed her cheek and I could see her giggling, and they held on to each other just a little bit too long . . . but she'd only called him a friend so . . . He was handsome, though. Almost as handsome as you.'

P snorted a third time. He smiled tightly. He knew he was handsome. He'd endured decades of people's confused reactions, wondering how they could both be so horrified and yet so attracted all at the same time.

'Your hair,' Cheryl said suddenly, leaning forward. 'Do you dye it or is that natural?'

'Natural,' he said neutrally, ignoring the chest she practically thrust into his face.

'Very Tan France.'

'Who?'

P snorted a fourth time. 'Ask her to describe the friend.'

'What did the friend look like? Other than almost as handsome as me.'

Cheryl giggled. P tutted.

'Well groomed. Dark hair swept back. Mid-twenties? In a navy suit, I think, with a leather briefcase. All expensive-looking. Looked like he'd just come from the bank. They looked good together. Young, stylish, full of ambition.' She turned sombre again, and slouched back. 'Such a shame.'

'First we've heard of a potential male interest?' P nodded from across the room.

'Yep,' he answered before he could stop himself.

'What was that?' Cheryl looked confused.

'Just thinking aloud,' he said hastily, painting on a bland smile as he got to his feet and held out a card. He kept a stock of them in his pocket. It was blank, but his magic shimmered across the surface and made her eyes see whatever he wanted her to see: today he was DI Robert Hanforth of the Greater Manchester Police. 'I've kept you long enough. If you think of anything else that might be relevant, this is my number. Leave a message.'

'Ooh.' Cheryl's face lit up again. 'I'll be sure to drop you one.' P rolled her eyes and zoomed through the window to wait outside.

But he hadn't missed the glint in Cheryl's eye either, and it made him think twice. They'd got everything useful from her already. With the tiniest glimmer of gold, he made sure the number on the card was fake. Like hell he was giving this woman a direct line to him.

He waved away his notebook. He enjoyed seeing P irritated. It'd teach her for turning up uninvited.

'Don't be a stranger.' Cheryl smiled widely as she opened the front door and beckoned him through with mild reluctance.

'Didn't like her, then?' he asked from the corner of his mouth as they set back off down the cul-de-sac.

'She didn't even bring the tea out in a pot. Never mind a tray! And when she gave you a biscuit on a napkin?'

It was his turn to snort. He could barely see her outline in the sunlight, just a glistening in the corner of his eye.

Then she laughed again. 'If she winked a second time I might've heaved. Wait until I tell Sage.'

12

OREN

He'd made it very clear yesterday he didn't want to come into their apartment. It was too . . . friendly.

'You're being rude,' P had chastised when he'd vocalized this outside the Arcānum headquarters.

'I don't need to. You can fill Sage in when she gets home tomorrow. That was the point of you coming today, wasn't it?'

But her jaw was set. 'We have something to show you. Come around six.'

And she'd flown off, leaving him in the middle of Downside watching her pearlescent body fade into Yuletide crowds.

Now it was six, and in spite of himself, he was here. Outside a surprisingly decent apartment block in a nice part of town. He wondered how the pair afforded it, since one clearly did everything she could to avoid getting a job within her actual means and the other was dead. Inheritance, perhaps?

He sighed and knocked on the door.

The lock clicked almost at once and P swung the door

open and took him in. He refused to acknowledge the faint smirk playing about her lips.

But this apartment had copies of every bit of paperwork they had . . . and he privately trusted that they'd have it more organized than he had his own. He avoided any paperwork unless it was absolutely vital. In fact, he'd thrown everything he had on his desk and not looked at it since.

He was still in a bad mood.

Most of his quiet time had been consumed with resentment over his argument with Sage. That she dared speak to him like that?

It was his own fault. In his quest to live a secluded life he rarely interacted with any one person as much as he'd had to speak with her and her housemate these last few days. Not outside his own race. And he wasn't used to someone who . . . clearly didn't know who he was.

A rare phenomenon these days.

That other werewolf knew. The geeky, gangly lad that'd turned up in that pub. The kid had turned white as a sheet. Had the look that said he'd read the textbooks shoved under kids' noses these days, documenting his name without his permission. Telling his story without his consent.

P hovered on the threshold, and he had no choice to stand there too unless he wanted to pass through her. Which he didn't. It felt disgusting to pass through any ghost.

She assessed him, taking in his clothes all the way down to his shoes. 'Have you eaten?'

He nodded, confused. He knew she couldn't eat.

She tutted like this was problematic. 'I'm trying out a new recipe.'

She stood back at last to let him in. It was bigger than he'd expected it to be. And comfortable. His apartment was full of all the practical elements of a house but this . . . with warm throws and flickering candles and framed pictures of smiling faces on the way, it felt like a home. His discomfort only hardened.

'A spicy meatball stew.'

'That . . . sounds nice.' He was surprised to discover he meant it.

And then he stopped again.

His mouth dropped open.

'What am I looking at?' He edged further into the room, staring at one of the walls.

The original archives file as well as what they'd gathered after visiting Cheryl Wentworth, the human police autopsy, everything from the newspaper offices . . . plus the crime scene photos Sage had snapped, all of it was now pinned on the wall. Arranged into sections, various bits were linked up with coloured string, and annotated with handwritten notes she and Sage must've made before the latter had left. In the centre was a map of Upside. A red pin was pushed into where he guessed Lucy had lived and died. And another string ran off towards a photograph of a smiling young woman with blonde hair that wasn't stained red at the tips. And eyes that weren't vacant and empty.

It was like something out of a detective movie. The kind of thing that no detective he'd ever known *actually* wasted their time with.

'Sage and I started filing it all into sections before she left. I've just finished pinning it all up. Thought it was easier to visualize it all.'

This poltergeist was ridiculous.

'Anyway,' P floated as if any of this was totally normal behaviour, 'Sage'll be back any minute. Come try a sample.'

'You cook even when she isn't here?' He followed her into a compact but immaculate kitchen, a small table in the corner.

'Bryce, the satyr two doors down, his wife died last summer. I make sure he gets at least one hot meal a day. He tries, but he's lonely. And a bit further up there's an elf couple with triplets, they're always happy to try new dishes. I think they're too exhausted to cook some nights so . . .' She chatted away as she stirred the pans and rattled in cupboards.

His eyes narrowed.

There was a point to all this. He just wasn't sure what it was, yet.

So he did what he always did. He stayed quiet, and switched on his senses, and observed.

It felt strange. He thought he'd forgotten what it was like to sit and watch somebody cook for him. The last memories of his mother doing that were so old they'd practically faded. Over a hundred and forty years. Had it been that long he'd forced himself not to think about her?

'You do a lot for others.'

'Dying puts a lot of things into perspective,' she shrugged as she fished about in the pan with a spoon, and leant forward like . . . she was going to try it?

He watched in amazement as she picked up a folded paper towel, held it under her chin and did just that. Tried to bite food on the spoon. It fell right through her chin and into the waiting tissue.

'You can taste that?'

She nodded, shaking out some salt. 'I was so sick of never being able to eat that one day I tried it. It must be a poltergeist thing because my ghost friends can't taste anything.'

'Can you feel the things you touch?' He watched the spatula she was stirring.

She raised a brow like it was a stupid question. 'They feel as they did when I was alive.'

'People?'

'You all feel like sticking my hands in a bag of hot jelly.' She shuddered. 'Ghosts feel like mist. Cold and damp. They say that two poltergeists can touch each other, like the living, but I've never met another. We're so rare. I'm the only one here.' She pulled a face. 'The two things a person needs to survive I cannot have. Food and basic interaction with the people you love. I sometimes wonder if it's some kind of punishment. A curse of the poltergeists.'

He didn't answer. He was taken aback by her assertion that basic interaction with loved ones was required to survive. He didn't agree. He'd gone most of his adult life without interacting with what was left of his family and he'd turned out fine.

She looked like she knew what he was thinking because she shook her head as she placed a bowl on the table. 'Honest reviews only.'

He took a bite, and his mouth exploded in flavour. He couldn't stop himself going in for another. She watched him in silence. Which truthfully, he preferred.

Then she asked something he didn't expect. 'Are you a dog person or a cat person?'

'What?'

'Do you prefer dogs, or cats?'

He considered the question. 'Probably dogs.'

She nodded thoughtfully. 'Hmm. That makes sense. Y'see, the thing about dogs, they're subservient. That's what dog lovers really mean when they say they love their dog's "loyalty".' She quoted the air with her fingers. 'A dog is loyal to the person who feeds it because they can't survive without them.'

'Your point?'

'Sage is so desperate for this chance, for you to throw her any small scraps of food, that she'll let you walk all over her,' she said bluntly. 'She won't say it to you, but the way you spoke to her yesterday wasn't OK.'

'But you're happy to say it?' he asked sardonically.

She gave him a tight smile. 'Ask a dog lover why they don't like cats and they'll tell you it's because they're aloof. But they're just self-sufficient. They don't *need* anyone to survive. What people mean when they say they don't like cats is that they're uncomfortable when the respect has to be earnt.'

He understood her point. It was polite, and she'd used the metaphor tactfully. He commanded subservience through power. That bought him loyalty: but it wasn't earnt. P was unique. She had no life left for him to protect. There was no way to intimidate or manipulate her into bending to his will. Her loyalty was a choice.

'You will be welcome here for the time you work with Sage,' she said quietly. 'But only if you can treat us, her, with respect.'

He had no interest in whether he was welcome in this apartment or not. He didn't want to be there in the first place. But he wasn't sure what it was about the poltergeist. He was so used to dealing with people who feared for their lives in his presence, he wasn't sure how to approach someone who didn't care at all.

And not just that.

The way she looked after not only Sage, but, apparently, everyone. Even him, for these brief moments. It tugged at something inside of him he'd long since learnt to ignore. In a funny sort of way, she made him feel more . . . human.

He knew what he was supposed to say, but he wouldn't say it.

He didn't apologize to anybody. Like he didn't smile at anybody. Or work with anybody.

He was just pissed off.

At everything and everyone.

At the world.

Always.

Oh, Oren. A voice he hadn't listened to in so many years echoed in his mind. *You can't have your own way all of the time. It won't win you any friends.* Sometimes he wondered if his mantra to live a solitary life had been out of spite. Revenge. When he'd lost his mother he'd raged against everything her memory had stood for, everything she'd ever said, all that he remembered. The only punishment he could offer for leaving him. A bitter, petty, vengeful son. That's what he was.

'Where has she been?'

He expected her to refuse to tell him. 'The Lake District.'

Good location. Lots of fields, small cliffs, tall hills. Easy for a wolf to get lost in. Plenty of livestock to feast on.

Ergh. Did she do that?

'She has a chalet. Rents it out the rest of the month.

~85~

Makes herself look like a hiker and sets off in the afternoon, gets far enough away and waits.'

'Why does she stay for so long?' He didn't particularly care that much, but . . . P looked thoughtful for a moment, and opened her mouth to answer.

She was stopped by the sound of the front door.

13

SAGE

'P?' She shoved through the front door. It was nearly evening and she was praying for food. Train delays Upside. Terrible weather. She was starved.

She felt like crap. Her whole body ached from the transformation and this time—

'Sage!' P gasped as she appeared through the closed hallway door. 'What happened?'

Then to her surprise the door opened and Oren was there too.

'What happened?' he echoed.

'Nothing.' She shoved past.

'You have a fat lip and two black eyes. Been getting in fights?'

'Well, if I have I'm obviously pretty *useless* at that too,' she snapped, kicking off her trainers.

'Sage.' She was surprised that it was P urging her not to start an argument. It shocked her enough to halt whatever was about to come out next. She rounded, eyes wide, but P just held out placating hands.

'Oh, *I'm sorry*!' She thought she might explode. 'You're defending him?'

'Sage.' It was Oren this time.

'I swear to God, if you roll your eyes one more time I'll give you a black eye—'

'Unlikely.'

She lunged.

She could still feel the wolf in her blood. It was too soon to be pushing her. Her head hurt, and her eyes throbbed, and her lip. She'd had enough. She wanted to curl up in bed and cry until it all stopped hurting. Then . . .

Before she knew it two granite arms were clamping hers at her sides. She screamed, but he was too strong. 'Stop, Sage!'

She fought for a bit longer just out of spite. Her body ached. She thought she might be whimpering. She gave in.

She wanted to kill him.

He let her go, then reached down and held her chin, examining the lip and the eyes. 'You don't remember how you did this?'

'Obviously,' she snapped. 'I was changed. I woke up like this.'

Because a turning on a full moon was the only time a werewolf had no memory of what they did. They became complete wolf, in mind and body and soul, and recalled nothing after. It was the only accepted method of creating werewolves, in fact – the accidental kind, when the aggressor couldn't remember attacking. She'd been turned on a full moon; it had been Lucy that'd sat down with her in the orphanage with a calendar and moon charts and worked it out.

If she knew who her sire was, felt they hadn't taken appropriate measures to get away from humanity before they turned, she could lodge a formal complaint with the Arcānum. But she'd never bothered. After experiencing full moon turnings for herself she completely understood they'd had no control over what they did to her and her family.

He nodded.

It was an effort to look anywhere but his face.

He passed a hand, faintly glowing, over her face. The one still holding her chin felt warm, really warm, and heat was seeping from the bottom of her face upwards. It went over her lips and towards her eyes. Then it started to travel down her neck too, in drips as if a liquid was melting down her insides. She stumbled back, staring down at herself.

'What did you do?'

'Numbed the pain, but it's better to let it heal naturally. My mother was a healer. She taught me to use magic to heal others as a child. Not many warlocks bother to learn how to fix anyone but themselves.' He grunted. He sounded a little bit annoyed. All this effort he was going to for her, just to piss his captain off. 'You're welcome.'

'I'll update you,' P cut across the tension. 'I'll put the kettle on, you sit.'

'Who is he?' she demanded. 'The man in the coffee shop?'

It was only after sitting that she had noticed the master-piece P had constructed in her absence. It was . . .

'P got carried away.' Oren's muttered explanation had summed it up well enough. She'd arranged everything neatly in piles on the coffee table before she'd left, hoping it'd be easier to rifle through for specific notes later if needed, but this was . . . next level.

Oren shook his head. 'No idea. Cheryl barely knew anything, most of what she gave us she saw through a window.'

'Oh,' P cut in. 'He's on first name terms with Cheryl because she fancied him. Isn't that right, *hon*?'

'P's annoyed I enjoyed a cup of tea made by someone that wasn't her.'

'She used napkins instead of side plates,' P hissed.

'We need to find him,' Sage said. 'He could have answers.'

P pointed to the wall. When she blinked, confused, P hissed again, raising into the air to point at a note near the top that she'd obviously added under a new section titled: *People of Interest*.

Of course. How stupid of her not to notice this small section among the overwhelming amount of detail pinned up there.

'The others on our list were nearly all human. They didn't have much to say.' P floated back to her spot on the sofa. 'All said she was professional and polite, but no idea who might want to kill her. There was one, a Thomas Richmond, who was interesting for, like, two seconds.'

'Why?'

'He's a werewolf too. We spoke to his human partner. He knew exactly what his husband was and said he'd been expecting the Arcānum to turn up. Tom'd heard about Lucy and warned we might appear while he was away for the full moon.'

'He knew?' she repeated, surprised. 'About us? About . . . everything?'

Oren pulled a face. 'It's not strictly allowed. But the Arcānum acknowledges it's not always possible to hide the truth. We make exceptions when Downsiders marry humans. Spouses only, though. He was obviously very stressed at the situation—'

'Uh, no, Oren.' P waved him away impatiently. 'You started speaking to me in front of him. When he clearly thought you were insane you told him there was a poltergeist in the room. *That's* what got him stressed.'

'You did *what*?'

'I thought he knew what the supernatural entailed!'

'Werewolves aren't a realistic fear to humans,' she said incredulously. 'Ghosts terrify them!'

He rolled his eyes. 'Anyway. They were away the day Lucy died. He had photographs, and receipts to prove it.'

She sighed. Another dead end, then. 'Anything else?'

P *hmm*ed as if to say, *Not really.* 'I found this stuck on the inside cover of her notebook.' She paused to hold up a post-it with a single word scribbled across it. 'MacAllister? It's a surname but not much to go on. It doesn't pop up in any articles she was working on or link to any scheduled meetings.' She shrugged. 'There are three MacAllisters in the Arcānum archives. Oren went down there to look it up. One is a long-dead selkie, another joined a werewolf pack twenty years ago and went off-grid. And the third is a twelve-year-old faun.'

'One *is* a werewolf, though?'

Oren shrugged. 'There's only one true werewolf pack registered in this city Upside, and that only formed nine years ago. Wherever MacAllister went, it's not the pack here. It's unlikely to be him. Not when her stories only cover local people and issues.'

'I didn't even know there was a proper werewolf pack living in this city,' P said.

'As opposed to a pretend one?' Oren asked sarcastically.

But she already knew P found the topic interesting, had made a point to know all she could about werewolves once she'd started living with one. She appreciated the effort. She did know there was a pack in the city, but she had been supernatural a lot longer than P. But by contrast, the thought made her uncomfortable. She was content to pretend she wasn't a werewolf for most of the month when she wasn't forced to turn involuntarily on a full moon. And packs were known to be *extra*. They lived together out in the wilderness, isolating themselves almost entirely from both human and supernatural society and just . . . wolfed about, she supposed.

It was her idea of hell.

P gave Oren a filthy look. 'It's fascinating. I'd love to see a pack in their natural habitat.'

She snorted. 'Their natural habitat?'

'You know! A real werewolf alpha? The pack dynamics? Loyalty bonds?'

'Pack loyalty isn't always a good thing,' Oren said quietly.

'What do you mean?' P looked curious.

He looked as if he was weighing up the merits of telling or refusing. Then sighed. 'Not too long ago there was a case of a werewolf pack that was too loyal. Their alpha, Amhuinn, was breaking the law but they wouldn't testify against him. In fact, each one said it was them committing his crimes. An *I am Spartacus* moment, if you will.'

'What happened?' P asked.

'Execution orders for those that stuck by him. Around half the pack.'

P looked horrified. And despite Sage's opinions on packs, even her own mouth dropped open.

'Was that fair? They were defending their alpha. Were-wolves will do that.'

He just shrugged, seemingly uninterested.

Then a phone rang.

14

SAGE

It was coming from Oren's pocket.

He stood to release the ringing from his jeans and pulled a face. She knew at once who it'd be. He tapped a few buttons and held it up as a voice blared out on loudspeaker.

'There's been another one.' Roderick's tone was aggravated. As if he couldn't believe the news had the cheek to impede on his day. 'Werewolf.'

Her heart dropped into the pit of her stomach.

'Where?' Oren's dark face met hers. 'We'll go now.'

'Too late. Humans have already got there.' She felt sick. 'The wolf died outside our city limits, the life force notification flagged up at the closest Arcānum branch to where the death occurred. It's taken them a few hours to check their records and figure out she wasn't local. By the time they got in touch with Hozier, the grandkids of the farmer whose land she was on found her around the back of a paddock. Human form, but ravaged. Farmer thought his dogs had attacked one of the livestock.'

P's hand flew to her mouth.

'That feels like a serious flaw in the notification process, Roderick,' Oren growled angrily. 'Why hasn't it been flagged before?'

'No idea. The spell might not have been cast correctly.' Sage could practically hear him shrugging down the phone. 'Just been the full moon, hasn't it? Probably explains why she was out in the countryside. Suppose there's also the chance she just got in a fight with another one through the night.'

She froze.

They all froze.

'Where did they find her?' Oren asked quietly.

Roderick paused, perhaps checking notes. 'Cumbria.' Then he barked a small laugh. As if nobody was dead at all. 'Place called Cockermouth. Anyway, I've pulled the file. Salina Gourlay. I'll send you her Upside address, you may as well go there instead. Check there's nothing supernatural on display.'

He hung up.

She stood in a daze.

'Sage?' P's voice sounded distant as she stumbled around the sofa. She wasn't going anywhere, she didn't have a plan, but she couldn't just *sit there*. Her chest felt hollow even as her heart pounded.

Her fingers came up to her lip. She could still feel it, the rip in her skin that'd barely begun to heal. She couldn't remember how she'd got it. Her hand drifted up to the skin around her eyes, still black and puffy.

Her worst nightmare. A werewolf's worst fear. Death at her hands on a full moon and she wouldn't remember it.

Had this one died on a moor just like her family—

No.

She just couldn't.

Her breathing turned ragged. Her knees buckled, and she grabbed the back of the sofa to steady herself. And then Oren was beside her demanding she look at him.

'Where? Where exactly were you?'

Her mouth opened and closed, but nothing came out.

He shook her elbow, and it wasn't gentle. 'Tell me,' he insisted. 'I can't help you if you don't tell me.'

'Windermere,' P said from behind. 'The chalet's in Windermere.'

'Get me a map, P. Now,' he demanded. 'Look at me, Sage.' Those blue-green eyes stared into hers. 'When you woke up, were you covered in blood?'

No. She wasn't. She blinked again. She wasn't, was she? Her breathing was still shaky, but she shook her head. 'Not much,' she rasped. 'I mean, on my face, but I thought it'd come from my lip.'

'Are you injured anywhere else?'

'No,' she said quietly. She felt dizzy. 'Just my face.'

'They're miles apart!' P said loudly.

Oren dragged her over to the laptop screen open on the coffee table.

He pointed at the map. 'That's good. That makes it less likely. And a fight to the death? You'd have wounds all over your body too. You'd be a mess. I very much doubt it was you.'

Relief crashed into her so hard she could barely breathe. She knew the hand on her back had to be Oren. God, she wished it was P. Wished she could hug her, just this one time.

When she looked up, P's eyes were lined with tears. Her friend nodded only once, but it was enough to say that she felt it too. That she understood.

Then, *crash*.

There was a bang from the hallway. They spun as a sharp, familiar-looking dagger erupted from thin air in Oren's left hand, the blade glowing with the faint golden light of his magic.

'Bloody hell, boys!' P almost screamed as Harland, Danny and Rhen fell into the room. 'You frightened the life out of us! What're you doing?'

All of them were gasping, as if they'd run all the way from the other side of the city. Harland clasped his chest with a hand as he gulped down air, his hair slick with rain, and sweat too, by the looks of it. His face was bright red, and his glasses were steamed up. He looked at P, then to her, ignoring Oren completely.

Oren swore under his breath, the dagger evaporating into mist.

'I told you,' Rhen said breathlessly, clapping Danny on the back, but he sounded immensely relieved, like he hadn't believed whatever he'd been saying himself. 'It's not her.'

'Everyone's saying a wolf was practically ripped apart in Cumbria last night,' Danny said. 'We know you, we thought . . .'

Harland bent double, hands on his knees. 'We ran straight here. But it's not you. It's not you.' It sounded like a prayer. But then he rose, and paused, looking startled. 'What's happened to your face?'

'Still figuring that out.' She swallowed.

'There's not enough damage for her to have been in a fight to the death. We don't think she was involved,' P supplied.

'Right,' he said, then pulled a face, as if what P had said needed a moment to register. 'What?' He looked back at her. 'You really thought you'd savage anyone to death? Come on, Sage—'

Oren tutted impatiently. 'A werewolf has been killed just as she comes home with a beat-up face and no recollection of how it happened. What did you expect us to think?'

Danny gave Oren a strange look. 'That the killer tried to attack her too?'

The room stood in silence.

In her panic she hadn't even considered it.

Neither had P, her mouth dropping open.

She swallowed. She couldn't remember any of it. Could

~98~

she have been face to face with the very person they were hunting, whatever monster was following lone werewolves out to secluded spots on the full moon?

'Others will think I did it too, when they see my face,' she said quietly.

'Well, he can hide it, can't he?' Harland nodded at Oren. 'Glamour it.'

She looked at Oren to see if it was true, to find his jaw clenched. 'Know a lot about warlock magic, do you?'

'Oren,' she warned wearily as Harland flushed a shade she didn't realize could exist on a face.

Oren sniffed. 'Fairies glamour. We *mask*. But there's little point. Her wolf blood will speed up the healing, her face will be mostly repaired by tomorrow.'

'Uh, what's that?' Danny's faint voice cut through as he noticed P's murder wall. 'That's . . . that's Lucy, isn't it?'

She swallowed, hard. 'Don't look at it.' She made for her friend at once, used her hand to turn his cheek away, to look at anything else, but he pulled out of her grip, staring, horrified. Rhen and Harland turned to look too.

Harland shuddered. 'Does this mean you've got a lead?'

'A lead,' Oren muttered. 'You didn't tell me you were Sherlock Holmes.'

Harland was puce again. She shook her head, determined to pretend Oren wasn't there. 'We have nothing yet, except a third of a shoe print.'

'You mean that?' He pointed at the close-up picture, his

shoulders cringing. He pushed his glasses up. 'It's a Converse shoe—'

'How do you know that?' P asked, surprised.

Harland looked back at her as if it was obvious. 'The pattern on the sole?'

'Explain,' Oren demanded with thinly veiled impatience.

'All Converse have that diamond pattern on the sole. Limited editions might have a different—'

'You're absolutely sure?'

He nodded, pushing his glasses up again. 'Look.'

He raised his own foot that wore a battered green Converse. And sure enough, there was the worn but obviously still diamond-patterned sole.

'Rhen.' Harland dropped his foot, stumbling at his own bad balance. 'Show them yours.'

Rhen lifted his own mustard Converse foot to reveal the same.

'Well, literally every nerd in the world wears them,' Oren gestured at the teenage trio, 'so it won't narrow down much. But it's good to know anyway.'

'A lot of fashionable—' Danny started.

'Any of that information winds up online or in the news-

ers.' Oren pointed at the wall as he glared at her friends.

l know where it came from.'

His phone let out another ping. He frowned at the screen. 'Business address only. Recently moved, hadn't updated home address yet.'

He looked up, a question in his eyes. And she knew, this was his real apology at last. He didn't know how to be sincere, to talk like humans – how could he? He had nobody to practise on. So he was relinquishing this power instead, the only language he really understood anyway. It was her call if they went right away or tomorrow, and he wouldn't judge her for it.

She nodded.

White teeth flashed. She hadn't realized it had also been a test until she saw she'd given the right answer.

15

SAGE

Salina Gourlay rented a decent-sized room on the second floor of an Upside building in the city centre, which she'd made into a professional-looking workspace. The floor below was home to a twenty-four-hour gym and Sage could hear the dull, repetitive thudding of someone on a treadmill.

Oren drew back a curtain hanging along one half of the room. There was a narrow bed, and other bits of exercise equipment she supposed meant something to someone trained in physiotherapy.

He crouched before a small sink and opened the cupboard doors below to rummage. She wandered over to a desk pushed into the corner, but a quick rattle of the cabinet handles beside it revealed them to be locked. The shelf on the wall above looked ready to buckle under the weight of the files piled there, but nothing particularly stood out.

Not like at Lucy's place. Though she supposed the absence of blood sprayed everywhere helped.

Hm.

She circled the room. She could barely scent werewolf

there at all. But it didn't mean much, so many different people passed through the room that it was a headache of different odours. It wasn't like a home where the scent was ground in.

The walls were lined with certificates for all Salina's qualifications, and it hit her in that moment just how finite life was. All that had been learnt, all the thoughts, and the memories . . . A person could spend a whole life compiling an encyclopaedia inside their own head, a library of knowledge, a wealth of history. Then *poof*. All gone into nothingness the moment death took them. As if none of it had ever been there at all.

Her chest swelled with overwhelming sadness. She looked at Oren's back. He was tall. Not overly broad, but she hadn't been able to help noticing the muscles that flexed under the fabric of his clothes when he moved. Eternally youthful. He'd told her he was nearly one hundred and fifty years old. He looked barely half a decade older than her. What would he look like in another hundred and fifty years? She'd be long dead. She wondered what he'd consider her as when her bones were dust, her memories of him long since evaporated into time. A blip in history? A face and a name he couldn't remember?

She said as much out loud.

'You'll be the first werewolf in Arcānum history if all goes to plan. I'll remember you for that.' He barely even glanced up.

'So much feeling,' she muttered. 'What an honour.'

'Makes life easier.' He shrugged. 'You should try it.'

'Be a cold husk like you, you mean?'

'Exactly.'

She tutted. 'Can you open these?' She rattled the top drawer of the cabinet again. He didn't answer, but a golden glow hummed around the lock and it clicked open.

'I've never seen it in gold before.' She rolled the drawer open and peered inside at the pile of files. The top one said: *H. Compton*. She pulled it out.

'Gold what?'

'Magic.'

Client notes, brief medical history. H. Compton was human. She threw it on to the desk.

'The warlocks I see around Downside are all different colours, but never gold.'

'The colour signifies the strength.'

'Let me guess, gold is the most powerful?'

He threw her a wry look. 'That's why you don't see it often. It's rare.'

'Still.' She threw *D. Nuttall*, *D. Bennett* and *D. Court* on to the desk in quick succession. More humans. 'There has to be more than just you. So where are they all?'

He didn't answer for a few moments. 'There are certain professions within the warlock community that require stronger magic . . . Gold is highly sought after.'

She raised a brow. 'But you're here . . . doing this?'

Uninterested in the contents of the cupboard any longer, he stood and flung the doors shut. 'I took early retirement.'

She didn't even know what that meant. She was about to open her mouth to ask, but he carried on. 'Blue is next, that's relatively rare, there are a few in Downside, though, Roderick is the only one in the Arcānum. Purple under that. There's a few more of those about. Berion, for one. Then red, green, orange, yellow. They're the most popular colours, you see. Still powerful by any standards. The weakest is still stronger than fairy dust, for example, and most witch spells. Other than anything cast by the witch mothers. They're our biggest rivals for power. If there were more of them they'd probably try to challenge us for our seat.'

The seat of power.

The supernatural world had no monarchy, per se. But in a supernatural settlement somewhere across the other side of the world were the Elders. A collection of the oldest-known warlocks. She wasn't entirely sure who had granted them the right to power, but whatever. They made rules, and at their behest, each supernatural city in the world was granted an Arcānum of warlocks to see that the Elders' laws were followed and peace was kept. Magic police for a supernatural government. That's how it had always been, for as long as anyone remembered.

'Have you ever met them?' she asked, moving on to the second drawer filled with stacks of leaflets as he wandered to the desk and started leafing through an appointment diary.

'What do you think?' When she didn't answer he looked and saw her watching him. He sighed. 'It was a long time ago. I haven't returned to Al-Khazneh since I left nearly a hundred and thirty years ago.'

'You're a long way from home,' she said, bending to slide open the bottom cabinet drawer. She could see it was territory he wasn't comfortable with. His spine was rigid as a board. She wondered if he knew he was so easy to read.

'I left early one day and refused to look back. I promised myself I would never watch the sun rise over the Stone City again.' He spoke so quietly she knew he wasn't speaking to her. 'It stopped being my home a long time ago.'

'Why?' she asked anyway.

'Olly Heywood.'

She blinked. 'Who?'

'There.' He was pointing at a page in Salina's work diary. Expertly avoided.

She leant in and under the same date she'd left Downside for the full moon was penned the name. And not only that, but an arrow went from his name and covered the next two boxes, indicating that this person would take up those days, too.

'Were they . . . going away together?'

'I don't know.' He frowned slowly. 'But a romantic getaway over a full moon doesn't sit right, does it?'

She shook her head. 'Unless they knew? You said spouses can know . . .'

He pulled a face that said, *Maybe*. Then closed the diary and put it in his pocket. A gift for P. 'We'll check the archives to see if we have Olly Heywood listed as supernatural.'

And something else.

'I know why she didn't register a new home address.' She pointed to the bottom drawer that was still open at her feet, a pillow and blanket stuffed inside. 'She must've crashed here.'

He pulled a distasteful grimace. 'Why?'

'Not everyone is as rich as you, Oren. She must've been struggling.' She kicked the drawer shut with her foot and sighed. There was nothing there more significant than that diary.

'Who says I'm rich?' He followed her back towards the corridor.

'You've got no mates and no social life. What exactly do you spend a century's worth of wages on?' she asked as she flicked off the light.

'Looking good,' he sniffed, and with a wave of that golden magic, the door locked behind them.

16

OREN

'It tastes better than I expected.' He examined the slice of Meat Feast in his hand. He wasn't hungry, but he'd heard her stomach grumbling across Salina's office. 'This whole place looks like it'd fail a food hygiene inspection.'

There were plenty of places they could've stopped at Downside, but he'd been watching her, and he knew that Sage had already started to notice the whispers and averted eyes she received courtesy of his company. So when she'd pointed at this human pizza place not too far from Dive Bar Upside, he'd reluctantly kept quiet. It wasn't anywhere near a five-star dining experience, but the fact they'd settled rather than look elsewhere was testament to how badly it was raining.

'Someone is picking off werewolves,' he said after a few bites. 'I'd expect you to be a bit more scared.'

'I have nothing to fear from a stranger, Oren. Nothing's more horrifying than you,' she said. But she was . . . deflated. There wasn't any of her usual bite to the insult. If only she knew just how much tolerance he was affording her little comments. 'Lucy died scared,' she admitted finally. 'Letting myself feel scared isn't as important as finding who killed her.'

His eyebrow twitched, but he said nothing. He could see something else was bothering her. It was on the tip of her tongue. He was just waiting . . .

'You said you'd help me.' There it was. 'When I thought I'd killed her. You said you couldn't help if I didn't tell you.'

'What's your point?'

'Shouldn't you have arrested me?'

He took a few more bites of pizza as he considered what she was suggesting. 'You'd have wanted me to?'

She looked down at her plate, and he knew she was avoiding looking him in the eye. 'Dunno,' she admitted. 'Maybe. I'd have deserved it.'

Ah.

And there was the heart of it.

'You wouldn't have even remembered doing it, Sage.'

'A life would still have been taken.'

He had to stop his head tilting as he examined this girl in front of him practically arguing that she should be punished. But what for? Because she hadn't killed that werewolf. It was clear she'd never got over the bad hands fate had repeatedly dealt her. Her family. Now Lucy. She tortured herself with it. It seemed to him that she mostly wanted punishing simply for being the only one to survive.

He understood that more than she'd ever know.

'I saw your face,' he said at last. 'The guilt would have been punishment enough. And you know there are exceptions for incidents involving werewolves on the full moon. You wouldn't be handed an execution order even if you had killed her.'

'Not like that Amhuinn pack, huh?' She glanced up, obviously wondering if she'd overstepped the mark.

It was at moments like this he understood P's fascination with loyalty bonds and pack dynamics. Despite having absolutely no idea of what really happened, she defended werewolves she didn't even know. It was just wired into her blood. Woven into her soul.

Yet . . . Amhuinn was one of a kind. Oren hadn't told them the whole truth. For starters, it was him that'd been sent to track the pack down. He cared little about the feelings of others but even he acknowledged how horrifying that case had been. It was infamous at the time. Because that alpha wasn't just wolf. He'd been warlock too. Warlock first. Approached a werewolf and asked them to turn him. He *wanted* to change, to be half-magic, half-moon. A warlock with magic who could also transform. Quicker healing, enhanced senses. Speed. Strength. It'd never happened before. And then he'd set about conducting experiments on humans, turning them on purpose, even when it wasn't a full moon, thus being in full control and aware of what he was doing. To see if he could pass on his magic as well as wolf blood. Even now, Oren wasn't entirely sure what Amhuinn had expected to achieve with his little hybrid army. Challenge the Elders for power, perhaps? That seemed the most likely goal. Though he still wasn't convinced that was truly achievable.

'Many of that pack were complicit, Sage. Amhuinn was . . . charismatic, charming, all the things a cult leader needs to brainwash his followers—'

She scoffed. 'Packs aren't cults, Oren.'

'Essentially they are.' He had to fight to keep the derision out of his voice. She was so naïve. So young. 'Amhuinn might have been the one conducting the experiments, but the rest allowed it. Some offered their own children. It was me that was sent to confront Amhuinn, Sage, and I have no regrets over the executions that happened that night.'

'No remorse at all?' she asked quietly.

He shook his head. 'Not that time. Not when it was so deserved.'

'Did any of them fight back?' He could tell she wasn't even sure why she was asking.

'Some. A lot of the younger ones panicked.'

'And the rest? You said you only killed half the pack.'

'I had them renounce their alpha and anyone I'd killed. Made them kneel and swear blood oaths. That they'd welcome death the next time we met, if it was under the same circumstances.'

'That was cruel,' she whispered. 'They didn't need to say all that.'

'Yes, they did. If I ever meet any of those werewolves again it won't be for the same crimes.'

Her expression was horrified. He smiled bitterly. 'I know what even the worst of my own kind think of some of the things I've done, Sage. And I've done far worse than you know.'

'Worse than that?'

He inclined his head.

'The kind of stories you wouldn't tell me about. In the archives?'

'Some.' He decided to tell her the truth. 'I'm not proud of a lot of them.' He shrugged, he felt so tired all of a sudden.

'I didn't think guilt would be your thing.'

He hissed impatiently. 'Pity isn't the same as guilt. Most think I do my job for enjoyment, but they're wrong. I do it because I'm one of the few that can. Someone has to keep order of the worst this world has to offer. But I also acknowledge that those I kill meant something to someone once, regardless of the crime, that's all. I pity those left living. Sometimes it's the only thing that stops me from getting carried away.'

A clear distinction. A line he knew she hadn't initially considered – that everyone who crossed the street to avoid them hadn't considered. They thought he relished the acts that'd made him infamous.

She'd thought it. Hadn't considered he might just do it to keep them all safe, because he was one of the few powerful enough that could. It wasn't an important difference to a lot of people. He was a killer either way. But it was a difference. And it mattered to him.

'Do you?' she asked. 'Sometimes get carried away?'

He pulled a non-committal expression. 'There was a point, a long time ago, that I did descend so far into a kind of darkness that I was the monster everyone still believes. From before I came to Downside to work in the Arcānum here. The worst stories are from that time; the ones I still hear whispered most often.'

'Why do you let everyone believe you're still all they say?'

'How do you suggest I change minds? All those stories are true, no matter how long ago they happened. And don't mistake me, Sage. I still have absolutely no qualms about killing, and I have very limited compassion.' He knocked back the last dregs of his drink. 'But playing on it keeps up appearances. There are still places that don't dare utter my name. The world is a better place when my reputation stops bad people doing bad things for fear I'll turn up and condemn them.'

She narrowed her eyes. 'You sacrifice yourself, is what you're saying.'

He laughed, the closest he'd give to any admission. 'It doesn't feel like a sacrifice. And the truth is, I'd do it again and again if it's what's required. So I don't feel the need to correct anyone. Nobody I pass in the street. None of my work colleagues. They're wary enough they mostly leave me in peace.'

'So why are you correcting me?' She finished the last bit of crust in her hand and sat back in her chair. 'To maintain the cover, don't you need me to be afraid of you too?'

'You're not afraid.' He looked at her, and he thought she understood this was the most honest they'd ever be with each other. Just this once he was allowing it. And they wouldn't speak of it again. 'And only someone who believes they're just as monstrous as I am, who thinks they've simply met not an oppressor, but their match, wouldn't be afraid of me. Someone whose first thoughts when a wolf turns up dead is to jump to the worst possible conclusion about themselves.'

She hadn't moved. But he knew she understood.

'Wolves are pack animals,' he said stiffly.

He'd laughed in her face when she'd first said it. But this time, offering these secrets, putting them on a more even footing with each other, was his way of accepting her offer of tolerance between them until this case was done.

She nodded.

He sighed. At everything. This whole mess.

He was Oren Rinallis.

The killer of monsters and demons and . . . werewolves.

All those werewolves tallied up on his long record of deaths. He still recalled some of their faces as they'd died. The feel of their hot blood on his face.

But perhaps it was P's mothering that'd guilted him into

thinking twice. Or maybe he just didn't want to admit that this evening, when Sage had thought she'd killed someone, and devastation had crumpled her face, he'd seen a younger version of himself in her.

'Who told you I won't change other than at full moon?' she asked.

Oh . . . *That* comment bothered her from their exchange in the archives? That was interesting.

'Roderick,' he said after a few moments. 'Obviously.'

'How does he know?'

He raised a brow. 'The Arcānum knows quite a lot.'

'Does he know why?'

'I didn't ask.'

'Why not?'

'Because it's none of my business.'

'You expect me to believe you're respecting my privacy?'

'More that I don't really care. But we can call it that if it makes you feel any better.'

She glared at him.

He shrugged. 'It really is none of my business. Unless it hinders this investigation.'

'Why would it?'

He got up off the stool and threw down a few notes, more than enough to cover whatever the bill could possibly be.

They stepped out into the night and cold blasted them. He pretended not to see her glance up at the dark sky and that pearlescent, glowing, beautiful, hideous ball, waning now.

He flicked on that sense he usually turned off when he wasn't at a crime scene, just for a moment. And just like at Lucy's apartment, there it was. Her heartbeat: fluttering like the panicked wings of a terrified bird.

Interesting indeed.

They walked in silence back to Dive Bar, until they reached the corner and he spoke at last.

'Just because I choose not to surround myself with friends, would rather be working alone, it doesn't mean I think you're a bad person, Sage.'

Because he wasn't sure if anyone other than P ever actually told her that, or even realized she needed to hear it. She seemed so small and pathetic that even he felt compelled to throw her this small bit of encouragement.

'Is there any point asking why you choose it?'

'No.' He smiled. 'There isn't.'

17

SAGE

The following days became monotonous.

She and P pored over the diary, obsessed with Olly Heywood and Lucy's mystery guy in the cafe. And when Oren wasn't around, following up on other cases he still worked around this one, they stalked the internet, trawled through endless follower and friend lists, but couldn't find anyone with the right names that lived in the right places. They couldn't also entirely discount the fact that, though the chances seemed outrageously slim, some people, both human and supernatural . . . just . . . didn't use social media.

It was torturous.

'It's not a coincidence.' She'd pushed her laptop away one night with a sigh. 'Two missing boyfriends.'

It was a truth neither of them had really wanted to voice, because the thought was so unsettling, so cruel, that they'd been clinging to the idea these innocent, unwitting, human men would turn up, distraught and grieving. But they knew deep down, if these deaths were linked, were committed by the same perpetrator, that he had likely got close to his victims in the guise of an admirer.

The missing admirer. Were Olly Heywood and Lucy's cafe guy one and the same? They had to be. When Oren had tried to recover the CCTV from the cafe, he had been rebuffed by an uninterested manager. All recordings were taped over every few days. Sorry, nothing he could do.

Sage didn't know what she'd do if she failed. She hadn't realized until it was too late how much she'd staked on getting this chance, and now she had it she was flailing. But the job at the end of it was starting to feel less important. It was for Lucy and Salina now.

'Sage!' a voice called as she walked through the centre of Downside with Oren and P.

They'd spent a long afternoon a few days ago down in the archives compiling the names and addresses of every werewolf in the city. Make sure they were on alert for anything suspicious happening around them.

But wow.

There were more werewolves Upside than they'd realized. They'd even enlisted Hozier's help – well, Sage had. Oren and Hozier seemed content to ignore each other. There were nearly fifty in the city centre alone. It'd taken three days to visit that list, even if only to post a card with their details on. With the werewolves who also lived out into the suburbs included, the task would take them weeks. Months. More time than they had.

That afternoon, Oren had barely contained his snarl in the face of an arrogant, twenty-something werewolf who declared he'd simply transform and kill anyone who tried to attack him, and she'd quickly ushered Oren away before he could do any more than warn that he'd be back if any human witnessed a transformation.

He'd straightened himself up and pulled out his phone to make a call. She was glad she couldn't hear P's reaction when he told her not to cook dinner. That he was sick of staring at that wall, now expanded with notes on Salina's death too. They were going out. They could talk about it somewhere he could get a stiff drink.

She turned, looking through the crowds.

'Juniper!' she gasped, finding her sphinx friend trotting up behind them, Harland trailing beside. 'Where've you been? You've not visited in ages!'

Juniper jumped to hug Sage just as they reached each other, lifting her heavy front paws to land on her shoulders.

She looked like just another teenage girl, her brown hair pulled back into braids, were it not for . . . everything else.

'I'm sorry we missed quiz night the other night, we've been so busy,' she grimaced.

But Juniper's eyes had already dropped over her shoulder, and her smile faltered.

'This is Oren.'

'I heard,' Juniper said stiffly.

When she glanced at Harland he was looking away. She

didn't want to know what version of Oren Juniper had heard about from Harland, Danny and Rhen. But her reaction confirmed her suspicions, that he was the reason their friends' visits were becoming more scarce.

'We're on our way to the Satyr's Arms.' Juniper forced a smile. 'Just for a few.' But her expression turned to horror. 'Oh, Sage, we would have invited you and P, honestly, but—'

She forced herself to smile too. 'You know we've been busy, it's fine.'

'It's not because . . .' She went quieter as her words trailed off.

It was because. They both knew it was.

It hurt, just a bit.

'Where are you going?' Harland asked. Clearly, the part he'd played in the decision not to invite them was regretful now he realized they were on their way somewhere with Oren instead.

'I . . . *invited* them to dinner.' Oren's tone said everything he didn't say out loud.

Juniper blanched.

'We're having a house party on Saturday.' Harland pushed his glasses up his nose, trying to make things better. 'Upside. My university flatmate's birthday. She said I could bring, well, you know, invite my own friends. Danny and Rhen are coming.'

'Apparently I'd stand out too much,' Juniper pouted. P

laughed and Juniper grinned too, but Harland still looked guilty.

'You could come too, P, if you wanted. You'd blend in, I mean, uh . . .' But the withering look she gave him was enough for the sentence to fade out into even redder-faced silence.

'No invite for me?' Oren asked sarcastically.

Harland tried to square his shoulders. 'You don't look like a student. Who would I say you are?'

'Don't worry, I have better things to do. Trust me.'

'I'll come,' Sage cut across the sniping. 'As long as there's not much else going on. Which it doesn't look like.'

He pulled an apologetic face. She knew Harland understood how much was riding on it for her. That it was personal. That Lucy had been her friend. Her chest swelled with appreciation.

'Well, we're late,' Harland said awkwardly, gesturing with his head to Juniper that they should cross the road. 'Enjoy dinner.'

She watched her friends start to walk away. Felt the pang in her chest again that they hadn't been invited.

It felt shitty.

It annoyed her. But . . . she also knew they probably felt neglected at the moment too.

Harland turned back, looking at her apprehensively. She panicked for a moment, imagining he could hear her thoughts.

'Can I . . . have a quick word?'

'. . . With me? Uh . . .' What could he want to say that he couldn't have just said a moment ago? 'Sure?'

P tactfully offered to wait at the restaurant, glaring at Oren to follow her. He rolled his eyes and sauntered off. Juniper glanced at Harland. 'Should I . . . ?'

He shook his head.

She had a feeling if he was OK with Juniper hearing then he wouldn't have minded P staying too . . . So this was about—

'About Oren.' He shuffled on his oversized feet as he glanced down at them awkwardly.

'Yeah?' she said slowly.

'I know he said it was none of our business,' he grumbled. 'But I was thinking . . .'

'Be careful.' She nudged his arm. 'You'll do yourself an injury.'

Juniper smiled, but as always, Harland's cheeks pinked.

'Chances are, the mystery boyfriends, I mean, y'know—'

'That they're the killer?' she supplied. She sighed. 'I know. We can't find them anywhere. It's like they've disappeared.'

'That's a weird coincidence, right? That both can't be traced at all?' Juniper looked between them.

'It's just . . .' He was going redder. She wished he'd spit it out. 'When he said he could glamour your face. Or mask it, or whatever he called it . . .'

Oh.

'Harland.' She started to shake her head. But her stomach fluttered uneasily at the mere suggestion. At the thought he could be fooling even her.

He leant in closer so that only she and Juniper could hear. 'Just hear me out. Sage, I know you'll think I'm crazy—'

'What motive would he have?'

'No idea. But I'm just saying, if somebody is going round dating multiple targets to get close to them, wouldn't they probably have to be able to alter their appearance?' She stared at him. 'This case was going to be dropped until you worked out the silver thing. It was only then he took it, even though their captain was angry about it. What if he realized he needed to cover his tracks better? And agreeing to keep you on the case is keeping enemies close kinda—'

He was getting into his stride again. Like when he pitched his other conspiracy theories, when his face lit up and she could practically see the fresh thoughts flashing through his eyes as he word-vomited it all out.

She looked at Juniper, whose face seemed to be purposely schooled into not giving an opinion. She knew the sphinx was just as aware what Harland, Danny and Rhen were like with their theories. But she also kinda appreciated Juniper's loyalty in not rubbishing his idea right away.

She sighed. 'I just can't see it.'

That wasn't entirely true, though, was it? Because why

else was her stomach still twisting into knots? At least, she realized that she understood why he considered it a valid suggestion. He had the ability, the lack of conscience? But . . .

'I'm not saying it out of jealousy, Sage,' he said quietly. 'We don't like leaving you with him.'

She looked up at him, and she could see that it wasn't jealousy. It wasn't just because he felt pushed out; like Oren had stolen their friends from them. His eyes were full of genuine concern.

'Just stay alert.' He stepped back at last, looking defeated. She nodded. 'And, well, I know what this means for you. If you need anything, just ask.'

But she already had a request the moment he said it. It probably wasn't as exciting as he would've hoped for, but . . . 'We're visiting every werewolf in the city. Warning them . . . The list is huge. You could help?'

She knew at once Oren wouldn't want to let him do that.

'He won't let me do that.'

Ha.

'Leave him to me.' She sounded more confident than she felt on that one. 'I could give you a list, if you're round for breakfast?'

He was supposed to be staying at their place, as he did every weekend or holiday that he spent Downside. But recently he'd found excuses to crash at their friends'. She knew that especially had hurt P's feelings too.

He looked sceptical. But he nodded.

18

SAGE

'When you wake up to him sitting at the end of your bed watching you sleep, I'll be ready to say I told you so,' Oren said when Sage caught up to him and P standing waiting for her in a small queue outside Northern Psyche: the premier spot in Downside for gourmet grilled cheese. 'He likes you, you know. And that selkie, what's he called? Rhen? The pair of them stink when you're all in the same room.'

'Shut up, Oren.'

'I'm serious. Did you not wonder what that smell was? The last time I smelt lust that bad I had to rescue some sailors from a siren in the Black Sea. And that was eighty years ago.'

'My love life isn't your problem.'

'You don't have a love life.'

'I won't if you scare them all away! Like you've clearly done with my friends.'

He snorted as a waitress with a magnificent set of dragonfly wings and a wide smile appeared and cut short their argument. 'Table for three?'

She led them into the bright restaurant; yellow walls and blue chairs, and . . . cheese never smelt so good.

Her stomach growled.

The restaurant was bustling. Couples, and groups of friends, and work colleagues on outings. The laughter and chatter was filled with the sparkle that only came with the excitement of Yuletide. Glittering fairy lights flashed and twinkled, draped over art on the walls and around the banister leading to more tables upstairs. A tall evergreen covered in tiny fireflies shone from the corner of the room.

They passed a table of kaperosas by the door – several women in white dresses with long, dark hair covering their faces. The pink lanyards around their necks signalled them as the women that ran the exclusive female-only wellness spa in Downside. Long, slender fingers pulled back the silky black curtains of hair just long enough for them to bite into their sandwiches as they nattered away.

The waitress led them to a table a little further down, and seemed unwilling to look Oren in the eye as she addressed Sage and P directly. 'Just so you know, the Baritone Banshees Choir have a table booked at nine. They're great fun but, ah,' she smiled apologetically, 'loud.'

She fluttered away, promising someone would be over to take their drinks order soon, as P snatched up the menu to discuss all the plates she'd try if she could still eat.

Half an hour later, two ginormous plates of grilled cheese and various sides – mac-n-cheese-topped fries, mozzarella sticks, chicken balls – had been piled on their table. P sighed as she watched Oren cut his sandwich in half. The phone in Sage's pocket pinged.

She pulled it out, and blinked, surprised. 'It's Hozier.' She read the message. 'She wants a word.'

Oren looked at her, then back at his food, then back at her again, incredulously. 'Now?'

'Says it's urgent,' she said, tapping in her reply.

'She's already here,' P said, looking over at the front of the restaurant.

'That was quick.' Sage greeted the tiny, red-headed warlock making her way through the crowded room.

'I track Upside werewolves as part of my job,' Hozier said brightly with a wink as she picked up a chip and popped it in her mouth. 'It wasn't hard to track your phone. I was already outside.'

'Not sure that's legit policy, Hozier,' Oren muttered under his breath as he stabbed at a bit of mac-n-cheese with his fork.

'This is P,' Sage cut across Oren to save Hozier from having to reply. 'She's my housemate.'

'We've met.' Hozier smiled at P. 'Only briefly. When you were away, Sage. I helped her find a file on a werewolf. And I come bearing another werewolf name. Darren Johnson. Does he sound familiar?'

'Should he?' Sage asked.

'Werewolf. Thirty-five. Maybe a little too old for you to know,' she added in an afterthought. 'He lived Upside too.

He died a few weeks ago.'

P's head shot around. *'What?* It wasn't in the papers?'

Downside Daily was much the same as every Upside tabloid, with the same kind of news, gossip, sports and adverts, just aimed at and featuring the supernatural.

'It was. Kind of. In the obituary section. He died of natural causes so it wasn't a story.' Hozier frowned. 'But I just . . . I was speaking to the warlocks that went to the scene today and it made me think. Sage, he had a nut allergy. He died of what appeared to be an allergic reaction to something he ate.'

Sage stared at Oren.

He stared back. His food, at last, forgotten.

'Exactly,' Hozier said softly.

'If, *if* this werewolf ingested silver,' Hozier said, 'then did Salina? She was ripped to pieces, but was she subdued first? If this is a trend then it's a proper link, it ties them together more solidly than before. Three is the threshold for serial killers. And you'd have one on the loose.'

'Was this werewolf injured in any other way?' Sage asked Hozier, frowning.

Hozier shook her head. 'But timeline-wise, Darren Johnson came first. Then Lucy, then Salina. If they can officially be linked to the same killer, it shows escalation in terms of violence.'

Oren nodded slowly. 'Losing control? Or getting more desperate?'

'Desperate for what?' Sage asked. 'If we're going with the theory that Lucy's death was a message, then we have to assume these other two deaths are too. And this is one hell of a warning.'

His expression was grim. He didn't need to say it out loud because they both knew.

They had absolutely no idea who that message was for. Every name, every source, every story . . . everything Lucy had been working on that could've landed her in trouble with the wrong people had been a dead end. As far as they could tell, she hadn't got herself mixed up with any of the 'wrong type of people' at all.

'If we can prove these other two are victims of the same killer, then there has to be another link between them,' P said. 'If their deaths are intended to frighten someone, that someone has to know them all, surely? So what links a journalist, a physiotherapist and . . .' She looked at Hozier questioningly.

'A delivery driver.'

'Right.' P shrugged. 'A delivery driver. Maybe we've been looking in the wrong places.'

'Well, where are the right places?' Sage asked her friend. It wasn't even a real question, not really. More exasperation.

P didn't answer. She didn't know either.

Oren grimaced at the food still covering the table. 'Eat up, Sage. We've got a house call to make tonight.'

19

SAGE

It was late, nearly midnight, by the time they'd decided it was quiet enough in the street outside for them to creep unnoticed into Darren's Upside home. It was still full of his personal possessions – his next of kin hadn't done anything with the house yet. Hadn't even visited, judging by three weeks' worth of mail they'd stepped over under the letter-box. But the lack of life, the lack of heating for weeks, made the property bone-cold.

The cushions on the sofa were perfectly lined up and spread out, and the coasters on the coffee table were the exact same space from the corners on either side. It was sparse. None of the usual clutter of a lived-in home. No piles of magazines or well-thumbed books. It was clinical. Unnatural.

'Obsessive,' Oren muttered as he stopped before the coffee table and stared down at the perfectly placed coasters. 'Did you see his coats by the front door?'

Sage doubled back to look. Four coats, hung from a row of hooks on the wall, the sleeves of each arm tucked into the pockets. Nonsensical. It was without any reasonable explanation other than what made Darren Johnson feel better. Just part of who he was.

'Must've been exhausting, to live like that every day,' she sighed, walking back into the living room, but Oren had moved on. She tuned in her wolfish senses. She could hear fabric rustling upstairs.

She found him in the bedroom standing in front of a wardrobe full of men's clothing; two of everything, all perfectly folded into piles so neat and tidy it was like looking into a shop display. Below, on the floor, was a long rack for shoes. Two identical sets of each.

'Why double?'

Oren made a non-committal hum. 'Probably couldn't stand getting dirt on his clothes. Back-ups?'

Exhausting, indeed.

He closed the wardrobe doors and looked around the room. She followed his gaze. The bed was perfectly made, even though Johnson had been found still in his pyjamas. He must've made it as soon as he got up that morning. 'I can barely even scent him, he's been gone too long. Never mind scenting anyone else.'

She nodded, dejected. Even her own sense of smell, stronger than his, had nothing.

She followed him back out into the hallway. 'Where did he die?'

'Presumably the kitchen, if he was eating.'

Even now, she could still hear the derision when he spoke to her sometimes, only thinly veiled behind half-hearted tolerance.

She pushed past with a pointed shove at the bottom of the stairs, and headed for the kitchen.

But she paused. Just beside the front door under the neat coats on the walls was a pair of shoes, perhaps the last ones he'd worn, kicked off as he'd arrived home for the final time. One was knocked on to its side. It must've happened as they'd taken his body away. A man like Darren wouldn't have left them untidy like that. It struck her just as the discarded remote control had done in Lucy's apartment.

She bent down and straightened it to just how Darren Johnson would have wanted it. It was the best she could offer his memory.

'No silver?' Oren asked moments later, as they stood in the middle of a small kitchen.

She tried not to sound too disappointed. 'The file Hozier gave us said that he had taken a bite from a croissant for breakfast. The packaging stated on the back that the pastry was made in a factory that used nuts in other products, and the assumption was . . .'

He nodded. 'But had someone sprinkled silver on to it?'

She sighed, shaking her head. 'Nothing here.'

He pulled a face as if to say it was still worth checking, but as she made to follow him back out of the kitchen again, she paused. To the left, beside the door, was a pedal bin. She let the toe of her trainer press the pedal and she peered inside. It was empty – not even a bin liner, so the whole thing must've been lifted and thrown out.

'Nothing . . . *here*,' she repeated quietly.

'What?'

'Where's the rest of the croissant? He only took one bite?' she asked.

'Not in that bin, I take it?' he asked sarcastically.

'Nobody has been here to collect the mail, what're the chances the outdoor bin hasn't been pulled out into the street for emptying on collection day?'

They stared at each other in the silence, then like a starter pistol had fired, they turned and raced for the front door at the exact same moment.

She hissed as he shoved her out of the way, not allowing her to barge past him a second time as he flung open the front door and strode into the freezing night. But at least it wasn't raining, so she'd take it.

Down a narrow pathway behind a wooden gate at the side of the property was a row of bins with different-coloured lids to indicate what could be recycled in them. Gold hummed gently on the rusting gate bolt and it slid back with a creak.

'Do you need to light it up?' She knew he couldn't see as plainly as her in the dark – and she also knew it would irritate him like hell.

'Even if I wanted to,' he said quietly, 'we're being watched.'

Her hand, on the lid of the black waste bin, froze as she turned.

A street lamp cast a soft yellow light down the deserted road. Three fat black birds sat on top.

'The . . . crows?'

'They're ravens.'

'Keen birdwatcher?' she hissed at the semantics of the *incredibly similar-looking* black birds.

He looked at her as if she were stupid. 'Ravens are magic. They follow me occasionally.' She stared at him. 'You didn't know they're supernatural?'

'Should I know that?' she asked slowly.

If she played it right and he started laughing, she could pretend she knew it was a joke all along.

'Even the humans have old legends about ravens,' he shrugged. 'What did they even teach you?'

So he was being serious. And she looked like an idiot.

Great.

'Maybe I missed that class,' she grumbled.

'They're of the old magic, they do the bidding of those like themselves.' But when he saw she was still drawing a blank he rolled his eyes. 'Dark magic, Sage. They're spies.'

'Spies for who?'

He pulled a face that said, *Who knows?* 'Whoever is willing to pay them. I've made a lot of enemies.'

'Have you ever paid them?' she asked. 'To spy on people?'

'Only once or twice,' he sniffed.

'Dark magic explains a lot.' She looked at him pointedly.

He tutted. 'I'm not a necromancer. Or the Faragahinde. Warlocks are new magic. We're . . .' He paused to find the right words. 'Despite how it must feel to you, we're not ancient. Or demons. We're not *that* kind of magic.'

She *hmm*ed as if she didn't believe him, and finally opened the bin lid.

Then slammed it shut as she heaved and gagged.

Oh, God. 'Yep.' She turned away, gulping down clean, fresh, silver-free air. 'It's in there.'

He grinned. 'You remind me of those pigs they use to sniff out truffles.'

20

SAGE

Sage had barely got out of bed the next morning when there was a knock on the door.

Was that Harland already? She grumbled to herself as she fell on to the sofa, the smell of toast teasing her nostrils. She'd have liked half an hour to come round though before he bounded in, overenthusiastic and ready to help.

P floated through the closed door and into the hallway.

She pulled her knees up ready to curl into a ball and snooze a bit more as she heard a vaguely familiar voice echo down the hallway.

'And you must be P,' Berion's deep voice purred. 'I've heard all about you.'

'You have?' came P's confused voice.

'Of course, one of the best chefs in Downside, apparently.'

Sage tutted. What a smooth-talker. She had no idea where Berion had heard that, in fact, but she could hear P giggling – *giggling*! What was Berion doing here?

'Is Sage about?'

'Uh, yeah.' P's voice was still high-pitched and pleased with herself. 'Come in, I've just boiled the kettle, do you want—'

He cut across her with a choke of laughter. 'Jeez, Sage. Didn't you sleep last night?'

'Oh, she always looks like that before she's brushed her hair—' P started, trailing off when she saw her expression. 'I'll just . . . Kettle . . .' And she disappeared again.

'We got back late,' Sage muttered, rubbing at her dull thudding temple. Because when she couldn't sleep, her head aching with everything in it they couldn't solve, she'd sat in front of P's detective movie wall with a bottle of wine and drowned her sorrows in it. 'Why are you here?'

'To discuss the' – his smile was tight – 'large outdoor bin full of half-rotted rubbish that I found stinking out my office this morning.'

Ah.

After his truffle comment, Oren had decided against bin-diving for the silver-laced croissant, and with a wave of his hand and a puff of gold, the whole bin had disappeared. Now she knew where it'd gone.

P was still beaming from Berion's compliments as she carried in her trademark tea tray. 'Oren told Sage to be ready to leave at nine. He'll be here to collect soon.'

'Nine?' he muttered as he sat down, quickly assessing which clues were left of one of P's discarded crosswords on the coffee table. He was in a suit of soft lilac velvet, the pewter chain of a watch snaking into his pocket. At his ears glistened two large diamonds and his fingers were again adorned with a selection of rings. 'You know, he used to be in the training rooms at five o'clock sharp every morning. These days he doesn't get there a moment before seven.'

'He trains *every day*?' P arched a brow.

'How else do you think we keep fit enough to fight monsters?' Berion pulled a dramatic face, his white eyes wide, then pointedly sipped his tea. 'If you saw him shirtless you wouldn't question it. Carved by angels.' Then he snorted. 'Of course he does. We all do. It's part of our contract. Bet you didn't know *that* when you pestered Roderick for a job, huh, Sage?'

Ergh. She hadn't, no.

But before she could say anything there was another familiar *tap, t-tap* noise in the hall.

'That'll be Harland. He's helping us today.'

'Does Oren know?' P's question echoed behind her. She chose not to answer.

Then she heard his voice, light and warm as he greeted P.

'Who's Harland?' Berion asked, his tone pricked with interest as he listened to him nattering away in the hall.

'Our friend,' she said quietly. 'Please be kind to him.'

'Why wouldn't I be?' He blinked, mildly affronted.

'Oren's awful to all our friends,' she grimaced just as the young wolf in ripped jeans and an orange hoodie fell into the room, laughing as he told P some anecdote from the pub night they hadn't been invited to.

'Oh.' He flushed at once as he turned and saw the

warlock. 'Sorry.'

He pushed his glasses up nervously as he straightened, the smile falling off his face. She understood. He expected another Oren.

But Berion got to his feet and extended a glittering hand, and with a wide smile he introduced himself.

'Pleased to finally meet you.' He inclined his head as Harland took the hand with confused uncertainty. 'Sage has told me about you already, of course.' It was a downright lie, but Berion exuded a mystical kind of confidence that made everything sound gracious. Harland flushed.

The sound of the front door opening a third time caused them all to pause again.

'How did I know you'd be here?' was Oren's greeting the moment he stepped into the living room.

But it was Berion who beat any of them to a retort.

'Because you urgently requested my services,' he said sweetly, raising his cup of tea in mock salute before taking another sip, his eyes glittering.

Sage grinned. *Thank you*, she mouthed.

'Breakfast!' P practically screamed. She could contain herself no longer. Berion looked up, startled, but was apparently wise enough not to speak. The corners of his mouth twitched as they put in their orders.

'Harland's helping us today,' Sage told Oren firmly as P floated away.

'No, he isn't.'

'Yes, he is.'

'Why would we need his help?'

'I'm giving him a list of werewolves. All he has to do is give them our contact details if they're worried or think there's anything suspicious nearby.'

Oren's nostrils flared.

'Danny texted me when I was on my way over,' Harland added. 'He's free today too. He can help, we'll get through even more if we split up.'

Oren looked ready to explode at the thought of more teenage werewolves.

'Come on,' Harland almost whined. He was looking at Oren like he was ready to beg, to give him just one chance to prove he wasn't such a loser. 'Even we can do that.'

'Sure they can,' Berion said brusquely as P appeared with one sausage sandwich wrapped in foil for Harland, and thrust an egg butty less politely into Oren's hands.

She was sure Oren had only agreed because handing over a list of names got Harland out of the apartment quicker, and he wanted to hear what Berion had to say.

'You didn't say you dumped the bin in the middle of his office.' Sage threw Oren a disapproving look.

He shrugged as he sat and propped his foot on the end of the coffee table. P clapped her hands loudly in his face. If she could have made contact she was sure the poltergeist would've whacked his ankle clean off. Berion watched her with admiration.

'Where was I supposed to put it?'

'Somewhere the smell wouldn't permeate my uphol-stery,' Berion smiled, but, oh, there was something feline and dangerous under his purr. 'Luckily for you, I was in the office early. I extracted the . . . well . . . it's a rotting mulch of mouldy pastry by now . . .' He held out an empty palm and in a whiff of purple, a clear ziplock bag appeared, some-thing blackened and crusty inside.

Sage acknowledged that since she wasn't heaving, Berion must be muting her senses again.

'Similar dosage?' Oren asked.

Berion nodded. 'Hozier filled me in on your conversa-tion last night,' he said grimly. 'It's not looking good, is it?'

Oren shook his head. 'We don't know if the third werewolf – Salina Gourlay – had silver in her system yet but it seems unlikely not to be related at this point.'

'Is there a link between her and the other victims?' Berion asked.

'If there's a link between any of the victims we've not found it yet.' P sounded dejected.

Berion frowned, and was quiet for a moment. Then he stood, and looked at Sage and Oren. 'You two had better be off, then,' he said brusquely.

'P, darling, come with me. Hozier will let you rummage through the archives as long as no other warlocks spot you and snitch to Roderick. Let's see if there's anything to find.'

21

OREN

The list of werewolves living Upside seemed to never end. Sage had handed the insufferable werewolf kids thirty names, barely a scratch on the surface. Their list was double that, and they'd grossly underestimated the amount of time reassurance took when they'd started the task.

Well. If it were left to him he'd hand over a card and leave. It was Sage who insisted on being friendly.

No, thank you.

He brooded in the background and left her to it.

By four-thirty, he was glad that part of their day was over.

Down in the archives with Hozier and Berion, P had found the contact details for Darren Johnson's only living relative and texted them the address: a residential home where his grandmother now lived. It explained why nobody had emptied his house yet, or even picked up the mail. Sage had sourced the visiting hours, and it was far enough across the city that she had been forced to agree to shifting, and he smothered a grin as they reappeared in some frosty-looking gardens, and she tried to swallow a heave.

'Imagine getting old,' he grumbled as they trudged up the pathway towards a beige-looking building. 'Must be awful.'

'Thanks.'

He shuddered, because he knew it'd annoy her.

'You age anyway,' she hissed as he hit his mark. 'Kind of. At some point you'll look older that you do now.'

'I'd have to live a very, very long time to look like an OAP. Fifty years and you will literally be one.'

She didn't grace him with an answer as they crossed the threshold into the building.

The home had *that* smell. Decaying old people. He struggled not to wrinkle his nose.

The walls were bland, decorated with shaky water-colours and sketches he could only assume were created by residents. The carpet was weathered with age, and what was once maroon was now a light, faded pink down the centre where years of footsteps had worn it out.

When Sage told the nurse at the reception who they were there to visit, she gave them a sad smile. 'She's been very quiet,' she admitted as she came around the desk to take them to Verity Johnson. 'We've had police here already.' She glanced back. 'Uniformed ones. To break the news . . .'

'We're just here for a social call,' Sage offered as they followed her through a light but equally beige communal room where some residents chatted, a few played cards or board games at tables, and a few just sat in silence. 'A follow-up. Check how she's doing.'

He was impressed how smoothly she was able to lie on the spot.

The nurse pursed her lips. Muttered something about 'finding them younger and younger these days'.

When Sage glanced back at him, fully aware he was double the age of most of the residents in there, he almost smiled.

They crossed the wide room to a conservatory. The sky was grey, the pitter-patter of fresh rain amplified by the glass ceiling. But there was something peaceful about the spot, he'd concede that.

Perhaps that was why Verity had chosen to sit there, alone, gazing out into the gardens obscured into a blur of muted colour by the downpour. In her hands were two needles, and a ball of white wool sat on her lap as her fingers moved. She didn't need to look at what she was doing.

'Verity?' Sage asked gently as the nurse left them to chat. 'Verity Johnson?'

She didn't manage to stop herself flinching at the milky-white film that covered the old woman's eyes, the cataracts obscuring what were once brown irises.

'Ah,' she sighed, closing her eyes and smiling. 'You smell like him.'

'Smell like who?' Sage asked, clearly taken aback.

'My Darren.' She opened her milky eyes again, putting her knitting on her lap as she gestured for the seat to her left. 'You are . . . like him?'

Sage glanced at Oren.

He shrugged.

'Like him?'

The old woman raised a nobbled hand, her fingers crooked and bent, and held it out. He watched. He resented admitting that having a partner with people skills got them further than when he demanded answers.

Like when he'd held that knife to her throat.

If he possessed just a shade less arrogance he knew he'd end up feeling ashamed of that.

Sage put her hand in Verity Johnson's, allowed her to encase her young hand in old ones.

'So soft. You'd never think. Never guess. Yes, my Darren was like that too. So gentle. So kind. Until that one night of the month he'd go out and not come home.'

He looked down at her knitting and realized what it was. A small, four-legged animal with a long tail.

'Where would he go?' Sage asked.

'Where do you go?'

'Far away,' she said quietly. 'Where I can't hurt anyone.'

'Is that why you've come?' Verity asked. 'Did you know him?'

'I'm with . . . our version of the police.' When she glanced at Oren again, he nodded. She'd found the easiest explanation.

It was the easiest part of the conversation, in fact, because it certainly wasn't easy for Sage to explain that they suspected her beloved grandson, her only grandson, who she'd been told had died of an allergy, had actually been murdered. She wept into a tissue for a long time.

He spoke at last. 'How is it that you came to know about your grandson's condition?'

'Oh.' Verity looked up. 'He speaks. I thought he was there just to look pretty.'

Sage was trying not to smirk. 'That's the only reason I bring him along. A distraction when the job gets tricky.'

'I'll bet, with cheekbones like that.'

He didn't know whether to laugh or frown.

'I've always known. The attack on a family holiday left him the only survivor. I took him in. Raised him. I had a choice to make and I made it to love him, no matter what he was. As long as he was happy, so was I.'

'The same happened to me,' Sage whispered. 'I was on holiday with my family. We were camping on a full moon. A transformed werewolf attacked our tents. I don't remember much. It was dark . . . The fur was drenched red with blood . . . A man walking his dogs found us the next day. It was too late for my parents and brother. I was the only one that survived.'

He'd never asked her what had happened, but it wasn't

hard to guess. Most werewolf stories were the same.

His memory flashed back to that night he'd gone after Amhuinn for the atrocities he'd committed. He'd thought about that night often lately, more than any other thing he'd done in his brutal, devastating life. All the werewolves tallied up on his long record of deaths.

'I'm sorry for your loss,' Verity said quietly.

'It was a long time ago.'

'It doesn't matter. It's the burden of those left behind, to pretend that the loss becomes less heavy with time.'

Oren could tell she was finding it hard to answer. He cleared his throat.

'We know remarkably little about Mr Johnson. We've gathered he had no family other than yourself, and no children. Do you know of any partners, ex-partners, even? Close friends we could contact? Any information we can gather will help.'

Verity looked thoughtful, but dubious. 'I've been in here for a long time,' she sighed. 'It's been a long time since I met any of his friends. He spoke recently of one, called it casual, but that he'd like to bring them to visit. He hadn't wanted to do that in a long time so I thought it must be . . . Oh,' she sniffled into her tissue. 'I never got the chance before he died.'

'Did this friend have a name?'

'Jamie, I think?' She screwed her face up, thinking. 'A man,' she added. 'Not that it mattered, I mean, I just know some girls have that name too.'

'Jamie.' He exchanged glances with Sage. She nodded. Another mysterious boyfriend.

'Anyone else?' Sage probed gently.

She made a confused noise, like she was trying to remember more names or details. 'He . . . The shop.'

'Shop?' Sage repeated, glancing at him. He frowned. 'He was a delivery driver, wasn't he?'

The old woman nodded. 'Exactly. More of a convenience store. Groceries, toiletries, but it made deliveries too. The owner is . . . like you, you see. Specialized in certain meats. Sold no products with silver in the packaging. And a lot of . . . *the community* shopped there. My Darren made the deliveries to the werewolf clientele. It wasn't much work. That's why he worked for other courier services too. To top up his wage, you know? But—'

He could see Sage trying to force her eagerness to remain calm. 'The shop, Verity, do you know the name?'

She shook her head. 'It's on St Stephen Street.' She looked at them hopefully. 'That's all I know. Will that help?'

'It will.' Sage nodded gratefully. 'We can work with that.'

She rose, ready to say her goodbyes. But Verity reached for her hand again.

'How did he die?' she asked. 'They said it was his allergies . . . but if you say . . .'

Sage clearly couldn't. She looked at him again with desperate eyes.

Maybe she was rubbing off on him, because usually he would've told the truth. 'We believe he may have been poisoned, and it was made to look like his allergy. It would've been very quick.'

The old lady looked horrified. 'Was he in pain?'

'No,' he lied. 'We don't believe so.'

She nodded and looked down at her knitting again.

'Thank you,' Sage whispered, touching the old woman's hand again. 'We're sorry to have upset you.'

'You offered me a small gift.' She smiled sadly. 'To be able to talk about him freely again. Take this.' She slipped a small pair of scissors from the pocket of her cardigan, and snipped the wool, then held up a small white wolf in her gnarled hands.

'Oh, I couldn't,' Sage tried to refuse, but Verity Johnson shook her head.

'I missed him very much when I woke up today. I thought it might make me feel closer to him. But you did that. I want you to take it.'

22

SAGE

'Where have you been?' a shrill voice demanded.

Sage froze.

So did Oren.

'What's going on?' Oren said slowly as they turned to see the kitchen table that had been dragged into the living room and laid out for a formal, sit-down meal. Around it sat Harland and Danny at either end, and Berion and Hozier on one side, facing them. Berion looked positively delighted at their telling-off. Danny and Harland looked awkward and uncomfortable, their presence at the table evidently forced by P.

'It's dinnertime,' Sage realized. She'd insisted they walk back to Dive Bar into Downside. They'd lost track of time. 'We forgot dinner.'

'Bloody hell,' Oren muttered.

'Yes, it is!' P snapped. 'We've been waiting. Sit.'

They straightened, like siblings in trouble.

'You could have started without us, P,' Oren grumbled. She ignored him and floated through the kitchen wall, her face full of furious irritation.

'You got an invite while in the archives, then?' Sage eyed Berion, who had tried his best to school his face into neutrality as P scolded them.

'It was more of a command, actually,' he said quietly.

'How did you end up here?' Oren asked Hozier. It almost sounded accusatory.

'Because I've spent my afternoon helping her too,' Hozier said pointedly. Helping *you* by extension, was what she really meant. 'She told me all about sneaking into the human buildings to steal information from Upside. Genius. We should tell Roderick to start employing poltergeists next.'

'He hasn't started employing werewolves yet,' Sage sighed as she unfolded her napkin. 'He's only humouring me.'

'Lots of races have aspirations of joining the Arcānum.' The tiny female shrugged. 'Nobody else has got this far.'

She smiled at Hozier. There was something predatory about her, but it wasn't cruel or sadistic. It didn't make the hairs on her arm prickle like Oren sometimes still did.

Harland muttered something under his breath.

'How've you done today, Harland? Why's your hair dripping?' Oren turned to him, leaning back in his chair and stretching an arm so that it rested over the back of Sage's.

She could kick him.

She looked at her friend, both of her friends, who had so far been completely and nervously silent, to realize that, yes, his hair was clearly damp.

'Because it's the middle of winter and this city never stops raining?'

'Why aren't you wet?' she asked Danny.

'We split the last couple of names to finish quicker. I got lucky.' He grinned, eyeing his unfortunate friend. 'All mine were cool. No questions. Just took the details. I got back here forty minutes before Harland. I just missed the downpour.'

The corner of Harland's lip still twitched. 'Not all of us have pet warlocks to keep us warm and dry with magic, see.'

Berion snorted into his wine.

'If anyone is a *pet*, I'd say it's— Ow! What was that for?'

She'd rammed her elbow into his side. 'Don't finish that sentence.'

'I was just—'

'I said, *stop*.' A slight on Harland or Danny for being a werewolf was a slight on her too.

'Apologies.'

She knew from the flash in his eyes he didn't mean it. But before she could say as much, P was back.

'Wow.' She whistled though her teeth as the ghost proudly presented a whole chicken surrounded by roasted potatoes and seasoned vegetables on a platter, and set it in the centre of the table.

'She does this all the time?' Berion's brows rose.

'You learn to roll with it,' she muttered as P disappeared and reappeared again with a bowl full of mashed potatoes and Yorkshire puddings, and then a large boat of gravy.

'Good lord,' Berion said as he piled his plate high. 'We'll come again.'

'Of course.' P practically shone, breathless, as she watched them all tuck into the food she couldn't eat. 'The more the merrier!'

'I don't eat for days when I know I'm staying the weekend.' Harland lifted chicken on to Hozier's plate. 'And I still end up taking portions back to my uni halls with me.'

Hozier laughed. 'P, this is fantastic. Thank you.'

If it were possible, P glowed even more.

Oren waved a hand and a glass of rosé wine appeared in front of Sage's plate, raspberries floating in the glass. Exactly what she'd ordered and drank in Northern Psyche. When she took a sip it instantly refilled. She wished she had magic just for that.

Hozier chinked their glasses. She could've sighed in relief that it turned out not every warlock was as grumpy as Oren or Roderick. She told her about their visit to Verity Johnson, and the shop they'd visit in the morning.

After a while chatter turned to other subjects, and as she sat laughing at Berion's tales about his failing love life, or Hozier's stories of a childhood sneaking into pyramids, for the first time in a long time, she almost felt normal. Just a normal girl with normal friends doing normal things. Not a werewolf hunting murderers, coming home ashamed of the black eyes and split lip she couldn't remember getting.

But of course.

It couldn't be that simple. It never was.

A nice dinner with friends?

Ha.

She didn't understand what was happening at first; one moment she was piling parsnips on to her fork, and then the room started to flash. Silence fell immediately. Danny jumped so hard his knee hit the table and his plate rattled. Oren stiffened beside her. Only Berion didn't seem to react.

'I know that when I see it,' he groaned quietly, looking at Hozier's left hand still holding her wine glass to her lips.

On her finger was a gold ring with what looked like a small white pearl in the centre setting, flashing a light so brightly it made white spots appear under Sage's eyelids even after she closed them.

Hozier swallowed, looking at her across the table. 'Portable alarm. I have a bigger one in my office.'

'Alarm for what?' But as her stomach dropped, she thought she already knew.

In a puff of her red magic, a small notebook appeared on the table. It wasn't like Oren's magical notepad: old and leather-bound and looked after for a long, long time. Hozier's notepad was crumpled and coverless. She tipped her hand palm up and tapped the notepad with the top of the ring. It stopped flashing. Red ink started to scribble itself across the page. Hozier ripped off the note and handed it over. 'Rosamond Drive,' she said grimly. 'You've got an hour.'

'Wait.' Harland looked up, his already enlarged eyes wide behind his thick glasses. 'That was one of ours, I think, hang on.'

He jumped up and hurried for the rucksack he'd left by the side of the sofa, and started rummaging through the front zip pocket.

'Here.' He pulled out a soggy-looking piece of paper, the one she'd given him with a list of addresses, some crossed out, some circled. 'Yep, after we split, I called but the driveway was empty and nobody was home. It's a dead-end road. Quiet. I posted a note with my number asking to arrange a time I could call back.'

'And you didn't think of going back to check?' Oren asked through gritted teeth.

'I was going to do the whole list then double-back at the end.' He held up his hands, his lisp getting stronger again.

'That's fair.' Berion cut between them as Harland's desperate eyes flickered gratefully. 'What's the name?'

'Mhairi Lindsay. I remember her because of the spelling,' he added, flinching as Oren tutted. 'Doctor.'

'Do you want us to come?' Berion was half out of his seat, Hozier not far behind.

Oren shook his head, his expression full of frustration.

He turned to Harland and Danny. 'This'd better not be the morning headline in *Downside Daily*,' he snarled, and strode from the room to wait for Sage outside.

23

SAGE

Oren shifted them Upside, outside a small two-up, two-down semi-detached with all the lights off. There was a car on the driveway, so Mhairi must've come home since Harland had called.

Oren raised a hand ready to unlock the door with magic, to discover it was already open.

The sound of a faint hissing met her ears. 'What's that noise?'

On a small table by the doorway there was a set of keys, and next to it the card Harland had posted through, his untidy handwriting visible. On the floor was a leather bag with three numbered dials to unlock it, and a dark coat hung by a hook on the wall above it.

'Come on.' Oren stepped into the darkness first.

'It's coming from upstairs.' She gestured to the ceiling with her chin. 'The sound. I think . . . it's water.' He was already on the bottom step when she shuddered. 'I can smell blood.'

'From here?'

She'd nodded. The wolf had been itching under her skin the moment they'd stepped over the threshold. 'It's not like Lucy's place. Not overwhelming. But there's blood some-where.'

'Silver?'

She frowned. 'Maybe. I don't . . . I'm not sure what I'm sensing.' It felt weird this time . . . like maybe silver had been here recently, but it'd been almost entirely washed away.

He frowned, but he didn't question her. He continued his climb and she followed. They stopped outside the closed bathroom door. The light was on inside, the strip under the bottom of the door the only light in the whole of the house; the sound, the hissing beyond, she realized, was the shower.

'She's in there. I can smell her.'

He nodded and pushed open the door.

'What is it?' she asked apprehensively as he swore.

'Well, the blood smells faint because the shower's wash-ing it away,' was all he said as he stepped into the room.

She made to follow, then froze in the doorway.

A woman still clothed, perhaps in her early forties, bound and gagged, was hunched over in the bathtub. She was facing them, her head and shoulders slumped forward, the shower above running cold water on to her.

Rope didn't just bind her hands and ankles but her whole body, and was expertly tied with complicated knots.

It would've been impossible to escape, she could see that already.

'Where's the blood coming from?' Sage asked, staring down at her dripping, mottled body as she edged closer. Her limp hair was dark and hanging over her face. She couldn't see her eyes but she hoped they were closed.

'Her arms.' Oren pointed. 'And her thighs. Look.'

She gasped. Criss-crossing slashes were all over the inside of the woman's arms, and right through the fabric of her trousers.

'The killer left her tied here to bleed to death,' he said darkly. 'The running water makes the blood flow quicker. She was a doctor. She'll have known what was coming.'

Sage felt sick.

'We can't turn the water off,' Oren said. 'The humans need to think they're the first to have found her.'

She nodded.

'The cuts on her arms and legs will send the humans into overdrive. They'll start all that occult bullshit. Ritualistic killings. Cults. Devil worship or whatever,' she said finally.

'Occult bullshit?' he repeated with a snort as he followed her back out into the hallway and closed the door on the tragedy of Dr Lindsay. 'Magic. Supernatural. We're the very definition of occult bullshit.'

She looked at him through the darkness as she got closer to the bottom of the stairs. 'You know what I mean. We're not satanic. You kill demons, for God's sake.' She raised a brow. 'Or at least, that's what the stories say. The ones you refuse to talk about.'

'Just don't want to give you nightmares.' She knew he was smirking from the tone of his voice.

'But they are real?' she pushed, lifting the medical bag on to the table next to the card with Harland's writing on. She could still scent him on it. It clicked open in a haze of gold without even having to ask.

'What are real?'

'Demons. Not just monsters.'

She didn't need to look at him to know that he was still smiling. 'I didn't have you down as the religious type.'

'As I lay next to my family's bodies this weird burning sensation on my chest got stronger and stronger.' She shrugged, but it felt . . . lame. It felt like bravado as she admitted a truth she'd never told anyone. Not even P. 'It was my necklace. A small cross. For years after I didn't realize it was the silver. I'd always assumed it was rejection for what I'd become. I suppose I've not had much faith at all since then. And Downside doesn't uphold human religions anyway.'

She rummaged in the bag. Bottles chinked and packets of pills rattled. There were pens and notebooks and blank prescription slips.

'Sage.' His tone was . . . well, she'd expected him to mock her. But the softness caused a lump in her throat she hadn't expected to feel. It mortified her. So she carried on. She refused to look at him. She pulled out an envelope that'd already been torn open. It was a wedding invitation, addressed to: *Mhairi and John.* He sighed behind her. 'You survived. That doesn't make you a monster.'

'It doesn't feel that way,' she said, pushing the invite back into the bag.

'I have killed demons,' he confessed at last. One small truth for the truth she'd offered him. 'As well as the monsters. I've come face to face with them more times than I can count, and I can tell you with absolute certainty that you are neither.' Then he laughed quietly under his breath. 'Not that I'm saying you're a complete angel, either.'

She turned to him. He was leaning against the wall, arms folded across his chest. She didn't realize she needed the answer until she was asking the question. 'Have you ever met an angel?'

'No.' He shook his head. But he was looking at her like he understood. Even if she didn't fully understand what she was asking for herself. Maybe he knew she just needed the idea of something that wasn't darkness or despair. 'But if demons exist and I know that to be true, mustn't I also believe in the existence of angels?'

She huffed quietly. Bitterly. He just nodded.

She looked at him. His beautiful face. His expression. 'What brings you peace, Oren?'

He didn't answer. Even through the darkness, she saw him swallow. Like an answer was there he had to force back down before his lips could dare to betray him. She knew she was looking at the real Oren again, not the bastard he usually hid behind.

Then he smirked, and the moment was lost. 'At the moment, whatever plate of food P puts before me every evening. None of my clothes will fit me by the new year.'

She had to force herself to smile as she watched him, the real him, fade. She cleared her throat. 'Why are you just standing there watching me do the work?'

'It's pitch-black.' He shrugged. 'I can't see a thing. It's easier if you do it.'

She tutted. 'It's a good job my eyes do work, isn't it?' She held up the leaflet in her hand she'd taken from the medical bag.

A leaflet for a physiotherapist. She had a few, perhaps to hand out to patients.

Salina Gourlay.

'She knew Salina, at least in a professional capacity. We've got a link.'

There wasn't much time left before the humans arrived. They needed to go. She handed him the invite while she pulled open the front door.

'John. More mysterious boyfriends, huh?' he said darkly as he slid it from the envelope and looked it over. Her foot had barely stepped on to the driveway when her phone pinged in her pocket.

There was no text to the message. Just a single picture.

Hozier's scruffy notepad now propped on what she recognized as the arm of their sofa back home. Another address scribbled in red.

She could've fallen to the floor.

It was the first time she'd heard Oren swear in genuine, furious anger.

Because on the screen was a single road name.

St Stephen Street.

24

SAGE

She gasped as she righted herself. She wouldn't ever get used to the feeling of the world slipping out from under her feet.

Oren had instantly shifted them there. Another dark, empty street. Ice-cold rain. Something was wrong. Oren's hand was at her elbow to steady her from the shift, but the second she'd found her bearings, she'd started to feel sick.

Not shifting sick. Or silver sick.

They were on a road with fences backing on to gardens on one side, the tops of houses just visible behind. Facing them was a row of shops. There was a barber's, a few takeaways, a laundrette and a couple of other empty stalls, all of them shuttered for the night. Most of them covered in fading graffiti.

Second from the end, next to a Chinese takeaway, was the address they were looking for. The shutter was pulled down, but she could see at once the lock that had been snapped off and left discarded a little way away, as if it'd been kicked to the side.

She sniffed the air.

Blood.

Lots of blood. More than at Lucy's apartment. Way more.

'Oren,' she almost choked, grasping for the arm of his coat as every hair on her body stood on end. 'Oren!'

'What?'

'Can't you smell that?'

'Smell what?'

'There's so much of it,' she whispered. She felt breathless. Utterly overwhelmed by the stench. 'So much blood. I can smell it from here.'

She gagged on the salty iron smell, so strong in her nostrils she could taste it on the back of her tongue. She heaved on dry air.

'What's wrong with you?' he asked, raising a brow.

'It's temperamental,' she swallowed. She realized she was shaking. 'It's woken up.'

'You know, if you changed more often, you'd be more practised. Have better control?'

She didn't even have a chance to snap a retort. His eyes went wide.

'Sage?' His reaction didn't correlate. She hadn't even spoken yet. She'd barely begun to point her finger at him when she looked down and realized that it wasn't a finger at all. Well, it was, but it was tipped with a thick, curling, razor-sharp claw.

The annoyance turned into panic, and she half-whimpered, half-growled as she raised both of her hands and stared at the talons.

She could still smell it. The blood. So much of it. It was getting even stronger as the wolf fought to escape.

Danger. It'd smelt so much blood and thought she was in danger. It was itching to get out, fighting to claw its way to the surface.

She was shaking so violently her teeth started to chatter. She could feel them elongating in her mouth. She could feel the sharp pain searing through her gums.

'Sage,' a sharp voice said as she watched the blood dribbling down her fingers from her destroyed nail beds.

She looked up but that face she knew had turned hard again, cold and furious.

'Look at me,' he insisted as her attention turned back to her hands. She was almost crying. Why wouldn't it stop? She wanted it to stop! Blood. Iron. It was all around her. The wolf wanted to explode from her skin and kill whatever the threat was.

She thought she mouthed *help* a few times, but she wasn't sure.

'Look at me!' A strong hand at her chin forced her gaze up into his own. 'Breathe.'

She did as she was told, but she could still taste the scent of blood on the air.

'Nothing can harm us,' he said firmly. 'Not while I'm here.'

'You don't understand—'

'I understand. The wolf wants to fight. But it doesn't need to. I'm here. I've got it. So tell it to leave, now.' He accentuated his words, slowly, quietly. Everything that was ever handsome was gone. His eyes had turned so dark they were almost black, and his own teeth had started to elongate again to match hers. The shadow of his own hidden monster was peeping out to challenge hers, to show her he was good on his word. 'You're in control. Push it away.'

'It's too strong—'

'It's not as strong as me. Control it, Sage.'

'I can't.' She was gasping, fighting, begging.

The hand at her chin came around the back of her neck, and she felt that warmth of his magic seeping under her skin again. Not to heal this time, but to soothe. The offer of a helping hand, if she could just reach out and take it.

'Breathe,' he whispered.

And at last she did.

At once, the claws retracted, and the teeth started to shrink again.

In a moment she was human again, her chest heaving. Her hands nothing but a shaking mess of dripping blood.

When she looked back, the monster on Oren's face had disappeared too.

'Thanks,' she whispered, her cheeks burning as she tried to swallow down the lump in her throat.

He looked at her for a moment, though what he was looking for, she wasn't sure. He shook back the sleeve of his coat and looked at his watch. 'Come on. We've not got long.'

'Wow.' Oren huffed out a disgusted breath as they reached the store front. 'Even I can smell it now. What the hell is in there?'

'Just open it,' she insisted. She could still taste the bile on the back of her throat. 'Get it over with.'

So he did. A soft golden haze sat on his fingertips as the shutter began to roll up.

But she could already see it through the darkness.

He couldn't.

She could see every last detail of the horror within.

The magic at his fingertips grew until it formed a ball of brilliant white light, and he floated it through the shattered glass door and into the shop.

It was trashed.

Shelves of tins and cans and packets of dried food had been shoved over, the contents scattered across the floor. The fridges full of milk and fizzy drinks had been scattered, as if something large had crashed into them. The shelves by the till that should've been home to rows of spirits had been smashed into pieces.

And everything else. Every last corner of the shop was splattered with blood. There were small clumps mixed among it. Stuck to the walls. The floor. The surfaces.

Torn flesh ripped right off the bone.

She recoiled, horrified.

This was brutal. Frenzied.

What Hozier had said about escalation . . . This was . . .

Oren didn't react other than to rub his smooth chin with a hand; as close as he'd come to displaying genuine shock.

Glass crunched underfoot as she stepped gingerly over spilt boxes of cat biscuits, the sleeve of her coat clamped over her nose to try and reduce the overwhelming smell. 'Where is he?'

'I suspect . . .' Oren said as he made his way round the other side of the shop, getting to the counter and peering over. 'Yep.'

'Is it bad?'

He nodded slowly.

She made her way around the edge of the counter.

And swore viciously.

'Told you.'

He hadn't told her at all.

He'd agreed it was bad. But then there was this.

The man was ravaged so hideously he barely resembled a human form. His face was a bloodied mess, so disfigured she wouldn't be able to pick him out of a line-up of mugshots. She couldn't even tell what colour his hair was supposed to be, it was so sodden with crimson. His limbs were covered in gouges so deep she could see the white of bone. Holes littered his body where flesh had been torn away.

This was a fight to the death, and it'd been a brutal one.

She backed away, horrified.

A battered old ledger was open on the counter, handwritten names and addresses of what she assumed were regular customers, stained with fresh, wet blood. The ink ran down the page, making most of the notes illegible.

She was about to point it out to Oren when the heaving sound of somebody being sick sounded just outside the doorway.

They both whirled.

She blinked, confused. How had her hearing, even more advanced than Oren's, not picked up on anyone approaching?

She sniffed the air again.

Oh.

That was why. Only wolf could sneak up on wolf.

'Oren,' she warned quietly as the figure stood hunched over, spitting bile into a gutter at the edge of the pavement outside the shop. 'Werewolf.'

Oren's face went dark again as he straightened, and as they made their way back to the front of the shop he waved a hand, their footsteps in the blood disappearing behind them.

'Who are you?' Oren demanded.

The hunched figure looked up.

He was a weedy youth. Young. Late teens. Glasses and lots of spots.

'Who are you?' he parried.

'Oren Rinállis. Arcānum,' he said bluntly. 'Why are you here? Do you know this man?'

'He sells supplies to our commune.' The young lad straightened, swallowing at the sound of Oren's name. 'We get a big delivery once a month. It was due this evening but it didn't turn up. I was sent to see why . . .'

'Commune?' she repeated.

He looked between them. She knew he scented her too. Knew she was a wolf. But as he looked back at Oren's towering, glowering figure, he didn't dare ask why she was there with the warlock.

He nodded. 'We're a pack. We live up on Winter Hill,' he stammered. Her heart skipped a beat. 'We have our own space there. Our own life. We use Patrick 'cause he's one of us, see. And Darren. The delivery guy. Never any hassle. Understand about the full moon. Understood, I mean.' His wide eyes flickered back towards the shop. 'What's happened?'

'Three guesses.'

'There's been a series of werewolf murders,' she cut across Oren quickly. The kid was in shock. Scared. He didn't need Oren's sarcastic backchat. 'We're here to check it out before the humans, which should be in . . .' She pulled Oren's wrist up to look at his watch. 'About five minutes.' She looked at his grey-white face with pity. 'Go home. Tell your alpha you need to make other arrangements for supplies. And that we'll be making a visit.'

He nodded, stumbling down the kerb in his haste to retreat as a raven cawed somewhere in the distance.

25

SAGE

Coffee the Vampire Slayer opened from dusk until dawn. P sometimes met her ghost friends there through the night while Sage slept.

It was four a.m. and Sage slid into the corner booth by the door while P ordered her a strong coffee. It'd been a restless night.

When she'd returned to the apartment, exhausted, Sage had found a note from P, saying she'd gone out somewhere. She'd gone to bed and tried to close her eyes, but if she got anywhere near drifting into sleep she jolted awake over and again from lucid dreams filled with blood and empty, lifeless eyes. By three-thirty she'd given it up as a bad job and rose to see if P was home yet.

She just wanted to get out. Didn't want to look at that wall. Didn't want to think about all that death.

The old questions plagued her, the usual since the day her family died. And then the day P died. And then Lucy. Why any of these people? What had they done for fate to decide that it was their turn to die?

No matter what Oren had said – that she wasn't a monster for outliving them all – she still couldn't shake the guilt away.

The cafe was artsy, a place to sit downstairs and drink coffee and eat cake, while upstairs boasted a small gallery displaying shots from prominent supernatural photographers.

'That werewolf outside the shop said the pack lives up on Winter Hill,' she told P. Her heart stuttered even at the name of it. But she was surprised to see that P didn't react to the news.

Winter Hill. Situated in the West Pennines, it was endless. Over a hundred and forty square kilometres of moorland. Great for hiking and dog walking and camping . . . And full moons. Easy to get lost in.

'I know,' she said quietly. 'After Oren mentioned there was a pack in this city I looked it up when I went to the archives yesterday. Only for my own interest, y'know, because I thought they must be pretty hard to hide, right? But I checked what Oren said. And he was right. The pack formed nine years ago.'

A full year after Sage had been found up there in the moorland, covered in blood and surrounded by her dead family. She didn't actually know exactly which part she'd been found in. She'd never gone back to look over the news reports to find out. Something told her P would know, but she didn't ask, and so P didn't offer.

She added some sugar to her drink and stirred it slowly.

And then her phone started to ring.

She was starting to dread the sound.

'If that's another one . . .' she growled as she pulled it from her pocket. And nearly crumpled in relief to see Danny's name flash up on the screen.

'Hey.' She put him on loudspeaker. 'You OK?'

'Uh, yeah, are you?' He sounded confused. 'I'm outside your door. I've been knocking for ages but nobody is answering.'

P's hand clamped over her mouth in horror. She'd all but given up on any of their friends turning up for breakfast any more. And the one morning she'd left the apartment one had turned up?

'I'm at Vampire Slayer with P,' she told him. 'Just wanted a change of scenery. You weren't calling for breakfast, were you?'

'Oh. No, it's OK. I'm heading Upside for some last-minute Yuletide shopping. You know how Juniper and Willow love anything human, since they can't go up there. I was just dropping in to check you're still coming to that party? Harland's Upside flatmate?'

She forced herself not to whine out loud as P scrunched her face in an expression that said, *You did promise.* But it didn't feel right after last night. Even if she could do with the distraction, to ward off the memories of Mhairi and Patrick's bodies, a party wasn't it.

'He's sent you to ask, hasn't he?'

Danny sighed. 'He didn't want to bump into Oren again after last night. And I think he's already said some of his friends are coming. And . . .' He hesitated. 'He said some cute girls live on his floor.'

P snorted. She rolled her eyes. Typical boys.

Typical spotty, gangly, awkward teenage boys. And she knew they had next to no luck with girls. They were like magnets to the slightest chance they might get noticed.

'He's worried about looking like a loser if we don't go,' Danny carried on. 'It's an all-day-and-night-er, starts at twelve, but we don't have to go until later. You only have to show your face for an hour or two, Sage, then you can go back to work. C'mon.'

She knew it was a guilt trip. But it worked. She conceded with minimal resentment. 'I'll come.'

'Cool!' He sounded relieved. 'I have the address. Me and Rhen'll meet you at Stellan's gate to walk there at four. I just thought, safety in numbers, since, you know—'

'I know.' She said goodbye, and clicked off the call.

She put her phone back in her pocket and refused to hear P's suggestions that she might actually enjoy herself.

'Long time no see,' Rhen grinned as she found him and Danny near the end of the dark tunnel that led out of Downside. His eyes stopped on the hem of Sage's dress, and his cheeks went instantly pink. In his hand, as always, was a giant golfing umbrella, despite the forecast – which she'd already checked – predicting no rain for the next two days.

Oren hadn't taken the news she was attending an Upside party lightly. He'd hissed about teenagers and reminded her they had five dead werewolves on their hands, then asked her if she was really taking this job seriously. They'd exploded into a vicious shouting match.

With P's intervention, a compromise had finally been reached, though it'd still ended leaving bad blood between them. She'd go for a couple of hours, and then they'd visit the commune that evening after dinner to ask them about Darren and Patrick. It'd give her a good excuse to leave the party. He'd stormed off in a temper, warning with a furious finger that she better not be drunk when he came back to collect her.

'It's you that's stopped turning up for dinner. We never used to be able to get rid of you.' She raised a brow at Rhen as they walked the last bit of the tunnel together. She'd known Rhen and Danny the longest, since her Downside school days, where they'd bonded over mutual appreciation of fantasy movies, and she was annoyed with them.

She smiled at Stellan sitting dutifully by his table. 'I'll tell P you were asking after her, shall I?' She glanced over her shoulder with a smirk for his reaction.

His translucent face lit up. 'Put in a good word for me, eh?'

'Yeah, well,' Danny said awkwardly, continuing their

conversation as they climbed up through the trapdoor. 'We weren't sure if you were too busy . . .'

'Rubbish,' she tutted. 'Is that the excuse you came up with for the nights at the pub you don't tell us about any more?'

She didn't need the fresh light from the barrel room to see both their faces going red.

'You know what they say about him, right?' Rhen asked as they stepped out into the barrel room. It was cold and dusty, and the air smelt stale and damp.

'OK.' She rounded on them, coming to a stop in front of the door to block both of their exits. She wasn't exactly on good terms with Oren right now, but her patience with her friends was really starting to wear thin. 'You two and Harland, you've got to stop with conspiracy theories!'

'They're not conspiracy theories!' Danny said, his hazel eyes wide. He looked like he'd got even taller since she'd last seen him, and his acne hadn't improved much. Both of them looked so . . . She had been spending too much time with Oren. She'd forgotten what real boys her age looked and moved and talked like. 'We researched—'

'You did *what*?' She almost exploded at the audacity.

'Harland said you told him he was being silly,' Rhen muttered, but his cheeks were going bright red. 'But we checked. Loads of the stories about him are true, Sage. He's done . . . terrible things. He's notorious even among the warlocks for not giving fair trials and passing execution orders instead of imprisoning people. He's' – he hushed his voice – '*killed innocent people*, Sage.'

She stared at them both.

'Stop,' she said. She didn't want to hear it. She couldn't.

'It's all true. It's on record,' Danny said, but he sounded sympathetic. He thought this was the first time she was hearing any of this, like she didn't already know what he'd done or his reasons for doing them.

But hearing their side still made her feel uneasy.

'We agree with Harland,' Rhen said. 'He's dangerous, and you should be careful around him . . . You know he single-handedly killed a chimera?'

'And?' She pretended that she didn't know chimeras were some of the deadliest supernatural monsters, almost hunted to extinction out of fear of them.

Danny gaped at her. 'Nobody can kill a chimera!'

She flipped at last. 'Then it can't possibly be true, can it?' she shouted, her voice echoing around the barrel room. She knew it was probably true. It was Oren. 'Look. It's none of your business, either of you. I . . . I . . .' She stared between them. They stared back, shock etched on their expressions. It wasn't their fault. 'I'm sorry,' she said. 'It's been a really long day after an even longer night. I am not even up to this party but . . .' She pulled open the door into the bar, if only so she didn't have to look them in the eye. The dulcet tones of whatever band were coming from the jukebox, and she forced herself to ignore the jeers at the dress that revealed a lot of leg.

'Is it really bad?' Rhen asked. 'I mean, I'm not a were-wolf but is it safe for you both to be out tonight? I told Harland I wasn't sure, but he insisted.'

In all honesty, she wasn't confident. 'We're safer together.' She swallowed. 'Absolutely do not go anywhere on your own, anywhere, but especially Upside. Even in the daytime, I mean it. Another was killed last night, after the one you know about, Danny. And not that far from here, either.'

Danny spluttered. Rhen swore.

They were out in the street and she was shivering. It was freezing. How quickly she'd got used to Oren's magic keeping her warm and dry. Now her teeth were chattering. From somewhere in the distance she heard a cawing, and when she looked across the street her eyes narrowed . . . yep, atop a street light was a raven, and it was staring right at her.

'And does he . . . does he not know who it is yet?' Rhen edged.

She rolled her eyes. 'You can say his name, he's not Beetlejuice, it won't summon him to us.' Rhen's cheeks went pink again.

But perhaps he could tell she didn't really want to say anything else.

He nodded. 'Well, then.' He threw an arm around her shoulder. 'You need a night off. And a drink.'

26

SAGE

'Is this it?' She came to a stop in front of a glass door, a large metal six in the centre.

Rhen shrugged. 'I guess so. Sixth floor? It's the only door here.'

She shoved it open and knew they were right. The alcohol fumes in the corridor beyond hit her enhanced sense of smell square in the face.

'Bloody hell,' Danny muttered, smelling it too. The sounds of chatter hitting her wolf ears led them to a door halfway down, the boys pulling to a stop either side of her, and she knocked.

A girl appeared. She was short with curly orange hair and a face full of freckles. She was wearing skinny jeans and a khaki crop top, with a big badge that said *Birthday Girl!* in tiny flickering lights.

'I'm Sage,' Sage introduced herself. 'This is Danny, and Rhen. We're Harland's friends.'

'Of course!' The girl grinned, standing back and beckoning them in. 'I'm Kat. I've heard so much about you all!

You're so pretty. God, no wonder Harland doesn't stop talking about you. Come in, come in, could P not make it?'

It was her turn to splutter, embarrassed, as she followed Kat into a communal kitchen space.

There was a table that had been covered with trays of standard party food and the whole side counter against the far wall was stacked with boxes, cans and bottles of all that alcohol she'd smelt from the hallway. Everything had the grimy student feel to it. Clean, but just not quite enough.

'She already had plans tonight.' Sage clutched at the closest thing to the truth she could find. 'She says happy birthday.'

Kat grinned. 'Some nights we wait to see if Harland brings anything back before we order takeaway. He said she's training to be a chef?'

She grinned at Harland's lie. 'If I tell her that, she'll make it a mission to send you more.'

'Please!' Kat laughed. Sage liked her. She was bright and easy. Some teenage girls weren't, some of them made her feel awkward. Or maybe just played on an already insecure mind. Sometimes she had to remind herself that humans didn't believe werewolves even existed, never mind harboured suspicions that she was one.

Then another boy walked in. He was, again, just like Harland. She couldn't help but smile. He was just so . . . ordinary.

He noticed her smile and thought it was for him.

'Hey.' He came right over. 'I'm Ben. Are you Sage or P?' He grabbed a can of beer and cracked it open.

'Sage,' Kat pouted. 'P couldn't come.'

'Oh, man!' Ben grinned. 'We wanted to ask her to send food round more often!'

'Kat was just passing on the message, don't worry.' She smirked at Kat as she opened her mouth to protest, embarrassed.

'Danny, and Rhen.' She introduced them again since it was obvious they were too shy to do it themselves. But Ben had already spotted Danny's T-shirt showing off some Japanese cartoon, and apparently that was all that was needed.

'Boys,' Kat sighed. 'I moved to uni up north to get away from my little brothers and I've somehow ended up living with even bigger kids.'

Sage laughed. And it felt so carefree. She suddenly felt so intoxicated by it – the freedom, here Upside, away from Oren and murdered werewolves – she wasn't sure she'd need any alcohol at all.

'Where's Harland?' she asked suddenly. She'd been so enamoured with the idea of real human friends she'd forgotten her actual one.

'Shower,' Kat said. 'Got back late from the library. He actually studies. Mental.'

She rolled her eyes but smiled. Harland had more dedication than her. She hadn't bothered with university. She knew that she wasn't going to live Upside, not without P, and human qualifications didn't matter Downside. They had their own universities underground: degrees in a whole host of magical fields that she could use in any supernatural dwelling across the world. But, well, the Arcānum had always been her dream. After the deaths of her family, she couldn't imagine any other purpose for herself than trying her best to ensure other children didn't grow up like her, orphaned and lost. It was ironic really, now that she had this chance, that she realized how much of her future she'd risked on one hopeful whim.

More and more students started to trickle in from other floors as Ben plugged a phone into speakers, and music started to blast out. He introduced her to a few more of his friends, and Rhen and Danny had loosened up enough they'd integrated well. All gangly boys desperately eyeing up some of the girls in their skimpy outfits, wondering whether they might try their chances.

Kat thrust a bottle of wine into her hands and stayed close by, perhaps sensing she felt out of her depth, but she couldn't tell her it was starting conversations with people her own age that scared her. That she was more accustomed to a one-hundred-and-fifty-year-old warlock. She wished Harland would hurry up.

As if her angry thoughts summoned him, he appeared, his hair still damp, but fresh-faced and smiling. He paused to greet some people by the doorway, and his laughter was so bright that for a moment he seemed older. And taller. And much less of the lanky, geeky teenage boy that went bright red whenever she even looked at him. She was glad to see other girls were smiling back at him.

'Hey,' he grinned, relieved. 'Didn't bring Oren, then? I thought you might.'

'Who's Oren?' Kat asked, eyes wide with anticipation of gossip. 'Boyfriend?'

'No.' She threw Harland a withering look. 'He's my . . .' But how did she explain a supernatural, crime-fighting, immortal work colleague?

Kat must have taken her pause, put two and two together and come up with five.

'Ah,' she grinned, 'it's like that? That's cool. Casual is cool.'

'No—'

Kat held her hands up and smirked, backing away into the crowd now Sage had her chaperone.

She turned to Harland. He snickered. 'I was interested to see how you'd describe an arcānas.'

She shoved his arm. 'P's training to be a chef, is she?'

He laughed. 'Basically. Not my fault I'm better at coming up with cover stories. How's it going?'

She sighed and shook her head. 'It's just so . . .' She struggled to find the words to express her exasperation. 'We can link most of them together, like . . . like the killer used each victim to lead him to the next. But we still have absolutely no idea why. It's driving me mad, Harland. I can't sleep. I feel like my head is about to explode.'

He was nodding, his face full of concern. He blew out a long, slow breath. '*Oh, what a tangled web we weave when first we practise to deceive.*'

She almost choked on the mouthful of wine she was swigging. And then burst out laughing.

'Was that . . . a Scottish accent?' she demanded.

'Walter Scott,' he said, instantly embarrassed, back in his own southern accent again. 'Scottish poet. Just thought it sounded better in . . .' He trailed off into awkward silence.

'Since when do you recite poetry?'

'I read a lot of books, Sage.' He made sure he sounded withering. 'I like literature.'

'I thought you only studied vintage video game encyclopaedias?' she asked, faux-confused.

His eyes narrowed, but he smirked. 'Those too.'

Twenty minutes later she was standing by the sink with Kat, Harland and two more humans called Pete and Chris from the floor below when Kat spluttered on her beer.

'Are you OK—' She slapped her on the back, but she was already shaking her head, waving her away.

'Who invited *him*?' Pete said begrudgingly.

'Who cares?' Kat's face lit up. 'He's definitely a third-year.'

Great.

She knew at once, without even looking, who would be at the open door.

27

SAGE

Harland groaned. And sure enough, as she surveyed the room, every girl had a face like Kat, and every boy had a disgruntled expression like Pete.

'Brilliant,' Harland said glumly. 'Of course Oren turns up to steal all the attention.'

Kat rounded on her. '*That's* him? Your boyfriend is that hot?'

'He's not my boyfriend!' she hissed. She knew he'd hear across the room and she refused to let him think she'd told anyone he was her boyfriend! Why was he there? She glanced at the time on her phone screen but she wasn't late. P wouldn't usually serve dinner for another hour at least.

'How old is he?' Chris asked uncertainly, watching Oren as he was cornered at once by the three girls closest to the door. Who was he? Was he lost? They could help him get to wherever he needed to be? Their rooms, probably.

Harland raised a brow that said, *You can answer that one.*

'Twenty . . . three?' She took a stab at a vaguely plausible answer.

Close enough. Kinda.

'Has he got any hot friends?' Kat asked.

Harland snorted.

Oren managed to extricate himself from the gaggle by the door and edge his way across the packed kitchen. He had a bag in his hand and she was sure he'd tousled up his hair just a little bit more than usual.

'You look . . .' he said as he reached the group. His eyes lingered on the short hem of her dress. 'You don't normally wear clothes like that.'

She narrowed her eyes, about to snap something rude, when Harland interrupted.

'I think she looks nice,' he said.

And instantly flushed beetroot. She was pretty sure he hadn't meant to say it out loud, and Kat's wide, surprised eyes darting between them clearly assumed the same.

Oren turned to look at him, his cruel lips curling, and Harland seemed to physically shrink.

'What're you doing here?' she cut in quickly before he could say anything else.

But he just smiled and turned back to Kat, who was trying desperately not to melt all over him. 'She thought I didn't know it was her birthday at midnight,' he said in a conspiratorially loud whisper. 'I was planning on taking her out. Surprise, y'know?'

She could have punched him. It was a downright lie; he knew exactly what he was doing. Kat practically whimpered.

'Obviously she didn't realize she'd double-booked herself.'

'A birthday surprise?' Kat repeated faintly. It was almost comical. She rounded on Sage, as if she'd been cheated out of something. 'Why didn't you say? We could've made it a double celebration.'

'I thought you said you didn't want us to organize anything this year,' Harland grumbled furiously, staring at her with an indignant expression.

'I didn't,' was all she could offer. It was true. It'd felt so inappropriate with everything else going on to celebrate her own birthday. She looked at Oren, confused. 'You've arranged something?'

He held up the bag in his hand. 'Trainers. Jeans. Favourite jumper. Biggest coat. Dress and heels in December, are you crazy? You'll freeze. And we'll be outside.'

Kat sounded like she might go into cardiac arrest. 'You see!' she hissed at the boys around her. '*That's* how to be romantic!'

'I do try,' Oren lied through his shining white teeth.

Sage knew for a fact that P would've been the one to have packed that bag. She snatched it off him. She'd kill P for this little surprise too, she'd already told her in no uncertain terms not to make a fuss.

She was almost ready to refuse to go with him, but she

wasn't entirely sure him turning up there, and certainly earlier than they'd arranged, wasn't an excuse to get her out and to another crime scene.

Her stomach started twisting into anxious knots again. She knew she couldn't risk it. 'I'm so sorry, Kat, do you mind?'

'No! You go!' She shook her head. She looked more disappointed to see Oren leave. 'Enjoy yourself!'

She turned to Harland, but he was scowling. 'I'm sorry. It just didn't feel right celebrating my own birthday with everything else going on,' she said quietly. He nodded, but he still looked annoyed. 'Please, be careful. Don't go out on your own in the dark. It's not safe for us. For you. I mean it, Harland. Please. Stay safe.'

He knew what she meant, and her genuine concern seemed to smooth his temper. He gave her a reassuring smile and squeezed her arm as she turned to follow Oren back through the kitchen of girls watching to see who he left with.

'What's going on?' she demanded as soon as they got out in the hallway. 'Another body? Where?'

'Nowhere. We've got a bit of time before we leave for the commune. It really is a birthday treat.' He pretended to look offended, but the arrogant drawl was back. 'And who says I'm an arsehole, huh?'

The insult she'd hurled at him when he'd stormed off before.

'Me,' she hissed as she pulled off her heels and started to

shimmy her jeans up her legs. 'How did you find out it was my birthday?'

How do you think? His expression said it all. 'She called me not long after you left. Told me the way I spoke to you was out of line.' He rolled his eyes, since clearly he didn't agree. 'I could tell she was dying to say why it apparently seemed to matter more now than any other time. I told her I'd kick you off the case if she didn't spit it out.'

'Oren!'

He waved her away. 'She knew I wasn't serious. She was just desperate and needed an excuse. She said you deserved to go to a birthday party since you'd so far deprived her of planning one for you. Told her to keep it a secret from me and let the day pass as if nothing had happened.'

She shook her head, at the both of them. 'And this is what, an apology?'

He laughed. She couldn't help but stare at him, how handsome he looked when he smiled. His face lit up.

'I don't do apologies,' he said. 'Not any I ever mean, anyway.'

She hit the ground again with a bump.

'Turn.'

'Everyone is so young in there.' He wrinkled his nose as she pulled the dress over her head, then put the T-shirt on.

'I'm that young.' She pulled the jumper over the top.

'You're not.' He turned back around, holding out her coat. 'You're nineteen tomorrow.'

'Oh, massive difference,' she tutted. He took her party clothes and they disappeared. 'You're just trying to find an excuse. You thought you'd hate me. Turns out you might even wanna be my friend.'

He huffed a small laugh. 'The day you change of free will, maybe I'll consider it.'

She glowered at him. He might as well have said, *When pigs fly.* And he knew it.

28

SAGE

Once upon a time, the Christmas market had been a few stalls, but over the years it'd evolved until the whole square outside the town hall was just the epicentre, as streets lined with wooden huts snaked off into other parts of the city. And they sold everything. Vendors came from across the seas, and the air was rich with smells of spices and foods from places she'd never visited in her life.

Roasted nuts, spicy sausages, vintage cheeses, there was a whole roast hog in the window of one of the biggest food stalls, strips of pork peeled off its back and handed out on little paper plates. In the centre were the bars selling mulled meads, spiced wines and a whole host of other beverages to be drunk under speakers blaring music.

'We're going to the market?' she asked, surprised that this was where he'd shifted them to.

'You talked about it at Northern Psyche, said it was tradition. You and P go every year,' he said as they turned the corner into the ginormous square. 'P said you hadn't been able to get away from work to go this year so . . .'

He pointed over her shoulder.

She turned, and just visible against the dark sky was a silvery figure of a girl, sitting on the shoulders of a statue on a high stone plinth. She hadn't seen them yet, was too busy watching the merry crowds below, twiddling one of her braids through her fingers.

He put his fingers in his mouth and let out an ear-splitting whistle. P's head – and about a dozen random other bystanders – snapped towards them. P grinned.

The ghost glided through the air. 'I've checked it out,' she said brightly. 'There's only one jewellery stall we need to avoid for silver, and I've already spotted another three or four I definitely want to browse first.'

Sage whined, patting her pockets. 'I haven't got any cash, I didn't know we were coming.'

P flashed a broad smile, but it was Oren who answered. 'She has my bank card.'

P held up a hand to show the small plastic card and a rolled-up tube of notes she must've collected before coming to meet them. Sage's eyes went wide. Not just at the money, but the fact that to everyone around them it'd just look like it was floating! She snatched it quickly as P giggled.

'Withdrew whatever you wanted, huh, P?' Oren's brow rose at what was clearly a couple of hundred pounds in her hands.

'It's expensive here.' She shrugged.

'I thought you said you weren't rich?' She rounded on him.

'He's eight-figure rich, Sage,' P tutted. 'Now come on!'

The atmosphere was merry, and the crowds outside the drink stalls were so thick they'd never get close. So they started at the outside edges. There were hand-stitched clothes, whittled ornaments, delicate pottery, ginormous blocks of home-made soap, children's puppets, jewellery. Sweet stalls piled high with sugar confectionery and chocolate-covered waffles.

Her eyes nearly fell out of her head.

P floated above, upside down, her head close so that they could hear each other without shouting. Sage grinned up at her. The glow from thousands of fairy lights strung between the wooden stalls glittered through her translucent body.

The crowds were thick, and it was a struggle to get through without bumping into every person she passed. Perhaps it was the atmosphere or the spiced wine, but nobody minded at all.

Oren gave barely any indication he was there, following through the crowd, letting them shop with his money; the only real reminder he was with them was the hand that reached down to take every new bag to carry every time they stopped at a stall.

'Oh my God, that's just,' she mumbled through a mouth full of toffee fudge from Laura's Confectionery that apparently made every possible flavour. And fudge was her favourite. The sample plates were her heaven. She held some casually aloft in her hand, pretending to browse the different flavours so that P, still hovering upside down, could lean in and lick the fudge, tasting it for the split-second it passed through her silvery tongue.

'That one's the best,' she agreed. 'Oren, try that!'

Sage held the sample up to him. She knew what he wanted to say but couldn't in front of the two girls behind the counter eyeing him from under their lashes.

You want me to eat that after P has been licking it?

Yes, she did.

'Try it,' she insisted.

Reluctantly he bit into the chunk of fudge. His expression transformed.

'We'll have that one. Two lots.'

'Oh, Sage, look! Mug coasters made out of old vinyl records.' P zoomed along to the next stall as she took their bagged treats.

Oren's tut was scathing. Clearly not to his taste. But on the best form she'd ever seen him, he said nothing. She looked back only once, and perhaps he could understand her thoughts, her silent thanks, and smiled a rare, real smile as he gestured with his head to follow P.

'I'm burning up.' She ripped her scarf from her throat as they nearly completed a full round of the outermost stalls. It'd taken nearly an hour, and the body heat was stifling. 'I need a drink. I love the mulled wine here.'

Oren looked over at the crowds surrounding the large wooden bar in the centre, and groaned at the size of them.

She observed the crowd too, and eyed Oren. 'You can use magic to make them move,' she suggested casually.

He knew the suggestion wasn't casual. He pulled a long-suffering face and thrust their bags back into her hands. 'Wait back by the statue so I can find you again.' He pointed to the bearded man on whose shoulders P had been sitting.

They edged to the towering monument, and now they were out of the crowd she could feel the cool air on her face again. Much better.

'How was the party?' P asked. She leant against the plinth of the statue and watched that black and white hair mingle into a slowly parting crowd.

She puffed out her cheeks. 'Danny and Rhen practically melted into the walls to avoid him when Oren walked in. And I thought Harland might spontaneously combust. The room literally froze.'

P started to laugh. 'Obviously.' Then her smile faded, and she sighed. 'He's just jealous.'

She scoffed. 'Harland doesn't like Oren just as much as Oren doesn't like him.'

P gave her a look. 'You know what he's jealous of.'

'Oh, don't start.' She waved P away, but she could feel her cheeks going pink.

She shrugged. 'He just sees you and a famous, handsome warlock disappearing off together every day.'

'It's work!' She wasn't sure why she was getting defensive. P came around to face her, blurring her view of the crowd. 'P, I love Harland, and Danny and Rhen, but none of them like that.'

'I know. I just think—' she started. Then she froze.

'What?' she said blankly. 'You think what?'

The sympathetic expression moulded into a frown as P stared at the stone next to her head. 'What's that?' she asked, pointing at something almost level with her eye.

She turned.

It looked . . . it looked like somebody had scrawled graffiti on to it, but the paint was still wet, dripping down the stone face. It wasn't huge – barely bigger than her hand.

A symbol.

She stared at it.

It took a moment. Sage had to sift through all of the scents of the market behind them, but there was no doubt.

'P.' Her voice shook. 'P, that's blood.'

And . . . the scent of something else, something familiar.

She looked down. At the base of the plinth was a bundle of sage.

She picked it up and gazed down at the small, tightly packed bundle of herbs in her hands.

'Sage . . .' P wasn't looking at her, or at the sage in her hand, or at the symbol drawn in blood. Instead she was looking at the statue of the man, the name etched into the stone at his feet.

OLIVER HEYWOOD
1825–1892

'P,' she said again, because she just needed to hear someone else confirm it. 'That says Oliver Heywood, doesn't it? Olly Heywood.'

P's eyes moved slowly down to the symbol again, and then to her, and the little gift left for them in her hands. And her eyes went wide as saucers as she realized what it was.

'You need to leave, now!' Her voice was frantic as she shot up into the air, shouting for Oren. Sage was already moving. Something inside her, some voice she'd never heard before, told her she needed that warlock if she was going to get out of the square alive.

She thanked God for supernatural senses, that a warlock's enhanced hearing was enough to hone in on a panicked yell across a crowded market square, because the second his face turned in the crowd, his eyes as wide as P's had been, he clearly knew something was wrong. It was like slow motion as she watched him barge his way back through the crowd, ignoring protests as he shoved two men out of his way. He pointed at P hovering over her head. *We'll meet you there.* P didn't even answer. Sage looked up but the ghost was already zooming off, back towards Dive Bar and home.

It felt like an age before they'd battled to each other through the crowds, though perhaps it'd only been moments. He didn't ask for an explanation. He wrapped an arm around her waist and with one quick jerk, whisked her away from the danger.

29

SAGE

When her feet touched solid ground again she was in the middle of their living room. The Yuletide tree P had decorated as Sage had slept a few nights ago glittered. The room was warm and cosy. It would've been perfect to come home to after some festive shopping. It all felt so meaningless now. Her chest heaved with a mixture of panic, and shock at the shift.

'The crowds,' she gasped. 'We just disappeared!'

'I masked us, nobody noticed. What the hell happened?'

She spun, looking around the room. Even with the head start, P wasn't back yet. She'd have probably done a better job at explaining.

'Blood,' she said faintly. 'On that statue. It wasn't there before. It was fresh. It was still dripping down the stone!'

'You're absolutely certain?'

'Yes, I'm certain!' she almost yelled in his face. 'It was a symbol.' She snatched up one of P's notepads and drew it, thrusting it in his face. 'It was this. And the name of the statue.' She looked up at him. 'It was Oliver Heywood, Oren.'

His whole body tensed in recognition.

She felt breathless. 'All the mysterious boyfriends we can't locate. Names plucked off the streets of the city.'

'Of course they are,' he said quietly. 'It's all one big game and now he's goading us.'

She swallowed. 'This was on the floor under it.' She held up the bundle of sage.

His body went entirely rigid as he took it from her.

'We'll need to go back,' she said as he inspected the bundle. He sniffed at it, but there was no other scent except hers on it. 'We just ran, we didn't even wipe off the blood.'

'I'll go. Now. Alone,' he said. 'It's not safe—'

'Bullshit!' she exploded, just as P zoomed in through the wall.

'What is?'

'He wants me to stay here while he goes back Upside!'

'Why?' She looked shocked.

'Oh, I don't know,' he seethed. 'Maybe the fact we've just been followed by the "Silver Serial Killer" or whatever they're calling him now!' He finger-quoted the name *Downside Daily* had used that morning. 'Half the city is gossiping about why she'd possibly be at my side every day.' He held up the sage in his hand. 'The killer obviously knows she's working the case with me. They left *blood* on *that* statue. This is a *threat* for her to back off!'

They glared at one another across the living room.

P swallowed. Then she grimaced. 'He's got a point.'

Another thought fluttered to her. On black feathered wings. 'Ravens,' she said quietly. 'I saw one watching me as I came out of Dive Bar tonight.'

He looked like he might combust. 'You knew you were *being watched* and you didn't come straight back?'

'No!' She flung her hands out wide. 'I'm not cowering at home!'

He ignored her entirely, and turned to P. 'A map for tomorrow. All the other statues in the city. We'll have to check they don't have any messages left in blood. But I'll go back to the square quickly and erase that symbol now.'

P nodded.

'But—'

He held up a hand and shook his head. 'When I get back, we'll go to the commune. Get ready. I won't be long.' She clenched her jaw in temper. He looked like he could hear all the names she was calling him in her head. Good. *You're being petty*, his expression said. She arched a brow: *So what?* 'And I'm putting a spell on the door until this is over. If they were able to follow us Upside they've probably followed us here. Know where you live.'

'Nobody can get into Sage's room while she sleeps without me seeing,' P said.

'And when you go out?' he demanded.

She opened her mouth, then closed it again. P gave her an apologetic look.

She was siding with him!

'So you're locking me in?' She laughed incredulously under her breath.

'If it keeps everyone else out, yes.' He lifted a glowing hand. But where usually his magic would sit in the air like shimmering gold dust, this time it started to come together, form the outline of a shape which solidified in his hand.

'What's that?' P blinked at the object he held out to her.

'One of my daggers, for the rest of the time you're alone here with all our evidence.' He gestured to the wall. 'The blade itself is silver. The sheath has a protective spell to contain the effects, so don't remove it unless you have to.' Sage flinched. He threw her an impatient look. 'All my magical daggers are silver, Sage, I've not had time to replace them.' He turned back to P. 'It's imbued with my magic. If you take it out, I'll know you've had to use it. I'll be here right away. I don't care who blasts through that door, you stab them. I'll get you off the murder charge,' he added, and though Sage was sure it was half a joke he didn't smile. He turned and pointed a finger at her. 'If you're here I don't give a damn about whatever problems you have with transforming, you change and rip their head off, understand?'

'Careful, Oren,' she said scornfully. 'You'll start to sound like you care in a minute.'

'Letting my partner get herself killed will only leave me with a shitload of paperwork. Forgive me for wanting to avoid it.'

'You can be a real prick sometimes, you know?' She

hardly realized the sofa cushion was in her hand before it was hurling its way across the room at his face.

He snatched it out of the air with one hand. He looked like he was ready to call her much worse.

P was fiddling awkwardly with her braids, making a show of looking at the notes on the coffee table as they snapped at each other. He threw the cushion back at the sofa, a haze of his magic ensuring it landed neatly back in the same place.

Then he half-sighed, and spoke so quietly her wolf senses had to strain to hear him. 'Please, Sage. I can't protect you when I'm not here.'

Her eyes prickled.

The unspoken truth she knew he'd understood in those terrifying moments at the market – the realization as they battled their way to each other through the crowds, that against all the odds, despite how either of them had felt towards the other the day they met, in that moment of uncertainty and fear, it was him she'd turned for. Not just because he was there, but because she did trust him. And she knew the moment that he hadn't just taken her outstretched hand, but instead thrown his arm around her and pulled her close – it was a decision too. He'd sensed her fear, saw himself be her answer, and responded by wrapping her wholly in his protection. She didn't know. She wasn't entirely sure what she meant. Just . . . that some things didn't entirely feel like obligation any more.

'Promise you'll stay here until I come back.'

She nodded resentfully.

He nodded back in acknowledgement, and then he shifted out into the night.

30

SAGE

She still wanted to punch him when he returned fifteen minutes later. He'd changed out of his trainers into sturdy boots and swapped his expensive-looking jacket for a waterproof coat. But she knew she was lucky he was still willing to take her anywhere tonight, so she bit back her temper and let him take her arm to shift them out towards Winter Hill.

She hadn't been anywhere near since she'd been turned, and she refused to look at Oren.

He said nothing, but she knew, whether P had told him or he'd looked in her file himself, that he was aware this was the place her family had died. Her heart was pounding in her chest so hard that she knew it'd be impossible for him to drown that sound out. Though she'd always purposely avoided tracking down the exact location, the thought of it too painful, she knew at least that she'd been found close to the little village of Rivington. And she only knew that because she remembered seeing the welcome sign through the car window as her dad drove them into the car park on the last day they'd spent as a family. They'd left the car there and only walked maybe forty minutes – though to her little eight-year-old legs it'd felt like hours – to the spot they'd stop and pitch their tents for the weekend.

She never found out what happened to the car, either.

She didn't even know why she was thinking about that car now as they walked quietly through thick, sodden grass. What a silly thing. She hadn't thought about that car in ten years. But now she could smell it. The musty upholstery, stained from the food and drink she and her little brother had spilt over the years. The crumbs near the seatbelt buckle.

Perhaps it was because Winter Hill was also situated in the Rivington Moor that all these things came flooding back to her. Some memories she hadn't allowed herself to remember suddenly were as clear as if they'd happened yesterday. She wondered if it was coincidence that a pack of werewolves had settled here not long after the attack on her family. But . . . as she looked around the dark abyss of emptiness, she understood. The chances of them being stumbled across were remote. Now she was looking across the moors with older eyes, the chances of a lone werewolf stumbling across their tent that night seemed pretty goddamn unfortunate.

'I know we check out most places at night to be low-key,' she said as she stared at the line of trees behind a barrier covered in hazard signs that was designed to keep humans out. 'But why did we think this one would be OK in the dark?'

Oren didn't answer. He lit a ball in his palm and lifted it up. The sky was already inky black. She knew once they stepped into the shadow of the trees Oren wouldn't be able to see anything at all.

'Come on.'

As soon as they climbed over the fence and crossed the threshold, she knew. Out of sight, between the trees, she could hear footfalls padding gently over mossy ground.

'Oren,' she warned quietly.

'Yep.'

'Do we turn back?'

'We need to speak to them,' he whispered stubbornly. 'We're Arcānum, they can't just attack us.'

'What if they don't believe we're Arcānum?'

'Why else would we be here?'

'Oh, I don't know,' she whispered sarcastically. 'Because maybe they've heard a werewolf killer is on the loose, what do you think?'

'They can scent me. They know I'm a warlock.'

Somehow, she didn't think it was going to be enough.

They got about ten metres before glowing eyes appeared in front of them.

One.

Two.

Six.

Seven.

Eight.

More and more.

Dozens of them.

One pair of amber eyes prowled into the flickering circle of Oren's suspended light. A black wolf, bigger than any of the shadowy figures lurking between the trees. Its head nearly reached her shoulder.

'We've come to speak to your alpha,' Oren said loudly and clearly for all of them to hear. But his words were greeted with snarls. 'My name is Oren Rinallis. The Arcānum is investigating—' He was cut off by more growls, a snapping of teeth so loud it shook her bones.

'Erm,' she said from the corner of her mouth. 'Not going well.'

'Nope.'

'Can you use magic?'

'There're too many.'

She startled at the news. '*What?*'

'It only stretches so far, Sage,' he said through gritted teeth. 'Why I have to be so good with a blade too, remember?'

'And do you have one with you?'

'Sage, if I stop them with that they die, and I don't really think that helps right now, do you?' She nearly growled at him herself. 'You remember me saying your no-transforming would only be my business if it got in the way of our

~208~

investigation? Well, now is about the time it's becoming a problem, by the way.'

'It doesn't affect the investigation,' she hissed back as more of the eyes edged closer.

'It affects whether you die!' His other hand began to glow with more magic. A warning.

'I'll take that risk.'

But before he could snap back the wolf with the amber eyes and black pelt lunged, snapping its ginormous muzzle at her arm.

She shrieked, jerking away from razor-sharp teeth. But she realized too late it had achieved what it'd been after. It hadn't intended to rip her arm off at all, rather just get between them. Even as she turned to dash back to Oren two more wolves shot forward and cut them off completely.

Oren's face had already transformed back to that monster again. Eyes inky black and fangs as long as any wolf around them. He snarled at the closest wolf, a grey thing with green eyes and a maw dripping with saliva. It stopped in its tracks, and she didn't see what happened next but then one was backing away, whining in pain.

'Oren!' she warned desperately as another furious beast filled the gap. But the three now facing her were herding her further and further away. She could see just fine with her own wolfish eyes but she knew if Oren's light went out he'd be blind. And then they'd attack.

She needed to get back to him.

Her heart fluttered with panic.

The wolves made no more attempts to hurt her; growled if she tried to stop moving, nothing more. But she understood. They knew what she was and hadn't marked her as a potential werewolf killer. Because what werewolf would go round killing their own?

'Listen, you've got it wrong—' She held her hands out in a desperate plea. A million crazy possibilities rattled through her brain. Perhaps they assumed she was a soon-to-be victim, captive to a warlock, and they were under the impression they were saving her?

They were mistaken, and if they killed an arcānas they'd all be sentenced to death. The whole pack.

Like that pack Oren had killed.

Shit.

Shit!

Harland had said the case was infamous. And Oren had told them his name! It didn't matter whether these wolves knew that pack or not. Wolf loyalty was different. They'd avenge their own simply out of principle.

She saw a flash of Oren's magic in the distance, then a howl followed by furious barks of anger.

Her chest constricted in instant fear.

She could feel it inside her. A panic so strong it was going to overwhelm her. If they didn't kill him *she'd* throttle him. She swore it to whatever gods might be listening.

'Please,' she tried to the black wolf. 'I swear to you, we're here investigating recent werewolf murders, two victims are known to your pack. We just want to ask about them.'

The wolf gave no reaction.

Another flash.

More howls.

And then she heard a cry that was human. Well, warlock.

'Oren, go!' she yelled through the darkness. 'Just go! Leave!' Shift away. It was his only answer, his one escape.

One of the wolves snapped a vicious maw at her, furious at the help she offered.

'Please,' she begged again. Not to the wolf. Just . . . the sky, the trees, just anyone or anything listening. *Please make them listen*. She knew that he wouldn't leave without her. She cursed him for it.

Then she heard him. The urgency in his voice was laced with panic of his own as he yelled her name. But it wasn't from the direction she'd been herded away from. She twirled on the spot, staring through the darkness, looking for any sign of wherever he'd heeded her advice and shifted towards.

'Over here!' she screamed, waving her arms over her head as the ground began to shake. The wolves that'd been circling him realized a second too late he'd evaporated into thin air, but his shout gave his new position away anyway. They turned as one.

If he could just land it right, just get close enough to brush even a finger against hers they'd be gone; shifted

~211~

away to safety. But he couldn't see her through the darkness. Had no idea where she was.

And she was trapped by bodyguards still herding her deeper into the trees away from him.

The air hummed with mounting tension as the sounds of snarls grew more and more frustrated, worked up into more and more of a frenzy as they darted back and forth through the trees.

More howls as he shifted again, and another shout came up from her left.

Her cheeks were slick with tears she hadn't realized she'd started to cry as she sobbed pleas to her captors.

So she lunged, desperate – if she could just get past, get close enough, he might see her outline through the gloom—

The grey wolf crashed into her back, knocking the breath from her as she fell. Hard. She yelled out in shock as her temple cracked against a root protruding out of the ground.

She could hear Oren shouting, but the blow to the head had disorientated her, and her arms shook as she tried to push herself up.

It all happened so quickly.

The air around her was deafening with snaps and snarls and howls, and the thudding of endless enormous paws. She could sense the wave shifting direction every few heartbeats, could feel the wind of their bodies hurtling past, and knew that he was shifting quicker and quicker, jumping from spot to spot with desperate haste to try and find her before fleeing at last. But she was on the floor out of sight, dazed and confused. He had no clue where she was and he sure as hell wouldn't find her down there.

She tried to stand, but a heavy paw landed just between her shoulder blades and pushed. Her chest thudded back into the mossy ground.

She heard him call her name one last time before a yell went up, and she knew he'd misjudged a shift. Come out too close, perhaps almost on top of one. A howl told her they'd missed. But only just.

In that moment, she hated him. Hated every moment she'd spent starting to give a damn about him. He was a bastard, and she hated him for what he was about to make her do.

For the first time in a very long time, she closed her eyes, and willingly spoke to the wolf inside her.

31

SAGE

And she'd forgotten.

Forgotten what it felt like for her human bones to shatter, and the wolf blood try to fix them as they distorted under her skin. The burning agony of that skin ripping under the strain of the new shape that was her morphing, changing body. She felt her clothes rip and tear, falling from her in scraps as white fur sprouted from her limbs. Blood poured from her nail beds where claws pushed through, staining her white paws red.

But the weakness and clouded thoughts had gone. She was *whole* again. And powerful. And full of such unending rage. She was glad she didn't have magic, because in that moment, she would've set the world on fire.

She hadn't changed of free will in so long she'd forgotten how it felt to be on all fours. She rose on legs that shook no more and turned on the wolves that'd just shoved her back down into the dirt.

But as another shout and a howl went up, she didn't care. She lunged. Her paw connected with the jaw of the wolf on her left, and she heard a satisfying crunch quickly followed by a whine of pain.

It was enough. She managed to dive past at last, and she was back through the trees, heading towards the crowd that was surging after Oren.

She tried to open her mouth to call for him again, and realized her howl was only one of many.

She snarled in fury as she pounded past, overtaking blurs of brown and black and grey pelts as she followed his scent through the trees.

Why the hell hadn't he just left?

But she could see him at last, his chest heaving as he gulped air, trying to hold down the bile she usually felt after just a single shift, never mind so many. He backed up against a tree while he tried to rally himself to shift again, three snarling wolves bearing down. He couldn't see the two behind him, creeping around the trunk, ready to pounce.

How dare they? How dare the wolves do this when they'd come to help?

The one that crept from the left lunged and Oren startled, staggering back as he tried to right himself. She knew the moment he hit the floor that was it. She had seconds. She pushed so hard she thought her chest might explode.

She leapt.

Her paws landed on the spines of two in front and she felt them buckle. It was enough of a springboard to clear the barrier. She landed in the centre of the ring just as Oren's back hit the floor.

A wolf with sapphire-blue eyes lunged, jaw open, teeth angled for his exposed throat.

But she was quicker.

Her own jaw closed around its neck and she tasted blood in her mouth. But she didn't care. Rage. She twisted and in one vicious tear of skin and bone, ripped the throat out of the beast's neck.

It crumpled.

The frenzy froze.

She froze.

She dropped the flesh from her mouth, staring down at the glassy blue eyes that saw nothing. Cold settled over her as she realized what she'd done, without even thinking, just to save Oren.

'Sage?' a voice said behind her, and it pulled her back into herself. She remembered that he'd never seen her like this, didn't know the colour of her fur. He wasn't even sure it was her. It reminded her why she was there, and she lifted her head to look at the wolf beside the one she'd just killed.

She'd just killed.

She felt sick.

But she couldn't falter, not now. Not now she had the power and this pack was ready to kill them both.

So she held the gaze of the next wolf, and the one after that as she turned slowly back towards Oren. He lay still on the floor, staring at her bloody, dripping muzzle.

She walked to him on four shaking legs, stepped over his body, and settled on his chest.

The meaning was obvious.

He was hers. And if anyone else touched him, they'd die too.

But she'd just killed that wolf.

'Sage,' he whispered again, certain at last that it was her. She felt his fingers in the fur at her neck twist into a fist. It was gentle, but it was enough. His warning: *keep in control.*

The amber-eyed black wolf prowled between the other wolves. They parted to let him past, and at last she knew for certain who she was looking at.

The alpha.

She snapped one more warning as he stared at her, and then at the warlock she was protecting from her own kind.

Her heart pounded, and some of it was guilt.

She'd just killed that wolf.

Then he seemed to melt. His fur started to drop out in chunks as his limbs cracked and shrank and changed until a slightly balding, middle-aged man stood naked before them.

Then more changed, and from behind trees they were pulling clothing they must've left for themselves. Naked men and women, young and old, were hurrying between the trees pulling on loose robes as two more draped a long shawl over their leader.

Finally she sat up and let Oren rise.

But she didn't change.

In truth, she didn't dare. Not because her clothes had been shredded and she didn't have spares hiding behind trees, but she was scared of what she might say if she did. This overwhelming anger still bubbled inside her, and honestly, she wasn't even sure who it was aimed at.

She'd just killed that wolf.

Even as he stood, one of Oren's hands stayed twisted in the fur at her neck. Her head came to his shoulder.

She'd just killed that wolf.

'*And come he slow, or come he fast, it is but death who comes at last.*' The alpha's voice was stronger than his stature had given her cause to imagine. His accent that gave away a youth spent somewhere else was stronger than Oren's or Hozier's, and there was something oily about his voice, or maybe it was the way he stared without blinking that creeped her out. 'Oren Rinallis. The famous arcānas. Killer of all things monstrous and cruel . . . and werewolves too, if memory serves correctly. Tell me, are there any supernatural species left you haven't yet killed?'

Oren didn't answer. Didn't even give the werewolf the courtesy of acknowledgement as he waved a hand and the mud that covered his clothes disappeared.

'Who sired her?' the alpha asked, his still, yellowing eyes watching her.

'She doesn't know,' Oren answered for her.

'She's—'

Oren cut across him with a shrug. 'She doesn't know.'

Don't push me any further, his tone said.

They looked at each other for a long moment. Sage knew some kind of deal was coming. She'd just killed one of their pack; if they reported her she could kiss goodbye to her job, at best.

'She works for the Arcānum. If you have a complaint about the wolf she killed you can put it forward formally. The Arcānum would, however, be required to investigate the circumstances that pushed her into such an action.'

The alpha's gaze finally shifted to the wolf on the floor behind her. His jaw tightened.

'Werewolves cannot work for the Arcānum. Nobody can, except warlocks.'

'It's a long story.' Oren waved it away impatiently. 'I will swear you an oath of truth if you require it.'

The werewolf and most of those around them startled, surprised. So did she. Oaths of truth required blood to be sealed. If the oath was false, or broken, the person that made it died. Not that Oren's word was false . . . but it wasn't the kind of offer anyone made lightly.

The alpha was quiet for a moment longer. Then he said stiffly, 'We did not believe that a true arcānas, that *you*, Oren Rinallis, would turn up here in the company of anyone but other warlocks. We thought her presence signalled a trap.'

'Under the circumstances, it's understandable if your guard is up more than usual.' Oren's tone was pointed. And that was the deal. He would forget what they had tried to do to him, if they would take what she'd done to protect him no further.

She'd just killed that wolf.

'He was a problematic member of our pack.' Formal words for his official statement. 'His attitude was lacking and he often overstepped his mark. For what it's worth, he was not ordered to kill this evening. There are few who'll miss him. On this occasion,' he paused, addressing Oren in that same pointed tone, 'I will accept his fate as a deserving punishment.'

Oren's fist loosened at her neck at last.

'We need to speak with you, urgently,' he said. 'Is there somewhere we can talk?'

'She said.' He nodded at her again. 'Before she came to your rescue. Come. My cabin isn't far.'

32

SAGE

*S*he'd just killed that wolf.

She wanted to collapse to the floor and cry as she crossed the threshold into the cramped cabin.

'True white wolves are rare. They say they're touched by moon magic,' the alpha mused from a small table.

It was one room, a bed in the corner and cupboards on the walls. There wasn't even a bathroom. The thought of a communal forest toilet made her queasy and God only knew how they bathed.

On an upturned box beside his bed was a faded photograph of a woman and two small children, but a sniff didn't reveal the scent of anyone but him. Maybe they were victims of his choice to live a pack life – humans left behind after his attack. Maybe they had no idea what or where he was at all.

'Moon magic?' Oren took a seat without invitation. 'Be careful. I'd have thought werewolf packs would make a point of trying not to sound too . . . *Amhuinn*.'

Her head snapped towards him. She recognized the

name of that infamous alpha who'd tried to mix magic with werewolf attributes to create a super-hybrid race. Whom Oren had executed. It was a low blow to use it as a casual threat now, regardless of what'd just happened outside. When she'd just killed one of them herself.

She hated him.

'Werewolves around the world denounced his actions. As did half of his own pack,' the man snapped back sharply, clearly considering it a low blow too. 'He was as much warlock as werewolf, so I'd thank *you* not to play that card with me.'

'My mistake,' Oren said softly, but his tone wasn't sorry at all. He glanced at her as she settled down on a threadbare rug. 'Aren't you going to change back?'

'Her clothes were shredded,' the werewolf said as if it was obvious. 'Neither of you arrived with satchels. I take it she has nothing to wear if she does.'

Oren's eyes went wide in realization, and fresh clothes appeared in front of her at once. Black leggings and a jumper she recognized from her wardrobe. 'Is there somewhere she can change in private?'

'Does it look like it?' He raised a brow and gestured around the small room. 'We can turn our backs if she wishes?'

Oren stared at her. Though she'd made no sound, he seemed to understand she was reluctant.

The alpha chuckled. 'Oh dear. She has things to say she

doesn't want me to hear.' He read her like a book. 'And she cannot trust herself not to say them as soon as she changes.'

'Fine,' Oren said in a way that meant it was not fine at all. She bared her teeth, and she supposed his blink was the closest he would ever get to showing surprise.

She wanted to lunge for him. But she needed to speak to this man. And she'd have to pray that she could swallow down the vitriol she felt for Oren until they got out of there. She gestured to the far wall with her head, a clear order that they both turn to face it.

The cracking of her bones was even more painful than before, now adrenaline wasn't coursing through her, numbing the pain of it all. It was all she could do not to scream as she cracked and popped and shrank back into her human form. Yet a small whine still escaped her lips before she could stop it, and the golden hum that enveloped her naked skin, warm and soothing and gentle . . . it made her even more angry.

How dare he? After he'd forced her to change in the first place.

She pulled on the clothes, trying hard not to let them hear her panting from the transformation.

'What's your name?' she demanded of the back of the alpha's head when she was finally fully clothed and human again. She stayed standing. The two men sat at the table.

He looked her up and down with his yellowing eyes. 'You don't already know who I am before turning up here?'

'This was supposed to be a casual call,' Oren said. 'To ask what you knew about other people we're interested in. I didn't expect to have to check our records before we arrived.'

The man's jaw was set, and his nostrils flared. He didn't like Oren, that was clear.

'Michael MacAllister.'

She frowned. That name was familiar. 'MacAllister?'

'That's what I said.' He almost sang his retort, but it dripped with sarcastic politeness.

She met Oren's eye at last. He'd made the connection too. He nodded once. *Go ahead.*

'We have five dead werewolves,' she said. 'Murdered. Darren Johnson. Lucinda Hague. Salina Gourlay. Mhairi Lindsay. Patrick Tapper.'

If he was shocked by this news, it didn't show on his face. His unblinking eyes simply flickered between them, waiting.

'Why is it that one of them has your surname scribbled inside a notepad?' She crossed her arms across her chest, if only to hide her shaking hands. All of a sudden, this man was connected to three of their victims.

'*Just* a surname? Then how do you know it's me?'

He was sharp, and quick with his answers. The yellow eyes were too keen. Then he mirrored her, folding his arms across his chest too. But it was mocking. Oren was an arcānas but she, she was a werewolf, and part of his pack or not, he was still an alpha. He expected deference. Not an interrogation.

Oren pulled a folded piece of paper out of his pocket, opened it, and slammed it down in front of MacAllister. It was the sketch of the symbol she'd drawn from the statue. It felt like a million years ago now. Not an hour.

'What's that?' he demanded.

MacAllister stared at it, his head tilting slowly to the side.

And he was silent for too long. She watched him, waiting for just one sign, one small movement to give him away.

Then he slid it back across the table towards Oren with his fingertips. 'No idea.'

He was a liar.

'The boy we met outside Patrick Tapper's shop last night,' she pushed. 'He told you what he saw there? That Patrick is dead?'

MacAllister's head bobbed, but still, pointedly, he refused to answer her.

'Did you know that it was his delivery driver, Darren Johnson, who was murdered a few weeks ago too?' Oren asked. She knew him well enough now to hear the shift in his tone. He knew what MacAllister was doing to her.

It was the first time the werewolf showed any kind of reaction, even if it was just a blink of those staring, cold eyes. 'He's one of your five? It was an allergy, was it not?'

'Poison. Made to look like his allergy.'

MacAllister's eyes narrowed, and he leant back in his chair, crossing his arms again.

'What exactly are you accusing me of?'

'I don't think I've accused you of anything yet, have I?'

Oren cleared his throat quietly. A subtle warning.

He turned back to Oren, dismissing her entirely. 'Tell me, Oren Rinallis, do you remember the faces of every thing you've killed?'

For all her other anger she still couldn't stop the small growl, even as Oren didn't react to the obvious slight. The corners of MacAllister's mouth twitched.

'There are far too many.' Oren shrugged, leaning back in his own chair and sounding for all the world like he was bored. 'And far too few that were important enough to be worthy of remembering.'

When MacAllister huffed a small laugh, it didn't meet his eyes. 'All that death. So little care.'

'Perhaps we're kindred spirits, then. I've just mentioned five dead werewolves which I'm certain you've worked out by now are all connected to you, even if you deny knowing some of them. Yet you're not being very helpful. Do *you* not care?'

'I don't know all of them,' he said. 'Not personally. Some of my pack have likely crossed paths with them. That doesn't link them to me directly.'

'Yeah. Right,' Oren drawled. 'Nothing happens in a pack without the alpha's permission.'

'My pack's safety is my priority,' MacAllister shot back, and his sudden sharpness betrayed him. Oren had heard it too.

'Indeed. And I suppose that's why the location of this place is so remote?' MacAllister didn't answer. 'Our records for you are twenty years old: when you left civilization to join a pack. We have nothing after that. But we do know this pack only came into existence nine years ago. Where have you been, Michael? Pack loyalty makes it highly unlikely you left one pack for another. So why have you felt the need to relocate? Who are you hiding from?'

MacAllister leant back in his chair.

'I think the next target is you,' she said. 'I think it's been you all along. I think all these victims that link back to you are a warning. I think that symbol you're pretending not to know is a message.'

'You think you know a lot for such a young girl . . .' he sneered, his lip curling, 'in over her head.'

It took every ounce of her self-restraint, and the gold hum glowing around Oren's fingertips, to stop her lunging.

He turned back to Oren and let out a derisive laugh. 'Well, if that's the case, good luck getting to me.' He gestured at them both. 'You're lucky to be standing here. We won't be so generous next time visitors arrive unannounced.'

Bastard.

She'd had enough. He wasn't going to help them, and

he'd shown little remorse for the deaths that'd occurred.

She stared at Oren. Time to go.

He nodded. He stood and reached inside his coat pocket, and threw a card on to the old wooden table. 'Contact details, should you have a brainwave please do us the courtesy of letting us know. If we need to speak to you again we'll come back, and hopefully nobody else has to die.'

He pulled open the small cabin door without so much as a farewell and gestured for her to pass.

She felt like snapping his hand clean off as she stalked past and out into the night.

'Keep that one close.' MacAllister's voice came from somewhere behind, but she refused to give him the satisfaction of turning back. 'If you want to keep her safe.'

'Is that a threat?' Oren's voice was deadly quiet.

'Not at all.' MacAllister's laugh was soft. 'But even the great wolf Fenrir did not survive Vidar in the end. And I don't doubt you've created a world full of vengeful sons. Good evening to you, Oren Rinallis.'

33

OREN

'He knew what that symbol meant.'

They broke out of the trees at last. They hadn't dared speak on the journey out of the commune confines. Too many eyes watching through the darkness. Too many ears listening.

His heart was in his throat. Though he refused to let it show on his face, or tremor his voice. They'd barely got out of there alive.

And after the market, when he'd promised to protect her, it was she who'd saved him.

She'd killed that wolf.

She'd transformed and—

Fists collided with his arm. He reeled around to find her furious face still covered in dried blood. But once she'd started she couldn't stop. Her fists pounded against him.

His arms.

His shoulders.

His sides.

Wherever she could lay her hands as she screamed at him.

She hated him, the refrain between every other expletive, he'd forced her into that position, she'd had to change to save him. She didn't seem to care that she had fought against her own kind. Her fury was born of the fact that he knew she refused to change of free will, at any other time but a full moon, and it was his fault she had.

He could see it on her distraught face, that no rationale, no arguing, nothing he could say would break through, and that she saw it as some kind of a betrayal. That he wasn't supposed to need saving.

'Sage, stop!'

Tear tracks ran through the blood still smeared across her cheeks.

'You could've shifted out! You could've saved yourself.'

'And leave you there?' he demanded. 'Give me some credit.'

'Fought your way out, then!'

'How? Kill them all in front of you? Because that's how it would've ended if I'd fought back!'

She laughed, high and hysterical. 'Oh, well, that makes it OK, then, to just let yourself die! And let me kill instead.'

'Tell me you'd have been able to look me in the eye,' he hissed furiously, grabbing her wrists to steady them. 'Tell me we'd ever be OK again if I'd just slaughtered them all?'

Because that was the choice he'd made. All the choices he'd made tonight. It scared him now, now that he thought about it, because it meant he had to admit that he gave a damn.

'You knew!' she gasped. 'You knew I didn't want to change!'

'I never would have put us in that situation if I thought they'd attack!'

'It is your fault,' she sobbed. 'It's your fault.'

At last she gave up and sank to her knees, cradling her head in her hands.

He stared at her, this girl on the floor, so lost in despair. It was such an endless well of pain, a black maw of sadness he hadn't thought possible anyone else could feel. He didn't know what to do as he watched all this pain and guilt and hatred, all these things she'd clearly hidden, come pouring out.

'Sage.' He crouched in front of her, reached for her arm, but she wrenched away from his touch.

He lost his patience at last. 'I'm sorry, but I didn't make you—'

'Yes, you did,' she whispered between her tears. 'Because if I didn't you would have died.'

'Then I would have died,' he said simply.

And that was the truth.

He'd nearly died so many times, in so many ways, and over so many years she could never comprehend. He wasn't afraid of it. And that was the line he realized he'd drawn: he would've rather died than allow her to see him become what he'd have to become to destroy that whole pack. He would rather die than lose the sanctuary of a place without judgement that she and P had offered him these last few weeks. Now that he'd come to acknowledge that . . .

He was Oren Rinallis. He was scared of nothing.

But that terrified him.

'You just don't get it,' she whispered hopelessly. 'I don't want any more of my friends to die, Oren! Good friends don't do that! They save each other.'

'Sage, I told you, I . . .'

But even as he started his old refrain, this time it felt hollow.

'*You don't want any friends!*' she screamed. '*I know!* But I do. *I do.*'

Oren Rinallis, lost for words.

'Would it really be so bad?' she whispered.

'You don't understand.'

'What if I don't care?' She looked up at last, her brown eyes ringed with red. 'I don't give a shit about stuff you did decades before I was even born, Oren! I don't care people avoid you in the street. Or are you genuinely telling me that after all this is over we'll just part ways as if none of it happened?' She looked down at her hands. 'I care what happens to you, even if you don't. I'm sorry. I'm a pack animal. That's just how it is.'

Before she could stop him he reached for her arm again. Everything went dark, and when she blinked again they were outside her apartment door.

*

'You're back quicker than—' P almost screamed at the sight of her stomping through the apartment covered in blood. 'Sage! Are you hurt?'

She didn't answer. She slammed her bedroom door without a word.

He followed her, ignoring P too. He'd already heard her bathroom door click. He strode into her room and shut the door in P's shocked face.

He sat on the end of her bed and waited until she walked out of the bathroom fifteen minutes later in a dressing gown and with her hair wrapped in a towel.

'You look like you again.'

'That happens when you change back,' she said curtly.

'I meant without the blood.' He gestured to his mouth.

'What do you want, Oren?'

He stood up. 'Take tomorrow off,' he said. 'You've hardly stopped since this all started.'

'No.'

'Yes, Sage. You need a break. From work. From . . . me. We won't find him if you burn yourself out. Just . . . just chill out.'

'Don't tell me to chill out.'

He held up his hands in submission. 'I'm going!'

He refused to look back as the door slammed for the last time that night.

34

OREN

It was the early hours of the morning, and he had had enough for one day.

He still felt sick.

Confused.

Furious.

He wanted to go back up that hill right now and kill Michael MacAllister for what he'd put them through. What his whole pack had put them through. He'd meant it when he'd told her he wouldn't have put them in that position if he'd genuinely thought there was any danger. In that case, he'd have gone alone.

And no werewolves would be left on that hill tonight.

'Oren, wait!' P's shrill demand followed him out on to the street. It was late enough that they were the only ones there, illuminated by a street lamp under the dark glamoured fairy sky above.

He'd already slammed their front door, but nothing as silly as a solid wall was going to stop the poltergeist. 'What?' he demanded.

She jolted to a stop, her eyes wide. And he realized the face he'd turned on her wasn't the one she'd become accustomed to, it was the one he reserved for everyone else.

He felt so bitter all of a sudden. He knew he'd made a mistake with Sage. He'd become intoxicated with her naivety. He'd let himself become enamoured with the idea of someone judging him without the past. He never should've let his mask slip.

An idiot. That's what he was. Because look what'd happened.

She'd become attached. Expected them to remain in each other's lives after this case was over.

And he'd—

P drew herself up until she was taller than him and he had to look up to see her face. 'You don't scare me, Oren.'

His back stiffened. 'That wasn't my intention.'

'Then put all that anger away,' she said, pointing at his face. 'I won't help you until you do.'

Dog person versus cat person.

'I'm not sure it's something you can help with this time, P,' he said.

She could work miracles with many things, he was pretty convinced about that now, but fixing him, inside? Unlikely.

She sighed, and lowered again so her head was level with his. He didn't know how, perhaps because she was the mediator in so many of their battles, but it was obvious by the pitying look that she knew something had passed between them tonight. Some argument that'd been about more than just the case and the killer.

'The supernatural world was thrown at me the moment I sat up from my body and realized I was dead,' she said. 'You have a little time, you know, to learn, then decide whether to stay or pass on. That's when I found out what Sage really was.' She looked down at her ghostly fingers, trying to hide fresh emotion in her voice. 'Suddenly it all made sense – why something always felt off. I realized all those times I was suspicious she was hiding something, that was true, but it wasn't about boys or stupid stuff like that. It was about this whole world down here. I was a few days short of eighteen when I discovered Downside and I was over-whelmed, but she was only eight, and she had nobody, forced to keep it secret for years. That's why I chose to stay. To stay with her. She didn't even know I was dead yet. I found her still sleeping and I waited, and promised that she'd never be alone again.'

He hadn't known. Assumed this was a convenient arrangement between two supernaturals around the same age. How had he not known that? How had he never thought to ask?

'You . . . knew her before you died?'

'We were four when we met. Human Upside kids in the same nursery school. She said she liked my wellies so I let her share my crisps. And even after she was turned, went

Downside, she would spend her weekends at my house having sleepovers. None of us knowing what she'd become. We grew up together, best friends, as human children. It was . . . chance we ended up supernatural together too.'

'I didn't realize,' he said quietly.

'What I'm trying to say,' she sounded like she was choosing her words carefully, 'is that a room can be crowded and a person still feel alone. She has supernatural friends now she's older, but the circumstance of her childhood left her lonely *inside* for a long time, and she filled all those gaps with the guilt and grief and self-loathing that comes with being the only one to survive. I sometimes think her desperation to join the Arcānum and prevent bad things from happening to other people is her way of taking back control.'

He could understand that. Was that not what he'd done with his life?

He realized P knew that too. She understood completely this furious inner battle he was having with himself. He forced himself to look impassive, even as his stomach jolted.

She gave him a sad smile. 'She sees herself in you, Oren, that's all. Someone who's been alone for a long time. And she can't bring herself to let one more person feel as lonely as she has. But every time you snap or make a snide comment, it's just a reminder that you don't want to be helped.'

'I don't need help.'

She shook her head. 'No. You've isolated yourself so thoroughly you don't *need* anything from anyone. But friendship isn't about needing things from people. It's about offering just for the sake of caring, and accepting because you acknowledge the kindness.'

He didn't know what to say.

He hadn't signed up for any of it; it was all deeper than he'd wanted to be bothered with all those long years of isolation.

Yet here he was. And this poltergeist knew him better than anyone he'd known for decades.

'P.' He'd always made a point never to ask. In the beginning it was because he didn't care. Then it'd just been obvious it was too personal. 'Why won't she change other than a full moon? What is it she's scared of?'

P shook her head, smiling, as if he should've known better than to ask her to spill her best friend's secrets. 'If she ever tries to explain why she doesn't change other than the full moon it's because she trusts you.' She finished her lecture at last. 'If you dismiss her like you do everything else, the damage will be irreparable. You'll lose us both. Forever.'

35

SAGE

She'd forgotten how it was to change outside of a full moon. It'd taken everything out of her. And when she'd finally woken to a knock on her bedroom door the next day . . . morning was long gone.

The knock on the door had been Oren. The last person she'd wanted to see. But the order to get changed sounded important, and she refused to miss out on anything to do with the case. Not after the last forty-eight hours. Like hell she wouldn't see it through to the end now.

Now they were Upside.

The moment she'd stepped out of her bedroom and her fingers touched his outstretched palm, they shifted.

And she found herself in a rooftop garden: the edges decorated with grass verges and small potted evergreens that were able to weather the winter temperatures, and a little hut that sold coffee was shuttered and closed. The logo on the closed sign was that of one of the human universities across town. A white dome sat way across the other side of the garden, behind a wrought-iron fence, the door leading inside padlocked closed.

But still . . . no body. No crime scene.

She sniffed.

She couldn't smell any blood.

So why of all the places had he brought her here?

She could see raindrops disturbing the surface of a small gathering of water in a partially blocked gutter, but Oren's magic was preventing rain from touching her. And though his magic warmed her too, she pulled her jacket tighter around herself.

He didn't speak to her at all, and that made it even worse. She still felt stupid. Embarrassed. The jacket felt like the only barrier she had to hold between them. As if she could hide all her shame beneath the fabric. She glanced up, as usual, but wherever the moon was, whatever wisp of cloud or tall building around them it was hidden behind, she couldn't see it. Thank God.

He dodged the metal table and chairs outside the coffee hut and led her towards a canopy at the other side of the garden, lights strung across the top for decoration, though they were turned off now. He sat on one of the cushioned sofas and gestured to the other, a request to join him. On the table between them, a small fire burst into light. There was no wood for it to crackle, nor did the flames damage the tabletop it hovered a few centimetres over, but she instantly felt a welcoming warmth on her face.

A glass of wine appeared next to it on her side, a glass of

whisky on his.

'Why are we here?'

'To talk,' he said awkwardly. 'In private. About last night.'

Oh.

She supposed she should be grateful there wasn't another dead werewolf around the corner, but this . . .

'Please don't,' she said quietly, looking down at the glass she picked up and cradled in her hands. She couldn't think of any conversation she wanted to have less. She wanted to forget that any of it had happened. What she'd done to that werewolf . . . and the argument after.

'The first time I—'

Was he going to try and tell her about the first time he'd killed? How many years ago was that? A hundred and twenty? A hundred and thirty?

'Oren.' Her tone was cutting, even sharper than she'd meant it. But it must've done its job because he stopped.

She stared into the flames. Let them dazzle her eyes.

She knew she was being a bitch, knew that he was only trying to help. But . . . She found herself laughing bitterly. 'You never want to talk about your past. It's funny that a story about you killing someone is supposed to make me feel better now.'

She knew it was a low blow. But if he thought the same he didn't react. His handsome face stared impassively back, the shadows from the fire dancing across it. 'Go on, then.'

'Go on . . . what?'

'Ask me. That's what you've always wanted. Ask me anything and I'll answer it.'

Sage stared at him. It was a trick, right?

'You've travelled the world. You've been everywhere. Yet you end up . . . here? Why? When?'

'Seriously?' He sounded disappointed. 'You get a free pass and that's what you ask?'

'You didn't say I only had one question.'

He huffed at her cheek. But he answered. 'I arrived in Downside to work for the Arcānum sixty years ago.'

'I thought time was a human construct you didn't abide by,' she said faux-innocently. 'Didn't you say that when P asked how old you were?'

He tried to look like he wasn't smiling. 'You're too young to understand any other reference. I have to speak in ways your limited lifetime understands.' He almost looked wistful. 'You haven't had the time to see the things I have.'

The vast gulf of time between them stretched out again. It caught her off guard sometimes, when she forgot and remembered again there were decades and decades between them. Only this time, she realized, it made her chest feel a bit hollow.

'Tell me something you've seen, then,' she said. Suddenly, she realized, she wanted to know it all. Suddenly, she felt a bit breathless. 'Tell me everything I've missed.'

His expression was unreadable. 'Everything?'

He leant forward, resting his elbows on his knees. He looked at the floor, and she got the feeling it was so he didn't have to look at her.

'Oren?'

'Have you . . . heard of the Cariva?'

She coughed, choking on the wine she'd started to sip. 'That isn't real.'

'It's real.'

Everything her friends had said came flooding back. Everything she'd dismissed.

And she refused to hear it. He was playing with her.

The Arcānum? They followed rules, abided by laws, everything they did was to *keep* the law. That was what she'd told Harland and Danny and Rhen when they'd repeatedly pitched this theory.

It was a good fairy story, she'd give them that . . . but it was a story. A myth. Nobody actually knew one. Nobody could name a single member. A group of warlocks, a group of *assassins* roaming the darkest corners of the world? The strongest, most fearless, most powerful, left to hunt down the kinds of creatures that created legends. They answered to nobody, outranked every position other than the Elders themselves, were said to have unrestricted licence to end life at their own discretion—

She closed her eyes.

Her own thoughts answered everything.

'This is what I don't understand, isn't it?'

He took another gulp and refilled his glass. 'My father was an advisor to the Elders. He . . . fell out of favour when he made an assassination attempt on one of the Elders, and as a result, since my mother was also sentenced as an accomplice, I was orphaned at a young age. Eight.' He swallowed as he met her eye again. 'The same as you. It was a scandal at the time. Even now, the story is infamous in the Stone City. And our name became famous across the world in the weeks the supernatural world followed the trial and executions. It was supposed to be a stain on my name forever.' He looked back down. 'But I was powerful. I was scouted for the Cariva before I'd even graduated, and moved to their private training academy. Cariva get a different kind of training. Not everyone makes it, even among those with gold magic; some are stronger than others. I was the best.'

'You're lying.' But even as she said it, there was little conviction.

It was more of a plea. She could feel a gaping hole opening, an endless well of history she couldn't begin to comprehend.

He shook his head. 'I built my reputation on the blood of others, until at last my name outshone the fate of my parents. That was what really drove me, in the beginning. Desperation to escape my past. But in the end my arrogance got the better of me, I was captured by a minotaur. The last of his kind in that part of the world. I'd already wiped out the rest of his family. Killed all his children, and his wife. For two years I was tortured and—'

He shook his head. The hollow shadows of memory just behind his turquoise eyes were remembering another time.

But then he blinked, and returned. He waved away the rest. 'By the time I escaped I'd lost the taste for it. I took an extended leave of the Cariva and travelled. After a few years I ended up here.' He shrugged as if to say he didn't know why. 'I think it just felt the furthest from home I could get. Roderick knew who I was.' He sounded bitter again. 'But the truth is, you don't ever really leave. I'm bound by an oath I took. So Roderick and I play a fine game. We both know I outrank him. I humour his orders because the Elders allow me to remain as long as I serve an Arcānum. Service is still service. Even if it is not strictly Cariva business.'

'You're saying you're trapped?'

'I'm saying I don't wish to return. So, knowing my unique position, Roderick forces me to carry out his worst tasks here. Keep his stats looking good. Any hopes of forgetting my early days are squandered by his insistence I kill everyone on his behalf instead. My one stipulation is that I work alone . . . It's why I do *everything* alone, Sage. So that I never burden anyone else with all that I am. All that I've done. All I'm still forced to do. Because anyone shackled to me would also be forced to face unconscionable tasks by my side.' He looked up at last with a grim smile. 'I promise you, Sage, all these times I told you I didn't want a friend, a partner . . . it was to save you from me, not me from you.'

He saluted her with his glass. But she didn't raise hers to meet his.

Everything had changed.

So he drank to himself alone. Waited for her reaction to the secrets he'd never uttered before. Secrets she'd brought to the surface, forced out, because of the things she'd screamed at him.

'Say something,' he said softly. And now he sounded breathless. Pleading. She looked at him across the table and realized that not only was he asking her to accept all that he was, hideous secrets and all, but worse . . . Despite all the times she'd asked for his friendship, now she knew the truth he expected her to reject him.

'I feel stupid,' she confessed at last. 'For not being adequately afraid.'

'Not being adequately afraid has always been my favourite thing about you,' he said stiffly.

'The other warlocks. They all know? That's why they treat you how they do? Why Hozier is so afraid?'

'Warlocks are the only race that know with certainty we're more than just a horror story. Keeping the mystery to everyone else makes us all the more terrifying. Makes the job easier.'

She gazed at him, but she just couldn't quite . . . She

walked around the table to sit beside him. Held out her hand, a request for him to show her his. She took it in her fingers. Examined the skin. Ran hers over the callouses. She turned them over and looked at his nails. Clean now, but how many times had they been soaked in the blood of others? She held that hand in hers and tried to find signs that they'd been responsible for so much horror.

But . . . nothing.

'This is what Roderick used to blackmail you? About me.'

He nodded. 'He'd terminate my contract. Send me back. If I didn't take you on and make your life so difficult you didn't want the job any more.'

'I'm sorry,' was all she realized she could whisper. All she could say. But he shook his head: she had nothing to apologize for.

He didn't speak. She knew he was offering her the chance to tell her real story too. The truth she told nobody. Nobody except P. But she couldn't. Her throat constricted. The nod was so small she might've missed it. *It's OK*, it said. *I'll wait*.

Cariva. It mortified her.

A horror story come to life in front of her. A myth made flesh.

And he was sitting there in jeans and a sweatshirt and one of P's knitted scarves.

He pointed to her glass. 'Drink up. I brought you here for a reason. We have one more stop tonight.'

36

SAGE

She was surprised to realize he was leading her towards that white dome on the far edge of the roof. He held out a hand to help her step over the low wrought-iron railing protecting it from casual roof garden visitors, and gestured to the thin metal ladder running up to it. It was perched on top of a circular wall, and the padlock on the door unlocked with a small click as he waved his hand.

He let a soft light float up to illuminate the room as she followed him inside.

'What is this place?' She'd found herself in a cramped space, a rusting spiral staircase towering up to the dome above.

'Go and see.'

He gestured with his chin expectantly.

The railing was cold under her fingers, the staircase so narrow she almost had to turn sideways, and when she came out on the small platform there was barely enough room for both of them to fit.

But her throat had already constricted.

And her eyes were prickling.

'Why have you brought me here?' she whispered.

She stared at the ancient golden telescope.

She couldn't look at him. Couldn't bear to see ridicule if he spotted her tears.

He tutted like he heard every panicked, heartbroken thought. 'Why do you really think, Sage?'

When she looked back at last, he wore a tender expression she hadn't seen before.

'I can't,' she said quietly as a tear she couldn't hide any longer rolled down her cheek.

'You can.'

She shook her head.

'You said once that nothing is as horrifying than I am,' he said quietly. 'And here I am with you. Nothing here can hurt you.'

'You don't understand.'

'Only because you won't tell me.'

Her heart ached. 'Because I can't stand to have you look at me with disgust.'

'Have we not just resolved this issue in reverse?' He stared, his expression that was usually so impassive, so impervious to anything, now riven by a frown. When she didn't respond he sighed. 'I've not broken us in for you to not even look, just once.'

She clenched her jaw.

'I'll go first,' he offered, turning to look into the sight of the giant telescope.

She didn't know how she hadn't realized until they were up there. She knew there was an observatory atop the university. It was famous. But she'd never dreamt of going, not when it was a gateway to her greatest nemesis.

He moved the telescope, guiding it around the narrow landing until he located what he was looking for and twisted a dial to focus. He pulled back and beckoned her to come close.

Her heart was pounding in her chest. She wanted to burst into uncontrollable tears.

'I'm right here,' he said into her ear as she moved into his space. And she knew he meant it. So she took a deep breath and peered into the telescope.

She gasped.

And let her endless tears keep falling.

And every thought she'd kept locked away inside, every bit of fear and guilt came pouring out as she gazed up at the moon. Bright and shining and almost whole.

She could see it in such detail, the grey markings tarnishing her silvery surface. She was so bright that the stars around her paled.

She didn't care that he was behind her, witness to her undoing as she stared up at the thing that haunted her nightmares, yet was so beautiful it took her breath away. She felt like a traitor to even find the thing that had ruined her whole life so beautiful.

She lost all notion of time as she gazed up, shoulders shaking with silent sobs.

She didn't even notice his arms were around her until he was pulling her back, and she was enveloped against his chest. What she'd refused to let him do as she'd unravelled last night. She was so lost in endless despair that she didn't even try to stop him.

It was so at odds with everything he was.

'It was me,' she said finally, her voice muffled against his shirt.

'What was?'

He tried to look down into her face but she held on tighter, suddenly wanting to be pressed against him rather than see his eyes as she admitted this deepest sin at last.

'Two years ago. P knew I'd been keeping secrets so she followed me. Out to the Lake District where I transform.' Her voice was raw and she kept her eyes tight shut, as if she could hide away from the hideous memories. 'It was almost time, I could feel it coming, and I turned and saw her across a field. It was like something from a film. Like slow motion. I looked to the sky just as clouds blew away, and the last thing I saw was the full moon. And then I changed.'

She pulled back at last and looked into his eyes, her own swollen and red.

She saw the moment he understood the truths she was admitting to him and him alone in that observatory above the worlds.

She could barely even nod her head.

Then she saw the pity. That emotion again so alien on his face.

'I don't remember it. I just woke up and she was there next to me, waiting. A ghost.' She choked on the memory. 'I wanted to die too. From that day I've hated the wolf. It betrayed me. I can't trust it. I can't trust myself. I will not change unless I have to.'

'Sage, when you change of free will it's different than a full moon, you keep your mind. Part of you stays human. You know this?'

She shook her head. 'The last time I changed of free will someone still died, remember? I'm a curse. I change, and people die. At least you kill people who really deserve it. I can't even claim that.'

'That wolf was about to kill me, you were protecting your . . . partner. And what happened to P was an accident. She wouldn't be in Downside if she didn't understand that. She stayed. *For you.*'

'I took everything from her. A future. A life. Children. All of it, gone.'

'Not if Stellan has his way.' He offered a small smile. 'You know he asked me to put in a good word too?'

Despite herself, she hiccupped a laugh.

He wiped the wetness from her cheek with gentle fingers.

'Do you think I'm a monster now?' she asked.

He was quiet for a moment as he wiped her other cheek and swept her hair behind her ear. 'Only as much as I am.'

'I don't know if that's a good thing.'

His eyes shone. 'It isn't. But if we're going to hell for our sins, Sage, at least we'll go together.'

'I thought you did things better alone.'

'I thought so too.' He swallowed.

She looked up into his handsome face and smiled.

He nodded. And with his arms still around her, he shifted them back to Downside.

In the barrel room of Dive Bar he pulled her back just as she was about to descend through the trapdoor towards Stellan's desk, and waved a glowing hand over her face.

'What—'

'Don't tell Berion but I'm actually quite skilled at fixing make-up. You looked like a hag.'

He laughed as she called him something vicious.

But she smiled. 'Thank you,' she said. 'For . . .' She shrugged. Everything, she supposed. 'Making the effort to fix things after last night.'

'I think we were meant to go there tonight,' he said quietly.

'What do you mean?'

'When you asked me if you were a monster . . . the truth is, there's nothing you could've said that I wouldn't have been able to accept. There are no sins that could outstrip some of mine.' He looked down. 'And I'm not proud of a lot of things. But . . . I find that when I speak of it all to you, you don't make me feel ashamed.' He sighed. She wasn't sure if it sounded like relief. 'Don't the humans say that a problem shared is a problem halved? The weight of my secrets feel lighter tonight than they have in a long time.'

She stared up at him. The one person in the world, she realized, who didn't make her feel ashamed either. Like the weight of his secrets, something heavy in her chest started to loosen too. 'Now I know what Roderick threatened, I understand if—'

He shook his head. 'I told you that to make you understand. If you really want this job, if you want to stick together, he will make you witness terrible things by my side. You will be held just as responsible as me. You will be judged as I am. And you won't ever be able to tell the world otherwise. My reputation has to hold.'

She swallowed. 'Me and P.' She asked the only thing she supposed mattered now. 'We can trust you?'

'Always,' he whispered fiercely.

She was quiet for a moment. 'Wolves are pack animals,' she said at last.

His throat bobbed, his eyes bright. He looked down and in his hand was a small box that hadn't been there a moment before. 'I wanted to give you this. Happy birthday.'

'Why didn't you give it to me earlier?'

'I wasn't sure if you'd want it,' he admitted as he placed

it in her palm. 'I wasn't sure if you'd still want me after . . . everything.' After the truth. 'Go on,' he urged, nodding at her hand.

It was a small, battered jewellery box, the hinge stiff as she flicked open the worn brass catch.

Then, she gasped.

A pearlescent white stone, perfectly circular, encased in platinum and suspended from a thin chain.

She gaped at it, glistening and shimmering. Perhaps she was still too intoxicated by the moment, but as she looked at it, she thought it looked exactly like the moon through the telescope.

She cleared her tightening throat. 'You didn't have to get me anything like this.'

'Technically I found it, in the late 1800s, and it's sat in my desk for decades. Forgot about it until a few days ago when I was looking for something else. Maybe fate nudged it into my hand to remind me it was there. I don't know. But it's moonstone, so I think it was destined for you.'

This thing in her hands was almost as old as he was. Maybe older. 'You believe in fate and destiny?'

'Of course,' he whispered. 'Perhaps it was fate that led me to find it all that time ago, and urged me to put it in my pocket. Perhaps destiny knew that one day my only friend would be a wolf. Shall I?'

She knew that accepting the necklace was accepting more than just a gift. She was accepting the terms of a new life, a partnership they would forge together. She handed him back the box and turned, pulling her hair aside to make it easier. He lifted the thin chain over her head, and the moonstone sat perfectly just under her collarbone. As if it had indeed been destined to rest there.

37

SAGE

'Morning,' a bright voice chimed.

She gasped, jumping up in shock as P sat on the end of her bed, smiling.

'What time did we get back?' Her throat felt full of razor blades. Her head was pounding. She groaned into her pillow.

Reality was beckoning. Murders. Not mojitos.

Oren had insisted on walking her home. Though they'd not mentioned the bundle of sage since she'd found it under that statue, she knew the audacity of such a threat would be quietly irking him. She didn't think they should be surprised the killer knew she was working with Oren by now, but when it came to choosing her battles, she knew allowing him to walk her home wasn't worth the fight.

Downside was heading into the last few days before Yuletide and the city was alight. Every shop front was lit up. Every bar played loud music. The Baritone Banshees stood in the square outside the town hall and howled Yuletide songs. Oren had muttered his opinion and quickly redirected them down a different street.

Burning logs was a tradition, and every premises they'd passed had a roaring fire in a hearth, fireflies glittering between all kinds of evergreens cut to decorate mantles and windows. And mistletoe. That was a *big* one Downside. Slightly embarrassed hopefuls out with their friends loitered nearby, eyeing their secret crush.

That always made her smile.

Then a sound had made her pause. Music, but not what she was used to Downside. She'd grabbed Oren's arm and dragged him with her before he could protest, around the corner of a street filled with restaurants and bars, and past the Hypogriff's Wings pub on the corner where a merry crowd of goblins were spilling out on to the street, until there, a few more bar fronts away, she spotted it.

A brass quartet of four fairies, floating a metre or so off the ground, the soft hum of their fluttering wings almost entirely drowned out by their instruments. A small crowd had gathered to watch, tossing a coin now and then into an upturned hat left on the floor. She knew, to them, all the supernaturals around them, this could be anything this band composed, they had no idea that what she was listening to was Christmas. Human carols she sang as a little girl, P at her side, alive and well and able to touch her as they giggled in school assembly. The quartet had no singer, but she whispered under her breath, and her heart felt like it could explode.

After she'd forced Oren to listen to her sing two more human carols, he'd tried to stop her nudging him towards a fancy-looking new cocktail bar behind them. 'It's late, Sage.'

'You ruined my birthday,' she pouted.

She knew the emotional blackmail had worked as his nostrils flared. 'One,' he warned. 'And I get to choose which cocktail.'

So they had one.

. . . And she'd emotionally blackmailed him into a few more after that.

'About five a.m. That was three hours ago,' P said.

Sage made a noise somewhere between a moan and a strangled whimper.

P gasped. 'What's that?'

'What's what?' She shifted the fingers that covered her eyes enough to peer through. P was pointing at her chest.

Her hand came to her neck, confused.

'Late birthday present,' she managed to grumble at P, covering her eyes again from the light streaming in through the open door.

'That's . . . fancy.' She could tell without looking that P was smiling. 'He'd better get something nice for mine.'

'P.' She pushed herself up, praying she wouldn't vomit last night everywhere, and forced herself to look into her friend's bright eyes. 'I told him.'

She wasn't sure if she should've asked permission first.

It wasn't just her secret to tell.

'I told him what I did to you.'

P's smile faded. Sage could hear the hammering of her heart thudding in her own ears.

'You didn't do anything,' P whispered, looking at a spot on the duvet cover her fingers had suddenly become very interested in. 'Not intentionally. Nothing I didn't deserve.'

Sage flinched. The movement must've caught P's eye because she glanced up, and tutted. 'I followed you, Sage. I didn't trust you and I crept around spying. I *stalked a werewolf*. It was a valid consequence of my actions.'

She stared at P, furious all over again, as she always was on the rare occasions either of them acknowledged that night. 'How can you keep defending it?' she demanded.

'It?' Her bottom lip wobbled. 'Sage, I'm defending you!' She looked up at the ceiling in despair. 'How many times do I have to tell you I don't blame you for what happened?'

Another stab to the heart, as always. She wanted P to blame her. Sometimes, she wanted P to hate her, so that all her own hatred didn't feel so out of place. She wanted justification for her own anger. She wanted P to rage. To shout. To call her all the names she called herself in the darkest moments of her sleepless nights. Her forgiveness robbed her of validation and . . . she resented that. She looked down to hide her own tears.

'What did he say?'

'Well, he wasn't horrified,' she said glumly.

P started laughing. 'Did you expect different?'

'That's not exactly a glowing compliment, is it?'

She sighed, but she was still smiling. 'Roderick called your phone.'

Sage groaned, collapsed back down on her pillow.

'He wants an update.' The whine that escaped her lips was self-pitying as she rubbed her face and felt last night's make-up still smudged there. 'Oren called too. He'll meet you there in half an hour.'

'Great,' she muttered, ripping off the bed covers at last as P rose and floated for the door.

She turned back just before she passed entirely through. 'I know there's a lot we don't agree on about the night I died, Sage. Stuff we'll never agree on. But I stayed for you—'

'P—'

'No, Sage, let me speak, just this once.' She held up her hands. 'The girl I remember, who laughed loudly and smiled often, I thought I'd lost her when your parents died, because I never saw her again after that. Only once I knew, and you didn't have to hide any more, did I see glimpses of the girl you'd hidden away again. There are a few things I haven't worked out how to fix yet.' She swallowed, and wiped a tear. 'I realize now that those last bits weren't for me to fix.'

'P . . .' She was wrong. Sage knew deep in her heart she wouldn't have survived without P. She refused to let her think she hadn't been enough.

But P smiled like she knew what she was thinking. 'I've been able to offer security and forgiveness and that was what you needed, but you've also needed someone who understood everything else . . . Those dark feelings you can't escape from inside. And so did he. And I hear that laughter again. It's fragile, and sometimes I think it's a little bit afraid. You both are, because you make each other vulnerable in order to mend.'

'You're still my best, best friend.'

Her tinkly laugh was like birdsong. 'I'm not jealous.' Sage could tell from her smile that she meant it. 'You're allowed another. So am I. I'm trying to tell you that it's fine, that I want us to keep him too. And let's face it, neither of you would manage without someone stable holding the madness together anyway.'

She started to laugh at last as P turned to float away, but she still heard her as she disappeared. 'He's even more handsome now I've got a few good meals inside him.'

38

SAGE

Half an hour later she could've cried some more behind the sunglasses she'd thrown on to protect her eyes from the watery morning sunlight. And it wasn't even fully light yet. But the bright white ceiling lights of the headquarter corridors burnt into her sockets. She turned into the corridor that housed Roderick's office to find Oren already waiting, the collar of his coat turned up as he slouched against the wall, frowning.

'My head's splitting,' was his only greeting. And he was a little bit green. 'I've not been hungover since the 1960s.'

'I'm not sure if I'm gonna be sick yet.'

'I was sick as soon as I shifted home,' he grumbled. 'I should've walked.'

She started to snigger. 'Did you shift here?'

'Didn't want to risk it,' he said darkly as he lifted a hand and knocked twice on the door, and shoved his way into the room without waiting.

'Well, you two have seen better days,' Roderick said dryly. 'Good night?'

'Can't remember.' Oren ignored his boss's gesture towards the chair opposite the desk.

'And there was me thinking you'd hate each other.'

'Hoping,' she muttered. She leant into Oren's side in an attempt to keep herself upright. The arm that came around her back to hold her up was tight, sensing she was a hair's breadth from keeling over and vomiting all over their feet at the least convenient moment.

Roderick could clearly see it too as he surveyed them both in disgust. 'Indeed.'

'What do you want, Roderick?' Oren snapped.

He sat back in his chair and crossed his arms. 'I want an update.'

'We know who the real target is,' she said, and she didn't bother to sound polite. She'd never liked Roderick but now she knew what he'd done to Oren, the blackmail, she could barely stand to look at him. 'We're working on a motive. And I have a plan to lure the killer out into the open in the next few days.' Oren tensed. She hadn't got round to telling him yet. She'd actually only thought about it on the walk over. 'Between us, and Berion and Hozier if they consent, we'll have it wrapped up by next week.'

'Oh, no,' Roderick laughed softly. 'You wanted to prove yourself. You fix it. You're banned from asking Berion and Hozier for assistance. In fact, if you do you can kiss your little dreams goodbye.'

'Are you joking?' Oren cut in. 'There's a killer on the

loose and you're—'

'Watch your tone.' Roderick accentuated his syllables with barely concealed temper as he leant across his desk. Then he straightened again. 'Finalize your plans. I want this dealt with by Yuletide or the deal's off.' He threw something across the desk towards them. 'Here.' A brown file with Salina's name stamped across the top that'd seemingly been left in his room for days. He hadn't even bothered to return it to the archives. 'I took it when she was killed to find you her business address. Read it. Return it. Whatever. I don't really care.'

Oren opened his mouth to retort that he should've handed it over days ago. He'd kept it on purpose, knowing it'd make life all the more difficult. It didn't matter they had five dead werewolves.

But it wasn't worth it. 'Come on,' she muttered, snatching up the file. 'Let's go.'

She pulled out her phone and texted P a request to join them as she led the way down through the headquarters towards the archives, and Berion and Hozier's offices. It was still early, but given the animated grunts and roars coming from the training rooms, she was confident most warlocks were already in the building.

'Morning.' She, at least, was polite enough to knock before shoving her way in. She gave Oren a pointed smile. He rolled his eyes as he followed her in and shut the door behind them. She dropped Salina's file on to a small side table and shrugged off her coat.

Berion was sitting behind his desk like a king on a throne, sipping from a takeaway coffee as he leant over a flaky pastry on a napkin in front of him. Hozier smiled from where she lounged on the chaise, her legs up, wafting the crumbs from whatever she'd been eating off her chest. Oren made a disgusted noise. Her eyes slipped to him, but whatever retort was just behind her lips, she kept it locked in.

'Wow.' Sage whistled at Berion's leopard print suit. 'You've excelled yourself.'

'I do try.' He bowed his head, gesturing at the scalloped chairs. 'What brings you here? If you have any more rotting rubbish, you can sift through it yourself.'

'You'll be pleased to hear we don't.' She threw herself down on the velvet, shell-shaped chair as Oren ignored the other, and magicked himself a stool by the door. He was there because it was work, and because she'd made him, but he still refused to join in the social banter. This wasn't his world and he wasn't comfortable being there.

'Michael MacAllister,' she said, rubbing her still-throbbing head. 'Suppose we've got to save him.'

'Oh,' P sighed as she passed right through the centre of Berion's closed office door. 'Do we have to?'

Hozier laughed. P threw her an appreciative smile. Oren looked inclined to agree with P.

She filled Berion and Hozier in – the barest details

anyway, of their trip to visit the alpha. She left out the . . . worst bits.

Hozier wrinkled her nose. 'Suspicious, no, that he appears reluctant to help?'

'Exactly,' Oren said darkly.

'There's nothing in his records that are less than twenty years old,' P said, and the poltergeist couldn't hide the frustration in her voice. She'd ranted about it enough times at home. 'He's fifty-six. Relocated to Edinburgh as a child. Turned at twenty-two on a hiking trip in the Isle of Skye. But other than that, there isn't anything to account for his time between then and when his name popped back up as the alpha of this pack.'

'Werewolves that form packs are notoriously difficult to keep up-to-date records on.' Hozier nodded. 'Because they isolate themselves so thoroughly from society, gaps like that aren't uncommon for people like MacAllister.'

As far as Sage was concerned, that was a massive oversight.

Werewolves that lived Upside had to declare their move to the Arcānum. And Michael MacAllister had done that: he'd allowed the institution to cast the standard spell on his life force decades ago. Fine. Great. But though plenty of the Upside werewolves did regularly update contact details, it didn't look to her like much was done to check up on those that didn't.

Still, though she was grateful to Berion and Hozier for their kindness towards her – she was well aware from the looks she got walking through the entrance hall that many of the Arcānum warlocks thought of her in the same way

Roderick did – she didn't dare raise any of these qualms she had to Hozier's face.

'And you say he recognized that symbol?' Berion asked, twiddling the rings on his fingers.

'Pretty sure.' She nodded. 'He played it cool, pretended he didn't, but he hesitated. And he didn't ask us about it either, if only as a cover. That's the key. The reason why any of this is happening.'

Oren pulled the scrap of paper that he'd shown Mac-Allister out of his pocket and floated it over to Berion on a gold mist. 'Do you recognize it?'

Berion frowned down at the paper, then shook his head. He wafted it over to Hozier, this time on a purple cloud, but she looked nonplussed too.

'I've seen it somewhere.' Oren frowned. 'But that doesn't account for much. I've travelled the world, human and supernatural. Could've been anywhere.'

'In that case, is it more likely to be human if they don't recognize—'

'Sage,' P's shocked voice cut across her.

She was still floating near the doorway, where she'd spotted Salina's discarded file and picked it up. It was open in her silvery hands as P's wide eyes stared at her.

'What is it?' She asked the question, not entirely sure she actually wanted an answer.

'Cheryl Wentworth. The human woman we went to visit while you were away on a full moon?'

'The one who fancied Oren?' she smirked. Hozier snickered somewhere behind her.

'Lucy wrote an article about her long-lost sister. She told us she was away. It must've been a cover—'

Her stomach dropped. 'Salina was Cheryl's sister?'

P nodded. 'Salina was killed later that night.'

The final link they'd struggled with – how Lucy had been connected to any of these people at all. And it'd been under their noses all this time, trapped in Roderick's office, thanks to his petty grudges.

The trail was clear enough now. The killer had used each victim to find the next. Found Salina thanks to Lucy, found Mhairi thanks to Salina. Patrick through Mhairi.

Oren called Roderick all the things she was thinking.

'Last night, while you were out, I cross-referenced the known pack members against Salina's diary. Eight of them were her clients, and appointments always fell just after a full moon. Presumably they used her physio to soothe the aches and pains of a true turning,' P said. 'They'll have used Mhairi as their doctor too.'

'And MacAllister still denied knowing them?' Berion sounded aghast. 'When they treated his pack?'

Sage understood. For a wolf, *an alpha no less*, his pack loyalty didn't seem worth very much at all if he could brush off his association to wolves that helped his people so easily. 'P's right. Maybe he isn't worth saving at all.' She hesitated. 'But I do have a plan.'

39

SAGE

'To find the killer, we'd have to use MacAllister as bait. And Roderick says if I ask you for help I won't get my trial period.'

Berion's smile at the thought of dangling MacAllister in front of their murderer faded.

She pulled a face that said, *What did you expect?* 'He's panicking. Thought I'd quit by now.'

'He's a bastard,' Hozier muttered under her breath.

'But if Hozier and I are just . . . there?' Berion asked casually.

She nodded. 'So the day before Yuletide Eve, it's the full moon?'

Silence.

'Right?' Berion said slowly, but what he meant was, *So what?*

She rolled her eyes. 'It's the last full moon of the year.'

P gasped so hard Hozier jumped. 'Why didn't I think of that? Sage, it's perfect!'

'What is?' Hozier whined.

'The night before the last full moon of the year is the moon ball.'

'The moon ball?' she repeated blankly. 'What's that?'

It was Berion who answered, his eyes wide, and he looked as delighted as P. 'The one night of the year every werewolf is invited to celebrate together. Traditionally it was a ceasefire, the one night different packs could socialize with no rivalry or fighting. Nowadays it's just a big party . . . It's considered incredibly bad form to fight though. So there is still a ceasefire of sorts.'

'How do you know that?' She was surprised he knew anything about the old werewolf tradition at all.

'I attended a moon ball once in the Jura mountains. It was . . .' He sighed wistfully.

'Did you really?' Oren asked. Even he sounded impressed. 'In the Jura mountains?'

He nodded. 'When I took a few decades out to travel before joining the Arcānum. Sweet-talked a werewolf into taking me as their date. Knew a moon ball there would be something to remember.'

Because the Jura mountains were something special to werewolves. There on the border between a small French and Swiss town, the humans had held werewolf trials in the fourteenth century. Forced to flee for their lives up into the mountainous terrain, too treacherous for humans to follow but easy enough to scale on four legs, the largest werewolf population still resided up there, consisting of multiple packs.

'And there's a moon ball happening here?' Hozier asked. 'In Downside?'

'They happen everywhere. Ours is in the town hall. Every werewolf in the city is invited, and nearly all of them turn up, even most of the Upside ones come back down for it.'

'I went as her date last year,' P said brightly. 'It was wonderful.' Her eyes glossed over in dreamy memory just as Berion's had done.

It had been wonderful. Every year an advert went out in the back of *Downside Daily*, inviting applications to join the organization committee that worked all year to pull off something spectacular. Last year's theme had been 'Winter Wonderland', and the town hall had been turned into an arctic masterpiece. Fairies had been hired to glamour the whole room, and when they'd stepped inside, they were in the ballroom of an ice palace. Everything, from the dance floor to the crystals of the chandeliers, was made of glistening, shimmering ice. Carved wolf sculptures decorated the tables and drinks were served in carved chalices. Even the instruments of the band were made of ice, the delicate hairs of the violin strings and the wires of the harps frozen into place. The view through the windows had boasted snow-topped mountains. Everything had glittered. It had been magical.

'I just think it'd be the perfect opportunity to get close,' Sage went on. 'Oren and I saw first-hand how dangerous it is to try and get into that camp, we know he's relatively safe hidden away in that commune. For one night, the killer will know exactly where Michael MacAllister is going to be. He won't be able to resist turning up. I'm sure of it. Attack when vulnerable.'

'I agree.' Hozier nodded. 'It's the perfect opportunity. He's proved himself to be expert at integrating into casual situations to gather what he needs. If the five of us can get in there, watch MacAllister like a hawk, well . . .' Her voice trailed off. They didn't know exactly *well, what*, but it was a fledgeling plan.

'Wait a minute.' Berion held up his hands. He looked at her. 'Sage . . . there's a difference between us just "being nearby" and attending an invitation-only *werewolf* event. Roderick will never believe in a million years we just happened to be there by chance. You know the risk if we agree to come. You're sure you want to make this plan?'

She bit her bottom lip. 'I know,' she said finally. 'But . . . it's more important than that now. Of course I still want the job, but that's not what all of this has been for!' It was for Lucy. And the other dead wolves. She shook her head, throwing out her arms in exasperation. 'How can I stop now, if this is the one chance we have? And if Roderick uses it as an excuse, then . . .' She sighed and flopped back. 'Then so be it. Fuck the job.'

She wasn't entirely sure just how much she really meant that. But it was bigger than the job now. She didn't know what she'd do if she failed, and the thought terrified her.

Berion watched her, his head tilted to the side.

'Fine,' he said after a few moments. 'Let's do it.'

She offered him a half-hearted nod of thanks. 'I have a ticket that'll cover Oren. P can float in through a back wall, so we'd only need to worry about you two. You can't buy tickets. The only way non-werewolves can get in is by invitation, as a plus-one.'

Berion tutted with more drama than was necessary. 'Well, Harland won't want to take me as his date.' He threw a glance at Hozier. 'He'd be too scared to take you. What's the other one called? David?'

'Danny. He's already taking one of our friends, Juniper. And Harland is taking her cousin, Willow. He told me he'd asked her last week.' P glanced at her. 'He did say he'd already assumed you'd be taking Oren, that's why he hadn't asked you. They've worked it out between them, I think they've even asked some other werewolves you went to school with to get in the non-werewolves as plus-ones. They'll all be there.'

She understood the mixture of hope and sadness in P's eyes at the prospect of their friends, who they'd barely seen recently, all together in the same room.

'What about MacAllister?' Berion asked.

She started laughing. 'He's not a catch, you don't wanna be his date.'

'No. But he might get some of his pack to name us as their dates. We don't have to interact once we're inside.'

'You're vastly overestimating how willing he is to help us,' she grumbled.

Oren made a sound like he disagreed. 'He was only so confident in the confines of his commune, where he knows his surroundings and his pack have obviously practised protection techniques. It might be different if he thinks he could be cornered in unfamiliar territory. And a place where his whole pack can't just transform and attack because of the ceasefire tradition.'

'Perhaps.' She still wasn't sure. But then she groaned. 'The theme this year, it's masquerade.'

Berion's face lit up. 'I love a mask!'

Of course he did.

'And the perfect cover for a serial killer to hide his face,' Oren said impatiently.

'Oh, yeah.' His excited expression evaporated. 'Well, someone should go to MacAllister tonight.'

Oren stood. 'I'll go now. No.' He shook his head as Sage readied to rise too. 'Berion will come. You stay here and . . . whatever . . . with P.' He waved at the archives through the door. She flared up at once, but he held up his hands. He knew she was pretty sure they'd try and kill him again. And then what? 'Sage, the last time we were there you tore the throat out of one of his pack, and there's only so many times I can bargain with them. Please, just let me do this one.'

'That was you?' Hozier rounded on her, eyes suddenly bright again. 'I got the alert, but we let packs deal with their own dead. Aren't you the dark horse, eh?'

'Long story.'

'You still have that knife?' Oren asked P.

'It's at home somewhere.'

He nodded. 'You know the rules.'

She muttered something about what he could do with the knife if he kept urging her to kill anyone who walked through the door.

'What rules are these?' Berion asked, confused.

She told them about the bundle of sage they'd found at the market.

Hozier gasped. Her eyes wide. 'Well, that's not a coincidence, is it?'

'I don't think it is, no.'

Silence hung between them.

She turned to Oren. 'Please be careful.' No matter how he phrased it, she'd only killed that wolf to save his neck.

'Don't worry,' Berion smirked. 'I'll keep him safe.'

Oren huffed, muttering something about purple as he turned up the collar on his coat.

'Good job the witch magic makes up the difference, huh?' Berion sniffed as he picked at his fingernails, the image of disinterested.

Her head shot up. P's head swivelled. Hozier made a little squeak at the sound of the secret they'd obviously kept for decades.

Oren froze. 'What did you just say?'

'You never wondered how I was able to last so long in the training rings?' Berion pouted. 'I'm disappointed, Oren. I hoped you admired my air of mystery.'

'You have witch magic?' he said slowly.

'Invisible witch magic.' His white eyes glittered as he held out a hand palm up on the table and let it start to hum purple. Then the colour started to disappear. But the magic hadn't gone. She could still see it rippling the air, like the haze above a bonfire.

She stared as the haze disappeared. 'That's witch magic?'

As if to prove the point even more, an umbrella appeared in his hands without a hint of purple mist in sight.

She thought Oren's eyes might fall out of his head.

'My grandmother on my father's side was a witch. Witch mother. She died a long time ago now, but it's from her, and not a physical trait of the warlocks, that these eyes are mine. White eyes are a Witch Mother trait. But it isn't endless. It wears down with usage and needs time to replenish after. If I use it I have to be strategic, but at full strength I'm nearly as powerful as you, Oren.'

'You just let people think you're prissy,' P said slowly.

'It gives me the element of surprise.'

'Who else knows?' Oren demanded.

'Hozier, officially.' He gestured to his partner with his head. 'But it'll be in my file so Roderick too, though he's never acknowledged it. Witch magic is invisible, nobody knows unless I tell them, which makes it easier for him to ignore.'

They all knew what that meant. Plenty of warlocks had a superiority complex, and mixing warlock blood with anything less magical wasn't favourable. And Roderick was the type that disapproved. He only ignored it so as not to risk Berion, a vital part of his team, being ostracized.

Oren looked at Sage, aghast, expecting an equally incredulous expression. But she didn't feel anywhere near the shock he apparently did. She was two races mixed into one. It didn't feel out of the ordinary to her at all.

'I didn't know, either,' P offered blandly, though she was smothering a smile. 'If that's any consolation.'

'No, it isn't.' He turned back to Berion. 'Why are you telling me now?'

Berion considered. 'Let's call it insurance. You keep my secret and I won't tell anyone that a werewolf and a poltergeist have you wrapped around their little fingers.'

It was sarcastic, and his tone was scathing, but it was an offer. His contribution to this secret little pack they were building together where trust and loyalty would be absolute. Oren's brow twitched, and he looked bored too – all part of the game. He breathed a small laugh as he turned for the door. 'Then you'd better be ready. This time, I really will kill anyone who gets in my way.'

40

SAGE

'Perfect,' Berion grinned as Sage stepped into the living room two evenings later. 'I knew it'd suit you.'

He'd nearly died when he'd learnt, upon returning from MacAllister's commune, that she'd left ballgown shopping to the last minute, and had only the following day to sort it. An hour later, a dress had arrived along with an appointment card for a salon in the centre of Downside.

And what an adventure that trip had been. By the time they left P was wiping pearly tears of laughter from her cheeks. The pixies that ran the salon were maniacal. No taller than a hand, they darted around on bright dragonfly wings so quickly they were little more than blurs of colour, tittering and giggling in high-pitched voices as they weaved strands of hair and sprayed tiny travel-sized cans of hairspray.

As always happened when any supernatural realized that P was not only a ghost but a poltergeist – such a rare sight most lived centuries without ever meeting one – they'd gone into overdrive when she'd picked up a magazine in the waiting area. They descended in a rainbow swarm, dropping the things they were holding and cheering every time she caught them.

'It's just a black dress,' Sage said now, embarrassed. 'It'd suit anyone.'

That wasn't true. It was just a black dress, but it was beautiful. The bottom half was layers upon layers of black floaty gossamer that felt weightless as it trailed behind. A tight silk band around her waist accentuated her curves, and from it came two strips of silk that got thinner and thinner until they joined with a small pearl button behind her neck. It left a plunging V down to her middle and her whole back exposed. It was braver than anything she'd have ever, ever chosen herself. The whole thing was embroidered with subtle interlocking stars. The material fell in such a way that her necklace took centre stage on her chest. A full moon surrounded by a sea of stars.

And the mask! It was made of delicate, swirling lace and moulded around her eyes.

'It's supposed to be black tie for the men.' P was still eyeing Berion's light blue suit, and the extravagant mask covering the whole top half of his face was made entirely of peacock feathers. 'You knew that.'

'I did.' He shrugged. 'Hozier said she'd be ten minutes behind me, so that means at least twenty—'

The front door clicked and Harland hurried into the living room in a black suit that looked a bit too big, and a

Phantom of the Opera-style mask in one hand, a rucksack in the other.

'Hey.' He was breathless as he waved the bag that had his overnight things in. He'd consented to come back to their spare room when P had nearly cried at his latest excuse to sofa-surf elsewhere. 'Just dropping this off for later.' He stopped in his tracks. She wasn't sure if her face went redder, or his. 'You look . . . uh . . .' He swallowed, as if he wasn't quite sure he was supposed to say what he was thinking.

And then movement from the corner of the room made everyone jump.

The gold mist hadn't even dissipated yet, but there stood Oren. He was in a black suit too but his was tailored well, and evidently much more expensive. His mask was basic. Just black, no embellishments, but he didn't need any of that. He never did. He looked . . .

She sighed.

He looked like Oren always did.

'It's so rude to shift directly into the living room,' P chastised him. 'Use the door!'

'I was running late.' But he couldn't stop himself smiling at her. 'Sorry, P.'

He didn't sound sorry at all.

'You're such a show-off,' Berion muttered.

'I'm the show-off?' He pointed to himself. 'You're going to a black-tie ball in baby blue.'

'It's powder blue.'

'Drinks!' P practically screamed in the face of the bickering the room was descending into. 'Come on, I've been practising! You have time for one, Harland?'

P beckoned towards the coffee table where a selection of liquor bottles, glasses and some chopped fruit waited, and Berion showed more interest than she knew he really felt, considering he could magic any drink he wanted. Clearly, he was trying to help P push past the awkwardness of Oren ruining Harland's attempt at a compliment.

Oren stayed where he was, a brow raised at P's brand-new cocktail shaker now rattling furiously.

'You approve, then?' Sage asked, going to him instead of the table. 'I can be seen on the arm of the *infamous* Oren Rinallis?'

'Perhaps I would have done your hair differently,' he admitted, his eyes studying the curls over her shoulder. 'Where I come from, there are women who braid complex designs. An ancient tradition of my hometown. They call them constellations, because they make as many braids as there are stars in the night sky. But I think it would suit your dress.'

'I doubt we'd find anyone willing to braid an ancient warlock tradition into werewolf hair,' she smiled.

'My grandmother was a master braider,' he said quietly. 'Everybody knew when Zosia Attaia worked a constellation. I'm sure she'd have done yours.'

Another small gift, a little bit more of his history he was still working on giving her.

'Is she still alive?'

'I believe so.'

She didn't ask why he spoke about her in the past tense, as if she were dead. 'Then there's still a chance yet.'

He smiled, but then Berion was demanding her attention, holding up one of his own cocktail recipes. She accepted, humming with pleasure as she sipped. Even Oren nodded and consented to a glass. Berion grinned in triumph.

'Is that the Magic Kiss?' Hozier's voice asked as the miniature warlock waltzed into the room in a shimmering golden gown. Her skin glowed, and the tight fabric accentuated every curve it clung to.

Well, she *was* Berion's partner after all.

Naturally she'd make sure she turned heads.

It was her mask that stood out, though. It wasn't the traditional masquerade shape, rather it came up to two tall, pointed ears. And the bottom, just covering her own nose, came out like a pointed cat's snout. If she'd thought Hozier looked like a pharaoh queen when they'd met, tonight she was an Egyptian goddess.

Harland looked like he couldn't go any redder as he tried to avoid the chest bulging out of the top of Hozier's gown. 'I'm gonna . . . I need to . . . be late . . .' he muttered, putting his cocktail on the table and starting to back towards the door.

And promptly crashed into the cabinet against the wall, knocking everything off the top.

Sage dug her nails into Oren's arm with such force he

flinched. *Do not speak*, it demanded, as Harland crawled around on the floor, picking up bits of scattered potpourri between spluttered apologies.

Oren muttered under his breath as he waved a hand, and the lamp that'd smashed as it hit the floor repaired itself while Harland snatched up papers, pads and stationery that had skittered across the floor too.

'Please, Sage.' Harland put a hand on her wrist as she leant down to help him. It was shaking. She looked at him and realized his eyes were watery. 'Just . . . don't.'

'Harland,' she tried, but he shook his head and straightened, putting the last of the papers back on the cabinet.

'I'll see you there,' he said, pushing his glasses back up his nose. 'You really do look beautiful.' He turned to Hozier and though he was trying to be graceful, his face was still too red. 'So do you.'

'Uh . . . thanks,' she said, watching the whole display with faint bemusement.

'Why didn't he compliment me?' Berion asked as Harland practically ran from the room.

Twenty minutes later they weren't far from the hall, Hozier by her side as P bobbed along upside down, her head just over theirs so the three of them could gossip. Approaching the square that led to the town hall she could just about see a small cluster on the corner, and knew they were waiting for them.

Michael MacAllister watched them. He wore a suit with a dark green sash tied across the front, as did the two that were with him. A man and woman, both younger than he was, and infinitely happier-looking. Their faces were bright as they smiled at each other, their expressions full of fresh, youthful bliss. A real couple, who would pretend Hozier and Berion were their dates to smuggle them inside, then go off to dance the night away together.

'He looks miserable, doesn't he?' P sniffed as she righted herself.

'Tell me about it,' Sage muttered. 'Everything about him looks miserable. I've seen him naked.'

Hozier snorted. Even Berion grimaced at the thought.

But they were close enough she couldn't risk more without their wolf ears hearing, so she locked her lips and gave Michael MacAllister a tight smile.

'You're so dainty as a human,' was his greeting as he looked her dress up and down. His eyes lingered longer than they should below her face. Oren cleared his throat pointedly. MacAllister flashed a small smile. 'I see why you keep her close.'

'So she can rip out the throats of people who offend me,' he said smoothly.

She decided it was too early to open hostilities. 'This is P.'

'You're a true poltergeist?' MacAllister asked, taking her in. His eyes lingered on P's injuries like they had on Sage's breasts. He still barely blinked. It made her want to heave.

P just lifted her chin and ignored the invasiveness of his stare, and instead of answering she just held out a hand, palm up. He looked at it, confused.

Oren obliged.

From thin air he produced a small bundle of pinkish-white flowers branching off a thin stalk, and dropped it into her hand. It landed on her palm. Proof that she could indeed touch solid objects as only a poltergeist could.

MacAllister huffed a small laugh as he picked it up. 'A keen botanist, Mr Rinallis, or simply a charmer?' When Oren didn't deign to answer he looked back at P. 'This flower is called *Lathyrus odoratus*. More commonly known as the sweet pea,' he said as he put it back in her hand. 'Shall we go, then? Come inside with me. Tell me about life in death.'

She barely had the time to look taken aback as he turned, gesturing for P to follow at his side. She wasn't sure if he'd simply forgotten, or couldn't be bothered to introduce the two werewolves beside him.

Lucky Berion was the king of charming introductions, huh?

'Your gown is beautiful,' he told the young woman, and started to say something about how the green brought out the shade of her eyes as he introduced Hozier.

Sage smiled up at Oren.

'A keen botanist?' she asked.

He gave her an indulgent look that said she already knew the answer. 'Simply a charmer.'

41

SAGE

Inside the wide, slightly dated entrance to the town hall was a table with two werewolf women and a spread of long lists. They had little badges pinned proudly to their dresses that said *Event Organizer* in gold font.

They looked up at their approaching party, pens at the ready to tick off their names on the lists of every werewolf in the city. The one that took hers nearly blanched when she asked for the name of her date to scribble next to her own. *Are you OK?* she mouthed, as if perhaps it was a hostage situation, as if for this one night only she might be able to rally enough werewolves to save her.

Oren was laughing before they even got away from the table.

'They all think you've kidnapped me—'

They stepped through the door into the main hall, and Sage's mouth dropped open.

'What the . . . ?' Hozier managed to provide some of the words she was struggling to find as she also came to a stop just inside the doorway. They'd somehow walked into the middle of another town square. But it wasn't Downside. 'Where are we?'

'The Piazza San Marco.' Berion gazed around the room. 'I've not been here for decades.'

Her mouth was still hanging open as she let Oren lead her further in. Berion was right. She'd never been to Venice, but she knew St Mark's Square. The campanile to one side, and the basilica beyond. All around were the tall walls of the buildings that surrounded the piazza, and at all the windows, thrown open, stood a plethora of musicians of all different races that made up a grand orchestra. It was conducted by a green fairy on soft golden wings as he flew up and down, waving his arms.

She knew it was all a fairy glamour, their services hired by the event organizers to build this small city just for one night. She'd seen the room in its true form, the bottom half a vast open space, while the second floor was one long balcony that ran around the whole room, where observers could stand and look down from above. Knew this was where the orchestra really gathered, looking down from the balconies that had been made to look like windows. But it was just . . .

She spun slowly on the spot, gazing up. The roof, glamoured to look like a clear night sky full of stars, and just over the basilica in the distance was an almost whole, glowing, silvery-white moon.

All around the edges of the square were street vendors

serving various foods, drinks, snacks and desserts for revellers to go and try their fancy. There would be no sit-down meal, as there had been last year. No, tonight the room was filled with the small tables and chairs you'd find outside cafes, somewhere to take a small break after a long day's sightseeing.

The centre of the square was empty as wolves still poured in, but as the night wore on it'd fill with dancers, whirling and twirling and spinning to the music, a wash of colour and feathers and sparkling, dazzling dresses.

There were sashes like MacAllister's in varying different colours. Members of very real packs had their own distinguishing colours. In the past, they would wear them as part of the ceasefire rules that came with moon balls, so that every pack knew who they were making the effort to be friendly with. Now it was just tradition.

The colours made her eyes blur, and the masks! Small, large, subtle like hers and Oren's, extravagant like Berion's and Hozier's.

'I'll get drinks,' Oren said in her ear, but she was still too busy gazing around the room to notice.

But he'd seen what she hadn't, and made an excuse to escape as her name was called. She turned to see their friends hurrying towards them.

Juniper and Willow: both of them had their hair braided into matching crowns atop their heads, and they wore masks with feathers that fanned out into ginormous lion manes. Danny and Rhen looked as uncomfortable as Harland did, in ill-fitting suits, and all three of them wore matching white masks that covered half their faces. But she was pleased to see they'd succeeded in sneaking him and Cypress in.

Cypress was the only one she hadn't seen since that night they'd toasted Lucy in the Faun's Head, before this whole thing had begun. She smiled nervously, her fingers twisting anxiously as she gave Sage an apologetic look.

She held open her arms before Cypress could even speak and embraced her. She hoped it was enough to say that it was OK, that she'd forgiven Rhen and Danny, so it wouldn't make a difference with her.

But any conversation was stalled by choking sounds. Juniper and Willow were staring at something, both of their front paws kind of . . . trotting on the spot, and they made strange noises. Even Danny and Rhen paused attempts to greet her to watch the strange display.

She turned and realized that Berion and Hozier had finished bidding farewell to their escorts.

'Bastet,' was all Juniper managed to say as they stared at Hozier in her golden gown and cat mask.

'Juniper and Willow,' Sage offered, slightly bewildered as the pair bowed. Actually *bowed*.

'Oh.' Hozier looked surprised, but she smiled. 'You never said they were sphinx. Then of course you'd recognize my mask.' So she had come as a goddess after all.

And why was she not surprised?

Berion and Hozier had her friends eating out of their palms, the table full of such raucous laughter that there were only mild flinches by the time Oren appeared with a glass of wine, and P, carrying two bright cocktails which she passed to the warlocks holding court.

'No idea what they are.' She grinned brightly. 'I told the server to surprise me.'

All her friends tried to pretend they weren't watching Oren from the corner of their eye as Sage took the offered glass.

'Have you got eyes on him?' he muttered as she murmured a casual yes. She didn't want her friends to know what they were really there for; mild hysteria rippling through the crowd and tipping off the killer was the last thing they needed.

'Far left. Near the purple stall with cheese nibbles,' she murmured. 'We need to edge closer. Come on.'

Wolves were still coming in, a small, constant blockage by the door as everyone paused to react the same way they had on realizing just what they'd walked into. She looked at Hozier. Hozier nodded subtly. She was watching and she'd catch up soon.

So she let Oren lead her out into the piazza.

A few couples had started to dance now, spread out across the ginormous square as they took each other in their arms and started to twirl across the cobbles. She'd never tried to ballroom dance in her life. She had no idea what the difference between a waltz and a foxtrot was but she knew with certainty she had two left feet. The thought of trying made her want to shrivel into a ball of embarrassment.

'He's moved to the next stall along,' she said, watching the small figure that was MacAllister pick up whatever he was examining and sniff it. 'He's got a few werewolves around him. I suspect they're his entourage.'

'Bodyguards. For someone who played down his concerns, he's more wary now.'

'Hmm. Did you see him looking at P's scars?'

She tried to sound casual, but she knew he heard it.

'He'll know what werewolf injuries look like, Sage, there's nothing we can do about that. That doesn't mean he knows it was you.'

She gave him a look.

She stopped at a stall that was manned by an orange fairy doing elaborate tricks with cocktail shakers in hands with seven fingers. The fairy handed over two glasses of a drink that was pink at the bottom and yellow at the top, with glittery umbrellas and straws poking out.

'He's coming this way,' Oren said after a few more minutes of pretending to observe the spectacle of the fairy glamour around them. But she already knew the beady eyes of Michael MacAllister were locked on her through the little holes of his mask. The three werewolves that had been with him trailed just far enough behind they didn't particularly look like they were following, and when he paused before them they carried on by to loiter at a nearby stall.

'Anything?' MacAllister demanded.

'Not yet,' Oren said. 'But it's far too early, guests are still arriving.'

He nodded, looking out across the piazza. 'I've told my pack to spread out so it's easier to get to me. They won't make it obvious they're watching.'

'You're making yourself a target?' She raised a brow, surprised he was bothering, considering the lack of effort he'd put into assisting enquiries so far.

There was no warmth in his eyes at all. 'If they're here for me they won't come out if they can't get close.'

'So, you're helping now?' she asked, stirring her sickly cocktail with the straw.

'I helped your colleagues get in here, didn't I?'

'And you still don't have any idea what that symbol means?'

He smiled tightly, then ignored her completely as a woman across the room at a table called his name, waving for him to join them. He bowed his head, but it lacked Berion's grace. 'We'll find each other if we have anything to report.'

'What did he want?' P appeared the second he moved on.

'Nothing interesting,' she said, watching his retreat.

'Hozier and Berion have made their excuses and are around the stalls on the other side, near the door. You stay up this end, they'll stay down there. I'm just going to look through some of the back rooms.'

She nodded. 'Anything with a locked door, make sure you check inside.'

But P was already zooming off with an expression that said, *Duh!*

Five or six stalls later she'd had her fill of sample plates, and she was feeling restless.

There wasn't much they could do but keep MacAllister in their sights and wait. But the waiting? It was excruciating. And she'd pinned everything on the assumption the killer would turn up tonight.

Oren's sigh, deep through his nose, made it clear he was feeling the same.

'Come on.' He slammed his empty cocktail glass down on a nearby table and held out a hand.

'What?' She looked at it blankly.

'Let's dance.'

'Dance?' she repeated.

'We're at a ball, Sage. We're supposed to, I think.' He took her glass from her and put it pointedly down next to his own.

'We're supposed to be working,' she said through gritted teeth as he led her towards the dance floor.

The orchestra was playing something slow enough that her cheeks were heating even before they'd stopped in the spot he'd decided was for them – right in the middle of the square for all to see. He lifted her hand to his shoulder, and when his came to rest on the bare skin of her back she almost shivered.

She hoped her face wasn't bright red. It felt like it was burning enough to combust.

'Relax.' He laughed at the expression on her face. 'It's an easy excuse to circle the room a few times, just keep your eyes open for anyone that looks out of place. Uncomfortable or standing alone. I've got sight on MacAllister. I'll lead.' He knew her embarrassment wasn't just over her dancing skills, but she let him pretend. 'Don't look now,' he said into her ear. 'Two werewolves and a selkie are watching. They'll be plotting my demise together before the night's out.'

She refused to give him the satisfaction of an answer. And she was concentrating too hard on her own feet not tripping her over.

But . . . one dance turned into two, and neither made any move to leave the dance floor as the orchestra ended one piece and started another. 'Shall we stay here forever? Pretend that nothing bad in the world is happening,' he said softly as they revolved. Neither of them took their eyes from the crowds, both of them were there to work and that's what they were doing, but . . .

'I wish we could,' she admitted. She wished they were there just to dance, with no other worries weighing her down.

'I have a confession,' he said. She could feel his voice reverberating through his body. The knowledge of what those arms could do, the terrible things they'd already done, but the trust that she was safe in them. She'd known for some time now, but it'd been a hard realization at first – that she hadn't felt safe for a long time. Not since she'd been an orphaned child, scared and alone and forced to fend for herself. 'When Roderick forced us together I thought you were karmic punishment at last for a magnitude of sins.'

She grinned. 'I thought the same. I'd been waiting for the world to punish me for what I did to P. I thought you'd find out and . . . game over.'

'Game over?'

'You know. Chop my head off. Burn me on a pyre. Whatever it is you do.'

It was the first time his eyes left MacAllister. Just for a moment, he tipped his head back and laughed. She snaked her arms around his neck and held him tightly.

It was the hardest thing about P being a ghost. She could touch everything but Sage. Perhaps, she thought, that was her real punishment, that she would never be able to hold her best friend in her arms again. She hadn't realized how long it'd been since she'd hugged anyone until she felt both his arms wrap around her too, there in the middle of the dance floor.

'We can't stay here all night,' she said resentfully. 'Most of the guests must've arrived now. We need to check in with the others, work our way through the room systematically. We might have to get MacAllister out in the centre, figure out where he's most visible.'

He nodded, and at last he let go of her.

She turned to scout out Hozier and Berion, and saw Harland standing at a nearby drinks stall with Cypress. When he saw she was looking over he beckoned with a hand holding up a fresh cocktail.

'Thanks.' She grinned as she reached him, sipping gratefully. She noticed that while there was a whisky glass in his own hand, he didn't offer it to Oren. She tried not to smirk.

'Not dancing?' Sage asked. She'd noticed Cypress eyeing him awkwardly.

'I don't dance.' His cheeks were pink.

'Oh, come on!' she sighed. She snatched his glass of whisky from him with her free hand and thrust it at Oren, and then took Cypress's cocktail from her. 'Go,' she hissed, beckoning with her arms, herding them out towards the dance floor. 'Go!'

Harland's face was bright red. But Cypress saw her chance, even if her own cheeks were flushed, and she took his arm and dragged him away.

Sage grinned as she watched them go.

'Ergh. Teenage romance,' Oren grimaced. He knocked back the glass of whisky with a spiteful salute to Harland,

and turned away with a sniff. 'You find Hozier and Berion. I'll go look for P.'

She watched him melt into the crowds. It was funny, she thought, that even with the mask on everyone seemed to know who he was, and get out of his way. But, she supposed, nobody else had hair like his. There was no hiding Oren Rinallis.

Like there wasn't much hiding Berion, either. The blue suit and peacock plumes stood out in any crowd.

'You know, in 1927 I was the Blackpool Ballroom dance champion,' he told her as she found him propping up a cheese sample stall, his white eyes casually watching the entrance doors. 'It's so rare I get to show off my skills, now.'

She wasn't sure if he was telling the truth at all. But, she realized, she'd love to find out. She was about to offer to go out there with him – to survey the crowds again, of course – when an urgent voice broke into their conversation.

'I need to speak to you,' P said, eyes wide as she appeared beside them, no Oren in sight. Clearly he hadn't managed to catch up with wherever she'd been. 'In private.'

'Now?' She glanced at Berion.

'Now!' P urged, and without waiting she turned and zoomed off.

42

SAGE

'Sorry, sorry . . . uh, excuse me, sorry!' was her repeated refrain as they hurried through the now ginormous crowds around the vendors. If P wasn't the only silvery person in the whole room they definitely would've lost her.

'Bloody hell,' Berion huffed as they practically fell out of a group of chattering werewolves. He straightened with a disgruntled sniff. 'Where's she gone?'

'There.' Sage pointed to the pearlescent shine disappearing through the main doors. 'P, wait up!'

Had she found something in one of the back rooms? She glanced back to scan the room and spotted MacAllister still at the table he'd joined earlier. He watched, nodding once to acknowledge that he knew they were leaving.

Berion frowned. 'Come on.'

Just as they got to the door she saw a flash of red from the corner of her eye – Hozier's hair visible in the middle of a small crowd around a gelato stall. Berion let out a loud, quick whistle that she supposed Hozier was familiar with, because her head snapped up at once. She gave a small nod as they disappeared through the doors into the corridor beyond.

It was considerably colder than it was in the dance hall. Goosebumps covered her arms at once as she shivered, and the sound of Hozier's heels started to click as she hurried up behind them. The table they'd signed themselves in at was empty and unmanned now, with nobody to witness as they turned and followed P down a corridor to the first empty room with a little bit of privacy.

'In here.' P beckoned them inside.

They stepped into what looked like a storage room, almost half the size of the dance hall itself. Thick red drapes hung down one side of the room and it was full of broken chairs and fading signs, and random objects and props that would have no reason to be there had she not known the hall was also used to put on performances by Downside drama clubs. Everything was covered with a thick lining of dust. The air felt heavy with it. So much was piled up that even as P turned on a flickering light it didn't do much.

She shuffled along a few rows of stacked chairs piled beside a woodland-themed painted board to reach the opening in the centre of the room.

'What's going on?' Hozier said breathily as Berion helped her step over a pile of jumbled-up wires without getting her heels caught.

'Where's Oren?' Berion asked as he stepped over the wires himself to join their little circle.

'It doesn't matter! We'll have to find him later . . .' P shushed with her hands as she hovered in front of them. 'Just shut up! Just . . . just let me speak.'

Hozier met her sidewards glance.

P took a deep breath, wringing her fingers in front of her again. Dust molecules floated right through her.

She grimaced. 'The symbol. I know what it means. I have since last night.' She blurted it out as if she couldn't contain it a second longer. 'And the killer. Oh, Sage, I know who it is. We all do.'

She froze. 'Explain?'

'I had to be sure first.' P looked like she wanted to cry. 'I knew I'd see either way, tonight. And I did. I've just seen him—' She shook her head impatiently. 'I had to know before I said anything. Had to be absolutely certain.' Her voice faded away, her eyes lined with silvery tears.

Sage stared at P.

'No.' She shook her head as she felt her chest go hollow.

No. She was wrong.

Even as Berion made small noises of disbelief, she knew as P didn't take her eyes from her that P knew she was delivering something painful. Painful to *her*. She knew she believed with absolute certainty what she was saying was the truth. That's why she hadn't insisted they find him before this big reveal.

'I'm so sorry,' she whispered.

She shook her head again. P just nodded.

'No,' she said defiantly, her sharp voice echoing around the room. 'P. I—'

'This is why I didn't tell you!' she pleaded, her hands clasped in front of her as she floated closer, her expression begging Sage to believe her. 'I knew I needed evidence. I knew I needed proof or it'd ruin everything between us if I accused him! Please, just let me explain—'

'No!' she screamed. It felt like a dagger through her chest. A dagger of silver. She felt an arm around her shoulder, Berion's, but she didn't care about anything but the burning tears rolling down her cheeks.

Something she didn't know was inside her started to crumble. A wall she hadn't realized had built itself up, a barricade of hope and laughter and trust, tall and protective.

'Let's hear her out,' Berion said quietly into her ear. 'She hasn't been wrong yet, Sage, let her speak.'

She clenched her jaw to hold back angry words at the fact that anyone might even think it was true . . . Of course they did. They didn't know him like she did. She was ready to scream it in their faces.

But P was already ploughing on. 'I didn't tell you because I knew you'd insist on proof, and I didn't tell Oren because I knew he wouldn't wait for any at all—'

She froze again. Berion's arm still around her shoulder went rigid too.

P hadn't seemed to notice. 'And I'd never forgive myself

if Oren acted rashly and it turned out I was wrong. But, oh, he knew, didn't he? And we brushed him off. Oren knew something wasn't right about Harland—'

'*Harland?*' Hozier gasped.

A second wave of denial crashed into her, drowning out even that of relief, and that of guilt that she could have ever thought P was talking about Oren. Another statement she'd refuse to accept. It was even more ridiculous than the suggestion that Oren had been killing all those werewolves.

P paused, her turn to look confused. 'Who did you think I was talking about?'

She almost sobbed his name, her hand clutching her chest as if she could reach in and soothe her pounding heart.

'Oh, God, Sage no!' Her eyes were wide. 'Never!'

But before any of them could speak, a voice mimicked her from the doorway.

'Never,' it repeated. 'Never Oren Rinallis.'

Harland stepped in.

43

SAGE

She knew at once that P was right.

The sweet, innocent, geeky boy with thick glasses . . . It was all gone. The glasses had disappeared, and his face was cold and hard.

As he stepped into the light he moved with a grace she'd never seen before. And the voice that mimicked P . . . it wasn't Harland's voice. The southern accent, the boyish lisp and nerve-filled stammer. Gone. And she realized . . . it'd all been fake. The voice she'd known . . . It was a lie.

'Of course.' The voice sounded alien on his lips. It was deeper, stronger, it was *Scottish*! That accent he'd recited poetry in – it hadn't been put on at all. 'The warlock that has committed crimes so unspeakable could never kill werewolves, but Harland . . .'

His spine was straight, shoulders back, and any traces of lacking confidence had evaporated. With his chin held high he looked taller than ever. And older. A lot older.

She stared at him. Amazed. Horrified.

It couldn't be.

He'd been in their home, lived with them, *helped* them—

There was a flash of Berion's purple magic, but then another crack, a blue flash, and it'd gone. A flash of Hozier's red, but with another blue crack that was gone too.

'What?' Hozier stared at her hands.

Harland let out a cold laugh. 'You aren't strong enough.' He clicked his fingers, where a blue hum started to glow. 'Red is pretty lame, but blue outstrips even you, Berion.'

'Impossible.' Berion stared at the magic.

But . . . no. She'd never actually seen him transform, had she? She gaped at him. Had he used magic to trick her senses and make himself smell like a werewolf?

'Where is he?' she demanded. 'They aren't strong enough, but Oren is. What've you done?'

A flash of annoyance. 'Somewhere sleeping off the tonic I slipped into that whisky. So predictable. Both of you. I knew you'd try and make me dance. And that glass, I just needed you to hand it to him. By the time he wakes up you'll be dead. I'll be gone.'

Hozier laughed, and it was derisive. 'There won't be a place in this world you can hide, Harland. He'll hunt you to the end of the earth.'

'I did well enough hiding in plain sight, didn't I?' he sneered. 'I'll try my chances.'

He waved a blue hand again, the implication clear. He'd used that magic to trick them all, but Oren most.

She just couldn't make any of it compute.

She looked at Berion. He stared right back. *I know*, his witch-white eyes implored. *Wait for the right moment.*

Because he would only be able to overpower Harland's magic for so long.

She felt dazed. Nothing made sense. 'You've been hunting MacAllister?' she asked.

He nodded.

'Why?'

He turned to P. 'Well, don't stop now. Do the honours, P. It's my time to shine.' P was gazing at him, her eyes full of horror and sadness. 'Come on!' he exploded. 'We all know how meticulous you've been.'

'Made your life harder, has it?' she asked quietly.

'Yes, actually. Do you know how infuriating it was that you had access to Arcānum archives and all the information I needed? Trust it all to be guarded by the one person I couldn't kill for answers! No.' He dragged out the word with an air of drama to rival anything she'd ever heard from Berion. 'Trust what I needed to be under the protection of a poltergeist that never sleeps!' Spit flew from his lips. His voice echoed through the silence. 'So come on, tell Sage everything.'

He shifted the folds of his jacket to display a dagger tucked into the side of his waistband.

And, oh, was it familiar.

P's eyes went wide. 'You took Oren's dagger when you knocked into the cabinet?'

'I was good, wasn't I? The tears in my eyes made me look so pathetic—'

'Just get it over with, P,' Berion tutted impatiently. She knew he only sounded bored to annoy Harland; his arm was still clamped around her shoulders tightly.

P lifted her chin, but her voice shook as she spoke. 'Darren Johnson's murder was so subtle it went unnoticed. You used silver in the food so the Arcānum, and by extension MacAllister, your ultimate target, would know it was a supernatural murder. But it was too clean. Nobody saw it for what it was. That's the real reason you made such a mess at Lucy's apartment. To make sure it couldn't be mistaken for anything but murder.'

Harland nodded. 'Darren looked like an accident. My mistake. But kudos to you all for spotting it.' He praised them with an air of sarcasm. 'Lucy's apartment was juicy, though, right? I was pleased with the finished look.'

'You left that footprint in the blood on purpose.' She looked back at Sage. 'I went to Darren's house the other night, after I started to suspect, when I started putting everything together. Neither of you noticed that in a house full of double everything there was only one pair of shoes by the front door.'

She froze. Her mouth dropped open. She'd straightened them and not noticed?

'He was a size ten, Sage. Converse.' Her throat had gone dry. 'I searched the whole house. He had double everything except that one pair of shoes. So where's the duplicate? Somebody must've taken them. The murderer had taken them, and worn them to Lucy's in the hope someone would eventually link the two and realize Darren was murdered too. And just to make sure, you told us the kind of shoe to nudge us in the right direction.'

'Like I said,' Harland held his arms wide, 'hiding in plain sight.'

Berion's arm around her was the only thing stopping Sage lunging across the room. She didn't care. She'd transform and rip his throat out like that other wolf.

'You're a bastard!' she snarled. 'Did you know, when you got her name from Darren? He delivered to her, right? He delivered to most of the werewolves Upside, you used him to find more victims. Did you know she was my friend, and kill her anyway?'

He blinked at her, surprised. 'Oh, Sage.' He laughed. 'Oh, no. No, no, no. I didn't get her name from Darren at all. I got her name from you.'

She stilled. And everything went hollow.

Then the ground started to shift, and suddenly it was as if she were standing in that corridor smelling Lucy's blood.

He nodded enthusiastically. 'You thought I used each victim to find the next, and in some ways that's the truth, for the rest of them. But Lucy was an unfortunate coincidence. That's why she was the most difficult jigsaw piece for you to fit into the puzzle.' He looked at her again and smiled. 'She was never part of the plan until you mentioned her. See, my ultimate target was MacAllister, you were right about that, and though I knew he was near the city I had no idea where to find him. But you told me you had a werewolf friend Upside, an investigative journalist. I looked her up. I thought I'd see if she could spare me some time, help me locate my target through other means.'

How that name had come to be scribbled on a post-it, but nowhere else.

She could barely hear anything for the roaring in her ears.

Another friend dead *because* of her.

'But I knew as soon as I said the name that she recognized it too.' He frowned. 'That was strange. You see, all those other victims were old pack members. That's what made them my targets. Wolf loyalty runs too deep. They never truly left the pack. They were given new names and sent out into the world to *help* the pack stay hidden.'

'Doctor, groceries, deliveries . . . All planted out in the real world so MacAllister didn't have to associate with anyone he couldn't trust,' Hozier said slowly.

'Exactly!' Harland pointed at her like a teacher praising a pupil. 'So how did Lucy know who Michael MacAllister was? She was a lot younger than the rest of them. She scribbled down the name and pretended it was new to her, and I let the lie play out, just to see where it'd take us.' He sighed. 'Then I found a box in her bedroom while she was in the bathroom. Cuttings from supernatural newspapers that she must've saved for years. And on one little piece of paper, torn from the corner of a notepad, was drawn a symbol I hadn't seen in so long I forgot it even existed . . .'

'Where's the box now?' P asked. 'It wasn't in her apartment.'

'I turned it to ash. When she came out of the bathroom her fate was sealed. I knew she knew Rob probably wasn't my real name. Knew she was a risk to my plans.' Harland's nostrils flared in irritation. 'I spent weeks volunteering at a soup kitchen to get to know her.' He grimaced. 'The soup kitchen stank. The homeless were disgusting. All a waste of time.'

Sage felt numb.

'But she gave me something new and exciting. The symbol was just a bit of last-minute fun. I already knew it'd been removed from supernatural records so that while MacAllister would recognize it, you'd struggle.' Harland's sigh was melodramatic. 'Anyway. It was a shame. I liked Lucy. And as she lay dying it clicked. I remembered who she was. We *had* known each other, as children. I'd already thought she was dead. But she must've escaped.'

The silence was so heavy she could barely breathe.

Lucy had escaped . . . from where?

'It was too late by then to save her.' He shrugged again. 'I think I had more of a chance with her too, Sage. The gaming tees were just a cover, trust me, I wouldn't be caught dead in half that stuff you saw me in. I'm a catch in a suit. I mean, look at me.' He held his arms wide as he looked down at himself.

'The symbol, what is it, then?' Hozier demanded as the tension in the room rose closer and closer to breaking point.

'P,' he commanded. 'I never expected you to figure it out . . . it was part of a crime so heinous that its use became restricted over a decade ago. But you said you know what it means? That it helped lead you to me. How?'

She folded her arms across her chest.

'Go on!' he screamed.

She took a deep, resentful breath. 'Oren said he'd seen it somewhere before but he couldn't remember where . . . but actually, I realized, so had I. I didn't mention it because I couldn't place it either. I didn't know if my mind was playing tricks. Then it just came to me.' She looked back at them, not at Harland, and she bit her lip. 'The day I met Hozier in the archives and she showed me around, she pointed out the restricted section. Secret cases, banned topics, and files on all the Arcānum staff. It's not available to anyone without permission from Roderick. But I went back the night after. I sneaked in,' she confessed. 'I went for Oren's file.'

Berion swore under his breath, but Hozier, she was grinning, a look of pride on her face.

'P, you didn't,' she whispered.

'I swear it, Sage. I looked at nothing.' She was pleading again. 'And I'll tell him everything. I only wanted the full name of the pack he killed, the one that was trying to create magical werewolves.'

The magical werewolves Oren had destroyed.

And the silence wasn't just deafening. It was soul crushing.

She looked at Harland. Looked for any kind of indication it was true.

'Once I got the name I shut the file without reading another word,' P went on. 'Then I went to the file for that pack, still in the restricted section. I was just interested more than anything, it wasn't even anything to do with the case. But that's where I first saw that symbol. It wasn't as a whole, though. It was broken down into pieces, each segment representing various elements. That's why I didn't put two and two together right away. Why, I suspect, Oren didn't, either. The humans call it the Monas Hieroglyphica. An emblem of alchemy. Magic. Power. Eternal life. Amhuinn commandeered it to represent his mission. Once I knew where to look, last night, I found it in a library Upside in less than ten minutes.

'I took a file on MacAllister's pack into the restricted section last night to cross-reference names. It'd bothered me that MacAllister was Scottish. Packs usually stay relatively local to their home territory. But I remembered what Oren told us. He killed half of Amhuinn's pack for defending their alpha and he let the rest of them flee. Sage, you thought they tried to kill Oren the other night to avenge their own race, werewolf loyalty runs that deep they'd do it even for wolves they'd never met. But they tried to kill him because *they were that pack*. Amhuinn's pack. What was left of them.'

'Michael MacAllister was Amhuinn's second,' Harland said quietly. 'He was the werewolf that consented to change the warlock Amhuinn in an orchestrated, intentional attack.'

An unethical, completely illegal changing that set the course of so many terrible things in motion. And despite everything, despite the horrors her supposed friend had committed, she realized that she understood why Harland had started this hunt. Why he held MacAllister responsible in the absence of anyone else to blame. That to be what Harland so clearly was, to be a hybrid: a magical werewolf, he would've had to have been experimented on. As a *child*. And all this, all this death, had been because he'd needed someone to pay for it.

'The file said MacAllister had a wife and two children, but that Oren killed them,' P said quietly. 'MacAllister was the only survivor.'

Goosebumps rose on her skin, and when she swallowed, her throat had gone so dry she nearly choked on it. It'd been there for days, another clue. And as Harland's eyes – eyes that weren't yellow, that must've been his mother's – met hers she knew at once it was true.

'He recited poetry to Oren. Like you did to me,' she could barely whisper. 'Family trait, is it?'

44

SAGE

'He would recite to us as we fell asleep as children. My sister and I.'

That picture on the bedside table in MacAllister's cabin. A woman and two children.

'He thinks I'm dead,' he said quietly. 'Even now, I doubt that he thinks the person hunting him is me.'

'How did you escape?' Berion asked.

'When Oren Rinallis turned up to kill Amhuinn ten years ago I was fourteen. So was Lucy, though I knew her as Lily, then. I know I look younger when I'm dressed up in tatty jeans and second-hand hoodies. Then he started killing everyone that wouldn't bow at his feet.' His mouth pulled into a grimace. 'They genuinely thought they could take him. I thought they could. He was just one, and we were so many. He stood there with nothing but a sword in each hand and exploded. He was so quick that some hadn't even fully transformed before they died. I turned to run and saw our neighbour – her head was still human, and one of her legs, but her other leg and her arms were wolf. And her guts were spilling out on to the floor. I managed to crawl into a small space under our cabin that I used as a hideout when playing with friends. It was just enough to cover me. I cowered, too horrified to do anything else. I saw my sister transform and lunge for his back, and the blood spray from her neck. I saw my mother dive in front to protect her from another blow, but the sword went through them both. It was my father who fell to his knees and surrendered first.'

She didn't watch Harland as he told the story. She watched P, and P watched her, as the pair listened to that which they'd chosen to accept as Oren's past, and wondered if it'd make a difference once all this was over.

'And then what?' Hozier demanded, maybe because she knew they couldn't.

'I watched him grovel, crying and whining. I listened to him renounce my sister, and me. You see, he and my mother met and married in that commune, they were both already wolves but we were born human, then they offered us to Amhuinn. Willingly gave us as babies for his experiments. He renounced us as monsters. As abominations of nature. After *he'd given us to him*!' He was shouting again, the spit still flying. 'After he'd made us what we were!'

'Harland,' she started. Because even after everything, her heart was breaking for him. So much pain. She could see it on every bit of his face.

'THAT'S NOT MY NAME!' he bellowed furiously.

'Liam MacAllister,' P said quietly. 'That's your real name.'

'Was Lucy . . .' she started to ask, but she couldn't finish the rest.

He shook his head bitterly. 'She came to the commune already turned, a runaway. She was one of the lucky ones. Amhuinn couldn't experiment on anyone already a were-wolf. He needed humans. But she knew what he was doing. What he was like. His . . . cruelty towards anyone who displeased him. I don't blame her for running too.'

'Salina didn't recognize Lucy?' she asked. 'They met at least once, for the article.'

She realized with a pang that Lucy must've hidden her true accent too. Like Harland had. For all those years she'd known her.

He shrugged, uninterested. 'Apparently not. I suppose it's harder to recognize terrified children once they're all grown up. Though, I personally didn't risk it. I used magic to alter my age and appearance.' Then his expression turned earnest. 'I apologize for the split lip and black eyes,' he confessed. 'You came out of nowhere. You were faster than I'd ever expected. I didn't know at the time it was you, of course, but you were trying to defend Salina. It was the best I could do to defend myself and not kill you too.'

Her mouth dropped open. Oren had insisted it was unlikely she'd killed Salina given the lack of serious injuries he'd expect in a fight to the death. They hadn't considered she'd been there to try and help.

She'd tried to save her.

But failed.

Another wolf.

Another death that was her fault?

She knew when she finally fell to the floor she'd never get back up again.

'I told you then, another clue, that perhaps you'd got into a fight with the killer that night. It was complete chance you turned up,' he admitted. 'I didn't even know it was you until I fell into your apartment in my staged panic that you might've been the murdered werewolf. It was genuine shock when I saw the state of your face.'

'Wait,' Berion cut in, holding a hand up. 'It was a full moon. The only night of the month you go full wolf. How do you remember any of it?'

He looked at Berion as if he were being purposely idiotic. 'I can channel the magic to keep my mind, even on a full moon. It was one of the first things Amhuinn taught us. A gift of our hybrid nature. And something he most cherished. While everyone around us lost themselves completely on a full moon, we remained whole. Superior. I befriended Salina enough for her to invite me to spend the full moon with her, waited until she transformed and attacked. I was far bigger than her. It was easy. Easier than if I'd attacked her when we were both human.'

'Why pretend?' she demanded. 'Why befriend them?'

He shrugged. 'I was always going to kill them for the part they played. They might not have experimented on us but they didn't stop it. Turning a blind eye made them just as guilty. But I didn't know where they all were. I still needed help locating each of them, and I knew they would all know where each other lived and worked. Darren was the most difficult, I killed him in the end because he gave so little. When you threw me the boon that was Lucy, she led me to Salina quickly, and the chain started from there. A few well-placed questions had them accidentally ratting out their friends' addresses. That's why the gap between Darren and the rest was the longest. It just got easier.' He smirked. 'I got better.'

'At dinner the night Mhairi died. You had wet hair. You said you'd got soaked in the rain and changed before heading back for dinner.'

'She was a wriggler. Splashed everywhere in that shower. It's a gift for your conscience that I'd already got the address for Patrick Tapper's shop from her, because you blurted it out at the table that night.' He started to laugh. 'I knew I had to get to him before you did. So when we left your apartment I let Danny think I wanted to be alone. I went straight there while you went to Mhairi's.'

'You didn't have to do what you did to him.' She shook her head. 'It was . . . unnecessary.'

'He was a fighter. And a good one. It was hardly my fault.' He laughed again. High-pitched and loud. 'The bastard made such a mess his blood destroyed his ledgers. With the addresses of all his clients. Including MacAllister.

Can you believe it? If we hadn't been so close to the moon ball I'd have lost my mind.' None of them spoke. There was nothing any of them could say. But he barely noticed as he rambled on. Now he'd started talking about it he couldn't stop. 'I made sure you saw me almost immediately before or after each body was discovered, so you didn't think to question where I'd been. I played my part, pretended to be horrified, offered to help where I could. Someone give this boy a BAFTA!'

'When did you first suspect, P?' Hozier asked.

'That night, at dinner,' she confessed. 'You said you remembered Mhairi's name because of the spelling. M-H-A I-R-I. That's the Scottish way. And it was only that morning I'd been tidying up my notes, and I reread some bits about MacAllister's childhood in Edinburgh. It was just a weird coincidence. And then the next evening at the market, Sage told me you'd recited poetry in a Scottish accent. We'd laughed . . . but it bothered me.'

'Oh!' His eyes went wide. Excited. 'Did you like the sage? I thought it was a fun little touch.'

'It was a waste.' She couldn't stop herself sounding spiteful. 'I was never scared, Harland. Even after I spotted the ravens you had following me.'

It hung between them, the unspoken words that made his jaw clench. She'd always been safe, not because Harland had chosen to offer the gift of sparing her, but because Oren had rarely let him get close.

'Rhen called late that night, when Sage had already gone to bed.' P pulled the focus back to herself. 'He wanted to know if you were at our place, because you'd left the party. They'd assumed you were sulking but when Kat checked your room she found it empty. They couldn't tell Kat why they were worried, but Sage had warned them not to go anywhere on their own. I'm guessing it was those ravens that told you where she was. Followed us to the market.'

He nodded slowly. He almost looked impressed.

'You've known all day?' she asked P. 'Tonight, even as he came into our apartment?'

P looked back at her with sad eyes. She knew it wasn't an accusation, of keeping the secret and continuing to be friendly with someone who had killed so many in such awful, terrible ways. She just couldn't bear the thought of P dealing with it all on her own.

'He couldn't hurt me,' she whispered. 'I was the only one that was safe. I wasn't even one hundred per cent, or maybe I just didn't want to believe it, until we got here. And he couldn't keep his eyes off MacAllister.'

'Oh, P—'

'Yes, yes, so valiant!' Harland hissed.

'You knew we visited the commune. You knew we got the location from the archives. Why didn't you sneak about when P left at night, kill me in my sleep, snatch the information and go?'

His nostrils flared again, but for the first time he hesitated.

'I couldn't risk that she'd come back before I found it and got away, and tell Oren.'

'Yeah, right,' Hozier grumbled.

'What was that?'

'Everything else might have been faked but the way you watch Sage isn't,' she said scornfully. She stepped closer, so small she barely came past his middle. 'Trying to plant seeds about Oren. The jealousy. You might have used it to your advantage but you sure as hell meant it. You didn't want to kill her because you still clung on to the hope she might want you back someday.'

'Hozier,' Sage said quietly as Harland's cheeks started to blotch.

Berion nudged her with his hip, the slightest of movements, but it was enough of a warning. She was doing something, and Berion knew what it was. Perhaps it was part of their partnership? Something they did when they were off working together. Berion was the stronger of the pair. Was she the distraction?

'No,' Hozier said defiantly. 'He's had his *time to shine*. But all theatrics get reviews, right? So now I get my say. Mediocre. One and a half stars at best. And I've only given that for the hard work of the supporting cast.' She waved a hand at P.

'Shut up,' Harland growled.

'Not to mention the staging is a little worn,' she carried on, wrinkling her nose as she looked around the grubby storage room.

'Shut up!' And with a sudden jerking movement the knife strapped to his side was in his hand.

Sage reacted instinctively, made to lunge and drag Hozier back, but even as she moved forward she jolted. It felt like a punch right in the stomach. She heaved, bending double.

'Sage?' P gasped, darting forward. 'What is it?'

'Silver,' she rasped.

Berion looked confused. 'It can't be, Harland isn't . . .'

His voice trailed off as they all looked up at Harland, and he did indeed look pale. He hadn't convulsed, hadn't stumbled or gagged, but the hand on the leather hilt was shaking. He was using what magic he had to block as much of the effects as he could.

It happened in slow motion.

Hozier's gaze fell on Berion, and she gave him the smallest of nods. Then she turned back to Harland, a sickly-sweet smile on her face.

But whatever Hozier said Sage didn't hear, because at that exact moment she retched so badly she started to choke on her own bile.

But it was nothing to what exploded around them. Hozier's goading had worked because Harland lunged, the dagger outstretched, and while he was distracted by the amount of effort he was putting into controlling his urge to vomit, Berion leapt. She stumbled sideways. Then a flash of purple, which was so bright as it exploded through the room that she couldn't see anything else.

She heard a howl of pain, followed by yelling as everything started to come back into focus.

Then she realized.

The howl of pain was coming from her.

45

SAGE

The silver dagger was buried up to the hilt just below her breastbone.

P was there, hovering over where she lay on the dusty floor, her mouth moving, but Sage couldn't hear anything over the roaring in her ears.

Then Hozier's face, and she thought she might be screaming too.

Only Berion was missing.

As she bucked and screamed at the burning agony, she saw two figures on the floor a little way away behind the stacked tables, and knew Berion was wrestling Harland for his life. For all of their lives.

'We need to get it out!' P was screeching at Hozier.

'I don't know if that'll make it worse!' Hozier screamed back.

'It's silver! That'll kill her quicker!'

And then she felt another unending pain so terrible she thought she might die in that very moment. In that split-second she saw Harland's eyes meet hers across the floor, saw him realize what had happened, and he went still under Berion's weight. She turned to see the dagger in Hozier's hand where she'd pulled it from her chest. Then in a red haze, it vanished.

At once with its absence the burning disappeared, to be replaced with the dull ache of everything else.

There was more purple in the corner of her eye and she knew that Berion had won. Harland was lying still under whatever bonds of magic were tying him down, and he wasn't fighting back. Just staring. At her.

'I need you to hold still,' Hozier commanded. Her voice was strong, as always – that wild fierceness she'd come to associate with her – only this time her eyes betrayed her. She saw the wildness of fear there too. 'I'm not good at healing others. I never—'

'Find him,' she rasped. She couldn't breathe. Her chest was on fire again. It was a different kind of fire, and now it felt more urgent. 'P. Find him.'

P gasped. 'Oren can! He's healed her before!'

'P.' Berion's urgent voice came from somewhere nearby as he left Harland in his little prison across the room. 'Come on! Go through every wall until we find him. I can probably siphon most of the drug out of his system. Quickly! Hozier, do what you can until we get back!'

Hozier nodded as they fled the room, but her expression was still horrified when she looked down again. 'You'd better hang on.' Her bottom lip almost dared to quiver. 'I'm *not* being the one to tell him you've gone.'

'Tell him . . .' She gagged on the breath she could barely breathe. 'I never cared—'

'I know,' she shushed her. 'He knows.'

Because if she went before she got to say it herself, she wanted him to know that whatever Harland had told them, it wouldn't have changed any of her choices.

She wasn't sure if it was minutes, or hours, or days, or maybe even years. She didn't know how long she lay there taking small, shallow breaths, surely not enough to sustain her much longer, as she felt her life waiting to wink out, desperate dregs of a fragile magic trying to force her to stay.

'I think it's too late,' she whispered as blood trickled down her chin.

Hozier shook her head furiously, her eyes screwed up, hands shaking against her chest.

She was ready.

She wasn't. But she knew it was coming. Knew she couldn't avoid it. She was ready to tell Hozier it was OK to give up. That it wasn't giving up. It was an impossible task she'd been given and she didn't blame her.

Then there was a crash. It sent more searing pain spiking down her body as she jumped. Harland was still trapped under Berion's magic. He was whining. Groaning her name. Neither of them looked at him.

P was floating near her head again. Another familiar

face next to her. His mask was gone, and horror distorted the beauty. He fell to his knees, staring at the blood pooling under Hozier's fingers.

'What happened?' Oren demanded, blinking furiously as if still trying to push away some grogginess.

'Silver dagger,' Hozier gasped through her concentration. 'It's missed her heart but I think it's pierced the top of her lung.'

'A silver dagger?' he repeated, bewildered. 'But none of us had—' He stared down, and his eyes widened with horror.

'Harland threw it,' Hozier gritted out. 'It was his.'

'It was mine,' he whispered.

He must've known that Harland was the killer already, P and Berion would've had to explain, but he still looked dumbfounded. A sight she never thought she'd see. Oren Rinallis shocked into speechlessness. He blinked down, taking it all in. Then his expression morphed into white-hot fury.

She grabbed for him before he could twist away and end Harland there and then. A tear ran down her temple from her eye as she realized the truth. That she was afraid. 'Stay with me.'

He swallowed, and that rage was gone, back to shock and frustration.

'I can't feel my magic,' he choked. 'Whatever he gave me has muted my magic too.'

'I don't know how to fix it, Oren!' Hozier snapped. Sage could feel her hands shaking harder and harder with the effort.

He made a furious, frustrated, strangled noise, and slammed his fist into the floor by her head.

'Berion!' he yelled, even though the warlock was right there.

But apparently Berion didn't need asking, because suddenly there were more screams. Not hers, but Harland's. P disappeared then too. Maybe to beg Harland. She didn't know. She didn't care about anything but the blood welling in her throat.

Her vision was blurring, her breaths smaller and ragged. Retching and gasping.

'Hozier!' Oren warned. 'Save her!'

'I'm trying!'

'Try harder!' He was shouting at her too. He must've known, even without his magic, must've been able to sense the end was there. '*Save her!*'

She meant to grasp his shoulder, but her aim was off as her fingers curled around his collar, pulling him closer until his face was right by her own. She could smell him. Cedarwood. The aftershave he always wore. So strange. Such comfort in a moment of such terror and pain. She didn't want it to leave, that feeling of safety. She didn't want to be parted from it. But . . .

'If I,' she choked through the blood. 'If I go . . .'

He shook his head. 'You're not, Sage. I'll fix it—'

She grabbed for his wrist, but missed again. 'What if you let me die?'

Her vision was completely blurry, his face and that hair of different shades of black and white and grey fading in and out of focus.

'Why would I do that?'

'If I die now I stay young,' she rasped. It was a secret truth that had been bothering her as time had gone on. She'd tried not to dwell on it but recently, it'd consumed all moments of quiet thought. Was this a solution? The answer to an impossible problem. 'I can stay with you and P forever. A ghost.'

Her thoughts were almost drowned out by Harland's screams as Berion tried to force him to reveal what he'd put in Oren's drink. She only had eyes for Oren. His expression was pained, but he shook his head. And she realized he'd been thinking about it too. She hadn't been the only one wondering how long they'd have before she couldn't match his pace.

'I don't want to get old while you both stay young without me,' she confessed as more tears ran down the sides of her temples.

'I know,' he said, and his voice sounded hoarse too. She felt his hand on her hair, felt it tremor as he tried to be gentle. 'I don't want it, either.'

'So let me die now.' She was OK with it. It wasn't ideal.

There was so much left she wanted to do first. So much life left to live. But she'd do it. She'd sacrifice this to stay young with them. 'I'll come back. I promise.'

'I can't.' He sounded wretched. He squeezed his eyes shut, forcing himself to do the right thing. If she could just persuade him. She lifted a hand to his cheek. Her blood smeared his skin. 'There has been little in my life that's been good, Sage. You have been my salvation. You, and P. You've both made returning to Downside feel like coming *home*. If I let you die now I'm only doing it so I can keep you forever.'

'That's what I'm asking,' Sage whispered. 'Please.'

Something dripped on to her face. Something wet. She flinched. How could the ceiling be raining? But when she looked up she realized it was Hozier. A tear for their whispered conversation. 'Oh, Oren,' Hozier whispered.

Oren ignored her. 'Good friends don't watch each other die. They save each other. That's what you said.'

She coughed. It tasted of iron. Something wet dribbled from her lips. His eyes went wide. It pulled him back to reality. And her chance was lost. She was going to let him talk for long enough that it was too late, but it hadn't worked.

'Please.' He turned desperate eyes to Hozier, his voice cracking as he reduced himself to begging. 'Please save her.' It splintered something inside her. Hozier was shaking her head. She couldn't do it. She didn't know how.

But . . .

'Oren!' Berion's voice came like a calling from God as he appeared, his white hair like angel wings, a triumphant smile on his face. 'Hold still!'

It sounded like humming at first, louder and louder as Berion summoned all that he had left. It made her arms start to goose-pimple. But then a purple haze, only slight, just a small shimmer, started to emanate from Oren's body.

He gasped, his chest heaving in pain, and Berion looked like he was about to collapse from the strain too.

As quickly as it started it stopped, and Oren breathed one last gasping breath of air.

He raised his hands, and at last they were glowing gold.

'One day you'll regret this.' She tried to force a smile. But it was bitter. Already the blood in her throat was starting to retract back down into her body, and she could breathe more clearly. 'On my death bed, I'll remind you.'

She could feel the warmth in her chest, that familiar feeling of his magic touching her insides as he moved to lift her bloody body on to his lap. His hand came to her wound, covering the spot where Hozier had just been, and when he pressed the hand against her skin, hot, red blood swelled up between his fingers.

She curled her hands around his wrist to brace herself against the full force of his magic about to course through her veins and force her back to life. Hozier's bloody hand squeezed her shoulder, letting her know she was still there too, for this final moment of burning agony.

'I'm sure I'll regret it then even more than I do now.' At last a tear escaped down his cheek, and he leant forward to brush his lips against her forehead. His apology for what he was about to do. When he pulled back, his smile was both hope and sorrow. 'But I want to see you *live* first.'

'Lung's healed. Wound's closed. But only just. We need to be careful we don't tear it back open before it can be properly dressed.' Oren's voice sounded distant. She could still feel his warm body against the side of her face as he cradled her to his chest. But something had changed. The fear in his voice had gone, replaced with something else. Rage. 'Take her, Hozier.'

She felt herself being jostled, but it also felt like she was someone else, like it wasn't even her body. The world swam. Nothing hurt any more, she just felt overwhelmingly heavy.

She didn't want him to let go. She was safe in his arms.

Then she smelt the flowery scent of Hozier's perfume, and settled again as strong arms came around her neck.

He was up in one swift movement, and even through her heavy lids she saw something materialize in his hand. A long silver blade.

At once, she bucked. She felt it zinging through her whole body even as the weight of impressing sleep crushed her. She wanted to be sick all over again.

'It'll be over in just a moment,' Hozier soothed as her

arms locked her firmly on her lap. 'Just a moment and he'll send it away.'

She could hear screaming again, howls of rage and fear from across the room as the blade swung through the air.

A thud.

And the screaming stopped.

And she floated away into sleep.

46

SAGE

'Oh, Sage!' P's voice drifted into her consciousness. 'Can you hear me?'

'P?' Her throat felt like sandpaper.

'I was starting to think you weren't going to wake up.' She sounded like she was going to cry. 'You've been out for four days. Oren said you needed time to recover but . . . I thought . . .'

'Four days?' The fog in her brain managed to decipher that, at least. Her eyelids still felt so heavy. She let them flicker and close again. 'The full moon?'

'It was awful,' she admitted. 'We didn't know what to do. It was Hozier in the end, she went to MacAllister. Didn't even tell us. Said she thought it was safer since Oren and Berion had . . . well, anyway, she explained you hadn't woken up. That we didn't know what to do about the full moon.'

'What?'

'He said that with the very old ones, when the transformation is too painful, they put them to sleep with tonics, so they sleep through the change and the full moon. Wake a day or two later. We didn't know whether to trust him, and if you had a true turning here . . . in this apartment . . .'

'Don't.' Another tear seeped out of the corner of her still-closed eyes. She wished she could stop crying all the time. It made her feel so weak. But she couldn't face the thought of P seeing her transform again.

'It's fine,' she whispered. 'Oren wouldn't let any of us come. He took you himself. Shifted out into the countryside and sat with you through the night. You didn't wake. When you changed back he wrapped you in a blanket and brought you back here.'

'Oh my God.' Instantly, even through the pain and the fog and everything else, she was mortified.

'He had the blanket over you before you transformed back.' She could hear her smiling. 'Modesty intact. And the wolf blood actually seemed to help speed all the healing up after that. Hozier's here every evening to clean and dress the wound. It's nearly healed now, the last of the stitches dissolved yesterday.'

She blinked through the grogginess, but managed a bit of a smile at last. 'I thought she wasn't into healing.'

P grinned. 'Both Oren and Berion went bright red at the prospect of touching your chest while you were uncon-scious. Oren's been loitering outside the door to come in if there's a problem, though the healing's been perfect.'

She tried to sit up, but the dull ache of her chest was too

much. She fell back down into her pillows.

She tried to work out the numbers. 'So it's . . .'

'Boxing Day,' she nodded, referencing the human day, but they both understood it for what it was.

'I missed Yuletide?'

'It was quiet. Berion and Hozier came for dinner. I invited everyone else but . . .' She shook her head. 'They're in shock too. Gutted they trusted Harland, nobody really felt like celebrating after what happened at the moon ball. Cypress sent flowers, though,' she added, trying to sound bright. But Sage knew it was fake. 'And Juniper and Willow dropped in on Yuletide Eve to see how you are. Danny and Rhen call.'

'They're not too scared now, then, huh?' She smiled weakly. 'Hoping to catch Hozier?'

'Juniper said . . . well . . . Harland had embellished a lot of stories, told them Oren had said things about them he hadn't. They all feel really bad for staying away.'

She sighed. She'd never blamed them. She just . . . everything hurt. Her body. Her chest. Her heart.

'You're probably the only werewolf in the world to survive a silver dagger. People will never believe it. And the scar. It's . . . I mean, wait till you see it.'

She raised a brow, and it slowly became a laugh, and P joined in, and through the winces and gasps of pain they were just two teenage girls giggling in her bedroom again. It was delirious. Hysterical. And she knew if she stopped laughing she'd start crying again, so it was the only option.

'I should've died,' she said after a while.

'I know,' P said. And Sage knew she understood.

It was the worst thing in the world not to be able to hold out a hand to her.

'What happened after?' She cleared her throat to change the subject.

'Oren shifted you and Hozier here while I flew, then he went back while we got you settled.'

'And?' She urged her to tell what she was clearly avoiding.

'Oren shut it all down. He set off the fire alarm to get everybody out but told MacAllister and his pack to hang back. He had Berion tell them everything Harland told us. MacAllister reacted how I suppose any father who'd assumed his son was dead, to discover he was alive, but now dead again after trying to murder him, would.'

'Then what?'

'Berion said he had them get on their knees and grovel.' She swallowed. 'Made every single one of them swear blood oaths that they knew nothing about Harland surviving Oren's first visit. That none of them had aided his escape, or anything he'd done since. He made MacAllister renounce him a second time.'

'Did any of them die?' Because a blood oath would kill them if they made it while lying.

She shook her head. 'They all spoke true.'

She nodded. She'd expected that, if she was honest. To assist Harland in trying to kill their alpha . . . well . . . it wasn't going to happen.

'What's Roderick had to say?' she asked. 'Managed to deny me my trial period yet?'

'Ah, well.' P cleared her own throat too. 'You have Berion to thank for that. He did most of the bartering. You know what he's like. He can out-charm anyone. Roderick has agreed to skip your trial period altogether.' She froze. And P's smirk turned into a massive grin as she clasped her hands together. 'You're in, Sage! You've done it!'

'No.' She barely heard the words. 'Surely—'

'He did!' She was nearly bouncing. 'Oren said he announced it in a team meeting and everything. It's official. You start full-time with fresh cases in the new year.'

'You did half the work, P. You figured it out in the end. You should get the job, not me.'

P only smiled in a way that she knew meant she'd only done it for her. 'Friends forever,' she whispered. 'That's what we said.'

On their first night Downside together, when she'd taken her home at last and they'd sworn new oaths of friendship. No more secrets. To always have each other's backs. She swallowed down more of that awful, thick emotion.

'Did he say how it went down?'

She shrugged. 'A few weren't thrilled, but a surprising number enquired about who you'd be partnered with. Oren shut it down, said you'd already agreed between yourselves you're staying with him.'

'How is he?' she asked. She knew he wasn't in the apartment or she'd have heard him shuffling about outside the door by now.

P's laughter faded. 'OK.' She paused. 'Now. That first night was rough,' she said awkwardly. She held out her hands, almost like she was trying to apologize. 'I can't touch him, can I? I couldn't comfort him. He refused to leave, or step foot in Har— the spare bedroom. By the time he accepted a blanket on the sofa the sun had risen and he smelt like the inside of a whisky bottle. I couldn't do anything but sit in here and pretend I couldn't hear him crying.'

She stared at P.

'I think it was the first time in his life brute strength wasn't the answer. His or Berion's. Harland wasn't talking, and they couldn't scare or torture it out of him. And that concept is alien to him, isn't it? An obstacle he couldn't fix with violence. And it just so happened that obstacle was his own dagger in your chest. I don't think he'll ever get over that bit.'

'That's not his fault.' She shook her head.

'No,' P agreed. 'That's mine. For not realizing he'd pocketed it. Oren left it in my care.'

'I didn't notice,' she said at once. She wouldn't let her take the blame either. 'None of us did.'

P still looked down at her fingers, ashamed.

Sage frowned. 'How did Berion figure out how to release Oren's magic?'

'He didn't.' P looked up again, and her expression was tortured. It said everything she didn't need to say out loud. It'd been her. Her pleading and begging one friend not to let the other die. P had done what all Berion and Oren's threats and brute strength hadn't been able to manage, and got Harland to reveal the release.

But then her stomach grumbled after four days of nothing.

P got up at once, the timing a perfect excuse to leave and let both of them recover. 'I'll get you something to eat.' She turned for the wall.

But as she started to pass through she looked back. 'I'm sorry, about Harland.'

'Me too,' she whispered.

'Some time, when we're both ready, we'll talk about it.'

She nodded. 'But not today.'

P smiled and shook her head. 'Not today.'

SAGE AND OREN WILL RETURN IN . . .

ALL
THE
LOST
SOULS

-2025-

ACKNOWLEDGEMENTS

Firstly: the Big Man in the sky for hearing my desperate prayers to get longlisted in the 2021 Chicken House Children's Fiction Competition, never mind shortlisted, NEVER MIND THIS ACTUAL BOOK.

Secondly: Barry Cunningham. Picking up the call to tell me I was shortlisted is still a blur, but I know for a fact I misheard something and started blathering away and realized after the call was over I must've sounded so stupid. It still makes me cringe. But, great news, you still let me PUBLISH THIS ACTUAL BOOK!

Thirdly: Kesia Lupo, who was the one to read my original competition submission and didn't immediately toss it, and was so kind and helpful after, with pitching rewrite ideas and all that.

Fourthly: (yes, keeping to this theme now) Rachel Leyshon. Because do you know how much this woman has put up with me, living in a perpetual crisis of faith in my work, never once having been anything but supportive when she could've easily lost patience with me? Sorry for missing deadlines. Thank you for *everything*.

Fifthly: everyone else BTS at Chicken House I've ever interacted with, who have put so much work and positivity into everything else. Other Rachel, Laura, Ruth, Elinor. And Micaela Alcaino for the amazing cover.

Sixthly: my agent Lydia Silver who is nothing but supportive, kind, only ever at the end of an email, and who I know has my back on anything I could go to her with.

Seventhly: many people at The Golden Egg Academy but specifically Imogen Cooper and Charlotte Maslen for their passion and dedication for creating a supportive and encouraging environment on their courses, and Tilda Johnson for her invaluable mentoring for the brief time we worked together.

Eighthly: a GEA extension, my beloved F-eggs. Hazel, Davina and the two Debs. I know I'm appalling at the group chat and go missing for MONTHS, but your endless support leaves me eternally in your debt. Love you guys long time.

Ninthly: Becky, for soldiering through the very first manuscript I gave you at sixteen that was terrible, and you'll still have enough grace to read this one. And Sophie for letting me pitch random hypothetical scenarios or help- ing reorder random sentences. Or offering different words in the style of a human thesaurus. I eagerly await you immediately pointing out that Oren's utter horror at human emotions is me, and I'll promptly redirect you to this comment.

Tenthly: my mum will be personally offended if I don't put her name here somewhere.

Eleventhly: Marvy. Our house is a zoo but you were here first, curled on the back of the sofa or at the end of the bed through every letter typed. You've come to purr on my chest as I've growled in temper or cried in frustration. You've listened to me read out lines over and over, trying to get them right. Really, you read this book before anyone. And Major, because our looooong dog walks helped me figure out plot holes. Marmalade and Perseus have been nothing but a distraction if I'm honest, but I feel like I have to mention all of you now.

Finally, Jasper. For every evening, weekend and school holiday you've let me sit quietly and type. For being the most understanding boy in the world, and always my biggest hype-man. For being the reason I do anything. Everything I do is for us. I love you.